Devil's Food

Books by Kerry Greenwood

The Corinna Chapman series
Earthly Delights
Heavenly Pleasures
Devil's Food
Trick or Treat

The Phryne Fisher series
Cocaine Blues
Flying Too High
Murder on the Ballarat Train
Death at Victoria Dock
The Green Mill Murder
Blood and Circuses
Ruddy Gore
Urn Burial
Raisins and Almonds
Death Before Wicket
Away With the Fairies
Murder in Montparnasse
The Castlemaine Murders
Queen of the Flowers
Death by Water
Murder in the Dark
Murder on a Midsummer Night

Devil's
Food

A Corinna Chapman Mystery

Kerry Greenwood

Poisoned Pen Press

Poisoned Pen Press
6962 E. First Ave., Ste. 103
Scottsdale, AZ 85251
www.poisonedpenpress.com
info@poisonedpenpress.com

Printed in the United States of America

This book is dedicated to Annette Barlow for her great kindness, gentleness, intelligence and unfailing courtesy.

With thanks to David Greagg, Dennis Pryor, Belladonna and all the fans.

With thanks to Jeannie, Alan, Dafydd, Dennis, Jaye Francis, Henry Nissen, Richard Tregear, Richard Revill, John Landau, Kellie Flanagan, Ed Jarrett, Michael Warby, Atli, Belladonna and Ashe. And to all who care for the lost, stolen and strayed.

In loving memory of Sister Connie Peck FM, who even now is giving God a hard time about his negligent care of the widow and the fatherless.

He hath shewed strength with his arm; he hath scattered
the proud in the imagination of their hearts.
He hath put down the mighty from their seats, and
exhalted them of low degree.
He hath filled the hungry with good things and the rich
he hath sent empty away.

—Magnificat, Luke 1: 51–53

Insula

Roof Garden	
8A CERES Trudi and Lucifer	8B PERSEUS Vacant
7A HERCULES Belongs to grazier family	7B PLUTO Belongs to grazier family
6A NEPTUNE Jon and Kepler	6B FLORA Vacant
5A ARACHNE Therese Webb and Carolus	5B JUNO Mrs Pemberthy and Traddles
4A DAPHNE Andy and Cherie Holliday and Calico	4B MINERVA Mrs Sylvia Dawson
3A DIONYSUS Professor Monk and Nox	3B MARS Vacant
2A PANDORA Kylie and Gossamer and Tori	2B VENUS Mistress Dread (Pat)
SHOP 1 CAFE DELICIOUS/ HESTIA Pandamus family	SHOP 3 THE SIBYL'S CAVE/ LEUCOTHEA Meroe and Belladonna
SHOP 2 NERDS INC/ HEPHAESTUS Taz, Rat, Gully	SHOP 4 EARTHLY DELIGHTS/ HEBE Corinna and Horatio

Chapter One

It was one of the most horrible sound-effects I had ever heard. A thud, then a sick, wet crack, as though the victim's skull had been cloven, spurting blood and brains as liberally as a Patricia Cornwell first chapter. I sat up straight in bed, grabbing for my lover Daniel. He wasn't there. Then I grabbed for my cat Horatio, but he wasn't there either. So lacking anything else to grab, I grabbed my furry boots, dragged them on—all the while the dreadful noise was making the hair on the back of my neck stand up like a yard broom—took hold of my remaining courage in both unoccupied hands, and started downstairs.

I live over my bakery in Calico Alley, in the city of Melbourne, generally not a place haunted by head-chopping fiends. Not historically, anyway. I knew I shouldn't have watched that old Hammer horror movie before going to bed at my usual early time, ready to rise at the bloody awful hour of four am to make bread. My bakery is called Earthly Delights and up to this moment early mornings had been the only thing to fear in it. Or maybe it was that They Might Be Giants song 'Dead' echoing in my head. Or memories of the French Revolution as delivered by Mr. Dickens in A Tale of Two Cities. He had described exactly how the severed head fell from the guillotine. I briefly wondered how he knew. Jesus, I was scared. But nothing was to be gained by staying where I was and being terrified. Meroe always said that the important thing about witches is that they didn't run away from what they were afraid of. Where was Horatio, my gentlemanly cat and attendant of my bedchamber? Had he, God forbid, been a victim?

That idea pushed me down another ten steps. Anyone who attacked my cats was asking for a Grimm fairytale fate, baked in an oven. Another sickening thud—how many people were being executed in my premises?—and I unlocked the bakery door with all the caution of a compassionate person opening the morning paper, the world being what it is at the moment.

The noise became louder and ever more disgustingly fleshy, and under it a male voice was muttering, 'Got you, you cunt!' The Mouse Police slunk to my feet and gave me that look which cats reserve for moments when they are finding the human world unbelievably trying and are about to call their union. Usually nothing worries the Rodent Operatives but this was clearly more than even they, ex-alley cats with very flexible standards, were willing to tolerate.

I relaxed a little because I knew the voice. Jason Lewis, my almost-apprentice, maker of the most glorious muffins to be unleashed on a morning-tea hungry world. But I wasn't entirely comforted, because Jason used to be a heroin addict and he did appear to be dismembering some unfortunate soul on my bakery floor. Which was also to the point, because bakery floors have to be really clean and how were we going to get the bloodstains off?

I found myself short of breath and cold as I pushed the door fully open to reveal the murder scene in all its horror. Body parts, indeed, were spread wide. Dark splashes decorated one of my pristine mixing tubs. Jason, dressed in his old trackie, was brandishing a short handled hatchet. His face was stained and distressingly organic fluids dripped from his adolescent cheeks and—erk—the blade.

'Oh,' he said, seeing me at the head of the stairs, dressed in furry boots, a heavy blue gown, and an expression of growing amazement. 'Corinna,' he added, as my expression hardened into anger. He decided it would be best to explain. 'I wanted to make some soup for the shop, see, to go with the herb muffins, and I thought I'd make some as a surprise, you know, to show you, and then...'

'Enough,' I said, holding up a hand. I could see it all. Jason, poor innocent, had decided on a simple soup, which was sensible as his reading skills still weren't too flash and he had never made soup before. Pumpkin seemed obvious, only two ingredients, one of which was pumpkin. And knowing nothing about the vegetable, he had gone and bought a Queensland blue pumpkin. These are covered with a hide which, like a saltwater crocodile (another Queensland native), repels bullets. If the navy ever cracked the secret of the Queensland blue, they would have a true unsinkable.

Which explained the series of blunted cooking knives, the shards of destroyed pumpkin on a clean garbage bag, the axe, and the embarrassment. Also the noise of cracking skulls.

Somehow it is hard to stay cross with Jason. No one else would have done this. Make soup to show me it was a good idea, I mean, and when foiled by the thickness of the obdurate veg, have had enough initiative to use the fire axe.

'And no harm done, really,' I concluded. 'So if you will agree to take some advice on pumpkins in future, clean up the mess, and take all my knives down to the sharpener's at Maison before you knock off, we'll say no more about it. What time is it?' I asked. It was black dark outside and felt far too early to be early morning.

'Getting on for four,' said Jason, dragging in a deep breath of relief. He has failed so often in his fifteen years of life that he still expects every mistake to lead to instant expulsion.

'All right, I'm going to make coffee. You want to have a shower, get the pumpkin juice out of your hair.' He ruffled his fair hair with his free hand and said, 'Gross.'

'And feed the Mouse Police extra munchies, they've had a fright. Get on with it,' I instructed. Then I came closer and held out my hand. 'And, Jason?'

'Yeah?' he asked, tensing again.

'I think you might give me that axe.'

He gave me the axe. I let out a breath I had been holding and went upstairs to prepare to face the day, which meant that while I was dressing my coffee would be brewing. You may keep your energy drinks with their strange over-scent of curried grass. I am faithful to the superlative bean. No coffee, no baking. It's a simple rule.

I caught the alarm before it went off, put on the life-giving fluid, made my bed, dragged on some tracksuit pants in size Extremely Huge and a top in Forget It No Human Is This Big, my very own sizes. I am fat in the way that Kate Moss is thin. Definitively. Even defiantly. The only diet I am ever going to undertake is the one which says stop eating when you are full, and I always do. Except for raspberries.

There is always an exception to every rule.

Horatio emerged from under my bed. He sat down in the kitchen, paws folded, tail carefully disposed, the picture of a cat who has been far too deeply asleep to come to the aid of his human, even though no one expects cats to do that stuff anyway, it being the province of pack animals of low intelligence, like, as it may be, dogs. Had he been aware of my need, he would naturally have given the matter some thought.

Perfidious beast. His shirt front was so beautifully groomed, however, that I forgave him and handed over his breakfast as I was toasting my own. A good solid rye sourdough with raspberry preserve, for what was probably going to be a trying day.

Small rain scattered across the windows like handfuls of sand. The indestructible plants which Trudi has placed on my balcony in big blue glazed pots bowed their heads before the gale. Not a nice day. But here with the pleasant sound of a cat absorbing milk and the coffee tasting fine and the heat coming up from the ovens, my kitchen is not a bad place to be, especially since the bakery isn't infested with serial killers after all. I wriggled my toes in my sheepskin boots and drank and ate and got my mind around the day's tasks.

It was Monday. I had no Daniel because he had been out on some surveillance task and said he would sleep at his apartment.

Daniel is a gorgeous Israeli, dark, with a mouth as sweet as honey. He thinks I am beautiful. He's a private detective, specialising in finding lost children. Grandma Chapman, who brought me up, would have said that he was a gift from heaven and not to be too closely examined. Once she'd gotten over him being Jewish, of course, which might have taken a while. My own parents, shown up as incapable of raising a child, still lived in a hippie holdout enclave somewhere near Sunbury, whence they had moved from Nimbin some years before. I hadn't seen them for an age, not since Grandma died and left me enough money to abandon my career as an accountant and, with my own settlement and untiring effort, to start a new one as a baker.

I had bought this bakery, and the apartment which went with it, in Insula, an eccentric building erected at the wishes of a man who Professor Monk suggested had been beaten once too often for mistakes in his Latin homework. And had fallen and hit his head. Insula was eight storeys high, had a collection of fascinating tenants, and was a charming place to live. Here I had my best friend, Meroe, a jobbing witch who ran a shop called the Sibyl's Cave. Here was the delightful Professor, getting on a bit but sharp as a tack. Our newest arrival had brought forth complaints from Mrs. Pemberthy, who lives to complain, because she had a big loom and, if you listened very hard with your ear planted on a glass held against the wall, you might have heard it clacking to and fro. I never had and said so. No one else complained. Therese Webb had taken Arachne, the spinner of the gods, a very suitable choice for her profession, which was spinning and weaving. I had bought a length of her fine dark charcoal tweed to make a winter coat, and it was very good, strongly woven without puckering, though from the look of the weather outside I might have left my coat-making run just a tad too late.

Breakfast over, I took a platter of toast down to Jason, to stay his stomach until he could get some real food from Café Delicious. The Pandamus family offered very good odds on Jason's speedy consumption of their Trucker's Special and he never let them down, finishing mostly just over his record time of three minutes and seventeen seconds. Which isn't long for three eggs, toast, bacon, tomatoes, mushrooms and potato pancakes or hash browns, depending on who had drawn the early roster, Yai Yai Pandamus or Hungarian Kristina.

I descended the stairs carefully, balancing the plate. The bakery was clean. Heckle and Jekyll were eating kitty treats before going out into the alley and standing over Kiko or Ian at the Japanese takeaway for raw fish scraps, their invariable morning practice. Jason had cut up the pumpkin and put it in the biggest pot to boil down to its constituents. No trace of vegetable massacre was evident. He had even had time to put on the downstairs coffee machine and now fell on my toast with a cry of joy. My need to feed hungry things might have met its fulfilment in Jason. He is still very thin, though not the skeletal creature he had been. His hair has thickened and fluffed out into a blond curly halo strangely reminiscent of Harpo Marx. It is sternly confined under a cap during baking hours.

'Rye,' I said, scanning my list. 'We need to make egg bread—did we get the eggs? Good. And the usual pasta douro. Have you decided on your muffins for today?'

'Thought I'd try that rosewater one,' he said, mouth full. 'And apple and spice.'

I left the muffins to Jason. His are better than mine, even though we use the same flour, oven and method. Cookery is a form of magic, of course, and if there were specialised wizards, Jason would be the Muffin Mage.

Having demolished the toast, we began to measure, pour and bake. It was night outside, not a creature stirring except the Mouse Police, and it was very soothing, the swish of water, the bubble of rye-bread starter, the warm electric scent of yeast and the sweetness of Jason's rosewater. Machines rumbled into life. The 'snick-snick' of the dough hooks. The roar as the ovens were opened. I stretched. The day which had started so unfavourably was improving by the minute.

Jason opened the alley door at seven and fielded a thrown newspaper. The Mouse Police stalked out to their predestined appointment with Endangered Species of the Southern Ocean. That was also the signal for Jason to go and pit himself against the clock at Café Delicious and me to sink down on my baker's chair and drink my third cup of coffee. Dawn was breaking, muted grey with charcoal overtones. People were stirring. Lights, which in some cases had never gone off in those tall buildings, were lit again if they had. Persons in suits with briefcases passed, heads glued to shoulders as they whispered urgently on mobile phones—what were they saying that was so important that it couldn't wait until they got to a desk? In my opinion only imminent war, shipwreck or heart attack ought to need the use of a mobile phone. Hadn't the poor bastards noticed that once they had one of the pestilential things they couldn't call a single moment their own? Not when sleeping or travelling or even in the previously safe refuge of the ladies' room could those sharply dressed women know the giddying pleasure of being alone.

Still, I suppose it makes people feel important. Needed.

I had enough things needing me, like Jason and bread and cats, without adding an importunate mobile phone. Sooner or later it would have to go out the window or down the sink, and that would be expensive. Though not as expensive as this season's fashion, pink and white checked bouclé jackets cut out of what appeared to be horse blanket. With a spade. Recycling them would cost the wearers a packet once the glamour wore off. Still, in my old blue tracksuit I was hardly a feast for the eye.

First loaves out, next lot in, everything shipshape and Bristol fashion, as Grandpa Chapman had always remarked when Grandma and I finished cleaning up the kitchen. For remarking it once too often I had thrown a dishcloth at him on one rather overwrought day. But he was a sailor and when Grandma had to hand the kitchen over to him after breaking her arm, he just murmured, 'Out of the galley you go, old girl,' and shut her out while he cooked and dished up creditable meals. But she never forgave him for setting fire to her favourite tea towel.

I tend to free-associate at seven in the morning. But on with the dance. Loaves went into the oven pallid and came out brown and shiny. The egg bread rose beautifully and smelt divine. It drew a wandering Jewish hunk in from the cold.

'Challah,' said Daniel on one hungry breath, reaching for a loaf. 'But it's Monday,' he added, pausing for permission before tearing it apart.

'Here every day is Friday,' I said with a generous gesture which strewed flour all over the immediate area. 'Hello, Daniel.'

He kissed me with the kisses of his mouth, which were agreeably flavoured with challah. Beautiful Daniel with his trout-pool dark eyes and his hair growing out from its short crop. Lord, I am not worthy, but speak the word only.

He hauled out the sack of bread which I donate every day to the Soup Run, said, 'Later, ketschele,' and was gone, hoisting the sack easily onto his leather clad shoulder. I sighed and got on with taking Jason's muffins out of the oven while he counted the loaves for various restaurants. I sell most of my bread to the trade, but I like having a shop as well.

I went into Earthly Delights to open the door and take down the shutters which defend my cashbox from all those people with tyre-irons who are supposed to haunt Flinders Lane after dark. I've never noticed any of them but they must be there or what is Neighbourhood Watch for? Except to keep Mrs. Pemberthy glued to her window, binoculars in hand, searching for malefactors. And lovers. And dog walkers. And drunks who piss on walls.

Dead-heating the door opening was my shop assistant of the day, Gossamer Judge, known as Goss, and Sylvia Dawson, the best dressed retired hostess in the city. Goss was wearing a fluffy pink bolero thing with matching goosebumps on her bare belly, and Mrs. Dawson was clad in a dark chocolate leisure suit, complete with scarlet leather gloves. And a very fetching cherry coloured woolly hat and scarf.

'Good morning,' I said to both of them, allowing Goss to slip past me into the warm. Mrs. Dawson shook her head affectionately. 'The young have centrally heated bodies,' she said. 'I would be too cold to expose my midriff, even if it was a midriff that would reward exposure. Which, at my time of life, it isn't. Ah, well. Do I smell Sabbath bread, Corinna dear, and if so can I buy some?'

'Wise of you to get in fast,' I told her. 'Daniel has already ripped off one loaf and most of it's for a wedding. I don't make it often because breaking all those eggs is very labour intensive. Here you are.'

Trays slammed into their racks. My assistant had started work. 'How are you, Goss?'

'All right,' said Goss in a forlorn tone. I wondered if it was due to a heavy night on the town or another one of her sad little love affairs. Goss and her friend Kylie are eighteen and wannabe actresses. Because of their near-anorexic stature, they don't eat if they drink, and this can lead to abrupt, violent mood swings to which even the most premenstrual could not aspire. I have mentioned that it doesn't do my reputation in the food industry any good to have shop assistants who look like they're near starvation but it hasn't done any bad. So far, at least. I hoped that if the newest fashions started covering up the navel I would work out some other system for telling Kylie and Goss apart as they were otherwise almost identical. Labels, perhaps? Brooches spelling out their names? That would be too, too day-before-yesterday for those two.

I had gone into the bakery to welcome the Mouse Police back into the warmth (even for tuna they don't hang around in a wind as cold and mean as this one) when I heard someone yelling in the shop. I sighed. Since the last government introduced 'community care' and shut most of the mental hospitals, we have our share of wandering mad persons, mostly harmless, poor creatures. I have instructed Kylie and Goss to give them a roll or a muffin and escort them out of the shop gently but firmly. Usually this works. That day—of course—it wasn't having the right effect.

'I demand to see baker!' said an Eastern European voice raised in protest. Jason was measuring cardamom pods to be pounded for his rosewater muffins so I opened the door and came into the shop. Horatio was sitting imperturbably on the counter in his usual place, which argued nothing very dangerous was going on, in view of his disappearing act that morning. A small bald man in a suit was having a screaming match with Goss.

'Good morning,' I said, and Goss flounced around to say, 'He wants to see the baker and I said you were busy and he yelled at me!'

'Yes, so he did,' I agreed, fixing the gentleman with an unimpressed glare. 'Well, here I am,' I said coldly. 'I'm the baker. Want to make something of it?' After all, I still had the axe upstairs.

Suddenly he was all smiles. His bald head gleamed and he flashed a mouthful, I swear, of gold teeth. 'Young lady,' he said to Goss with what was almost a bow, 'So sorry to raise voice, but I get so…'

'Frustrated?' I asked, taking in the pantomime of grinding teeth and clenching fists. He was actually quite sane, it appeared. At least for this part of the city at this time of the morning.

He nodded emphatically. 'Frustrate, yes, yes. When no one understand. My English very bad, I regret. But need to see baker before buy bread!'

'Why?' I asked suspiciously.

He took my floury hand and kissed it. 'Your young lady,' he said. 'So thin. I worried. Your bread seem good, yes. But. Saying in my country. Never trust thin baker. You baker. You not thin.' He kissed my hand again. 'Order, restaurant of my brother. Here.' He peeled off notes from a wad which might not have choked a horse but would have seriously inconvenienced it. This he stuffed into my floury hand, together with some sort of order form. 'Payment on account. Deliver tomorrow.' Then he vanished before I could write him a receipt.

Goss looked at me. I looked at Goss. We burst into a slightly hysterical fit of the giggles which lasted through two hours' trading, on and off. Jason's rosewater and cardamom muffins were exquisite, tasting of a Thousand and One Nights. Like Turkish delight without the glue. I was eating one with great pleasure before the hordes bought them out when I almost choked on a crumb and all thoughts of laughter fled out of my mind.

Standing in the doorway of my very own shop, a bundle of cloth at her feet and a look of resolute disgust on her face, was my mother.

Chapter Two

I don't know how long I stood there, coughing and staring. Probably far too long for courtesy. Goss was gazing at me with that wide eyed expression which should get her a job in a soap soon. Jason had come out of the bakery to ask my opinion of his rosewater muffin. He, also, stood and stared.

'Hello, Starshine,' I managed. 'What brings you here?'

'Your father,' she said hoarsely.

'Sunlight isn't my father except by an accident of biology,' I told her. 'What about him?'

'He's gone,' she said, as if it was well known that it was all my fault.

'Gone where? Do you mean dead?'

She scowled at me. Her hair was streaked white now, and her face had sagged into disappointed lines. 'Left the collective. Left me.'

I was left in no doubt which desertion was important. This conversation was going as well as conversations with my mother always went. That's why I had as few of them as possible. By the special intervention of the Goddess, to whom I now owed a big favour, Meroe came in at this point. If ever I had needed a witch in my life, I needed her now. Meroe could be any age between forty and sixty. She has long coarse black hair and always wears a long black skirt and a black top, covered with some sort of drape or shawl. In deference to the weather, today's shawl was a huge muffling one made of stripes of purple, silver and black feathery wool, in which she looked like a minor Maori deity. She took Starshine aback, which was always a good thing.

'My mother, Starshine,' I said reluctantly. 'Meroe.'

'I've heard of you,' said Starshine in her flat accusing tone. 'You're Wicca. A solitary.'

'Blessed be. That's right,' said Meroe equably. 'And I've heard of you. You're Starshine, one of Cath's coven. Until she ran away with that surfer. I don't know who has taken it over now. Never very effective. What are you doing here?'

It seemed that witches didn't have a lot of time for tactful indirection, either.

'I need somewhere to stay,' said Starshine. Still arrogant. Still sure that she had a right to command my life. I was about to riposte that Jason would escort her to his backpackers' as soon as he had time and that Satan would be skating to work before she set foot in my sanctum, when I was saved—again. This time by Therese Webb, resplendent in an orange tweed cloak of her own making, who pottered into the bakery in search of a muffin or two. She screamed with delight when she saw Starshine. She flung herself forward and enveloped her in a huge, woolly hug.

'Jacqui!' she cried. 'How lovely to see you! Have you come to visit me? I haven't seen you in an age! Such a cold morning, too. I'll just get us a few muffins and you can come right up to my apartment. You must be frozen, my dear, come along.'

'No,' said Starshine. 'I came to see my daughter.'

'Corinna's your daughter? How wonderful!' exclaimed Ms. Webb.

I stuffed muffins distractedly into a paper bag and thrust it at Therese, an unlikely saviour. 'Morning tea,' I said blankly.

She patted my cheek. 'Thank you, Corinna. We're all so lucky to have Corinna's bakery here. Imagine her being your daughter!' she said chattily to Starshine, leading her by an unresisting hand and picking up her cloth bundle. 'I'm just up here, and I'm sure that Corinna will come and see us after she shuts her shop.'

'I'll be there!' I said. The scene which Starshine had meant to stage in my shop had been entirely obliterated by first Meroe and then Therese, and I felt weak. Possibly with relief, but also with oncoming anxiety and rage.

'Come back here,' said Jason's voice in my ear. He drew me into the bakery and sat me down in my own chair. Goss turned to satisfy the demands from the shop and Meroe closed the door between the kitchen and the public domain.

'Jason, some of that brandy,' ordered Meroe. 'And for a change I think we shall all have some coffee, even me. Goddess, what very nasty vibrations, I shall have to cense the entire building.'

'Yeah,' said Jason's voice, seeming to come from far away. 'What a stone-cold bitch! Here, Boss, you drink this.'

I gulped. It was hot coffee, heavily sugared, with brandy in it. The world came back into focus.

Jason was smiling at me anxiously. 'Cheer up, Corinna, she can't take you away,' he said. 'You don't have to say squat to her.'

'Thanks, Jason,' I said. 'By the way, those muffins are amazing. Call them Kama Sutra muffins and double the price.'

'I'll tell Goss,' he said, and got out. Jason finds emotions icky. Meroe, on the other hand, thrives on them. She took my hand in both of hers.

'She's always been like that,' I said bitterly, tongue loosened by brandy in the morning. 'She just thinks she can walk into my life, take whatever she wants, and walk out. Between them she and Sunlight almost killed me when I was five and they never wanted me, never loved me, they were relieved when Grandma Chapman came to get me.'

'Why?'

'Because they were totally wrapped up in each other,' I said, reasoning it out. 'They adored each other. There wasn't any room for anyone else.'

'Yet Sunlight has left,' said Meroe gently.

I pulled myself together. That was odd. 'Yes,' I answered. 'That is very, very unlikely. Really.'

'I believe you,' said Meroe, relishing her coffee. She seldom drinks the coffee made of coffee beans, preferring dreadful stuff made out of roasted dandelions or carobs. I personally consider there must be something else you can do with dandelions. Let them flower into clocks to tell the future, perhaps. 'This week, next week, sometime, never.'

Sun, leave Star? Their collective held them up as an example of devotion. I had never seen them apart, actually. When Star came to blight my life with a demand for something—fortunately, in my accountant days, it was usually money—he would be there, nodding as she denounced my way of life, my husband, my diet, my body weight, my use of chemicals in the washing-up and my ownership of a car. Then they would take the money and go. It was never very much. Cheap at the price to get rid of them. I said as much to Meroe.

'Well, she was right about the husband,' she observed.

'That's true. James was a waste of space. Something very strange must have happened. Thanks, Meroe, I feel better now. I wonder where Therese knows Star from? She'll hate being called Jacqui. She hasn't been Jacqui since—I don't know, school?'

'I don't know much about Ms. Webb,' said Meroe, 'but if you like I'll call a friend in that collective and find out what she knows about Sunlight's departure. I didn't like the Wicca they were practising in Cath's coven. Too dark, too demanding, leaning towards compulsion. Pure food, pure water, pure thoughts—trying to be too pure in an impure world can easily lead to a loss of compassion.'

'Just as an occasional cup of coffee doesn't tarnish your chakras too badly,' I said, yawning. Emotion makes me sleepy.

'Exactly. Now, if you are all right to be left, it is time I opened my shop, and Belladonna is waiting for her breakfast.'

'And that would never do,' I agreed, getting up and shaking myself. Meroe's partner in the Sibyl's Cave is a plump, night-black, intransigent feline called Belladonna, who would demonstrate her displeasure in some noticeable way, like leaving a disembowelled mouse in the window amongst the Celtic jewellery. This always had the strongest effect on vegans and strict vegetarians. Some had been known to faint.

Meroe went and I drank the rest of the coffee and put the last of the loaves in. I sorted out the remaining orders for the day as my carrier, Megan, arrived with her rickshaw, and we counted and loaded.

'I've got a new customer,' I told her. 'For tomorrow. Rye bread loaves with caraway seeds. Café Vlad Tepes.'

'Just opened,' said Megan, tossing her coppery hair. No one knows the city's businesses like Megan. She is an ambitious young woman who started her own motorbike rickshaw business and will, undoubtedly, be running transport in Australia before she is forty. It is good to be kind to the young, for they will be Prime Minister when we are decrepit and in need of help. 'In Exhibition Street. Very tasty Rumanian food. They are Café Simisoa in the day and a goth club at night. They stay open late for the goths, who go there because of the name.'

'Name?' I asked vaguely, though a lifetime of horror movies should have informed me.

'Vlad the Impaler,' she grinned. 'I'll remember for tomorrow. That all? Bye, Corinna,' and she was off down Calico Alley and into Flinders Lane, gunning her engine. The future of transport, in my view, was in good hands.

I pottered around the bakery, cleaning up and putting things away and checking stores until the last loaves came out of the ovens, the flames sank and died, the air conditioning shut itself off, and the shop bell could be heard clearly again as a little 'ting' whenever some hungry customer pushed the door open and smelt that fine, heartening scent of new baking.

The ten o'clock rush was over and it would be quiet now until noon, when the early lunchers poured out in search of either (1) enough calories to sustain their thought processes through yet another meeting or (2) a reason to go back to work in the afternoon. This was the time when, if all was well in the shop, I went upstairs and changed out of my baking tracksuit into something more suitable and freed Goss for her break. So

I did that, though my feet seemed hard to lift and I was still recovering from that burst of emotion. I'm like Jason. I don't like emotions. I don't trust them.

I looked at my face in the mirror as I brushed my hair, now shoulder length and not as mousy as it was since I started using Meroe's camomile rinse. I was as white as a sheet of ivory laid Basildon Bond notepaper. This wouldn't do. I took some Rescue Remedy and a long drink of mineral water, splashed my cheeks and gave myself a severe scolding. So what if your mother has turned up? Is that a reason to have conniptions?

Well, yes, actually, it was. But I was going to have to get on with the day nonetheless. And when I went to see Starshine, perhaps I could try not to lose my temper with her, perhaps we could make some sort of truce. I went downstairs repeating this like a mantra, but I did not believe it. The trouble was she despised everything I believed in, everything I did, and everything I was. That didn't allow a lot of common ground. And I felt the same about her.

Jason was serving and Goss was drinking her decaf non fat milk latte and nibbling a quarter section of the Kama Sutra muffin. She was saying to Jason, 'Real good,' when I came in. Both of them looked at me. I tried to answer the look.

'Yes, she's my mother, and we get on very badly. I wasn't expecting her and I don't know what she wants.'

'But you don't like her,' said Goss. I nodded. To my surprise, they both seemed to understand this.

'I can't stand my mum,' said Goss. 'Or her new bloke. He's gross. I refused to live with either her or Dad's new girl, so he let me live here with Kylie.'

'But she can't do anything to you,' Jason repeated. 'You're a grown-up.'

'She can do things to me,' I said grimly. But Jason was, of course, right. I laughed. 'No, she can't make me go with her to her godforsaken collective in the mud. She can't make me live on turnip peelings and collected rainwater.'

'Sweet,' said Jason. 'Tell her to get stuffed and let's get on with the baking.'

'I do love you, Jason,' I said, and he blushed. 'As you say. All the loaves are sent and gone, we just need to sell out the shop and we'll be closed for the day.'

'I gotta finish the soup,' he said. 'And take the knives to Maison.'

'You can go now,' I told him. 'Goss and I will do the lunch-time rush. Just turn off the heat under your pumpkin pulp and you can blend it when you get back. Tell Maison to put the sharpening on my account.'

He ducked his head at me and went off to slide the knives into their leather roll, chopper on one end, carving in the middle and vegetable knives at the other end. You could equip a reasonable riot with my knife roll.

Nothing else happened for two hours. Lunchtimers flooded in, bought rolls and loaves and muffins until we ran out, and ebbed back to their desks. Goss and I were just putting the last of the loaves I'd put aside into the Soup Run sack when Jason came back, strangely and pitiably resigned, in police custody.

Two police officers, both young men with John Wayne swaggers and new guns on hip. They set every hackle I had to rising as they shoved Jason into the shop. He stumbled but did not even direct an indignant glance at them for their roughness. This serve of indignation, then, was going to be on me. It was going to be a heaping one.

'Can I help you?' I asked in my most middle class voice. My girls' school might not have taught me much about education, but it was excellent on snobbery, class and arrogance. And intimidation, bullying and violence.

'He yours?' asked one police officer.

'I beg your pardon?' I raised an eyebrow. I did not begrudge the hours of practice I had spent on learning to do this. It had its usual effect. He looked away and his mate said in a more conciliatory tone, 'This young man says that he works here. We hear that a lot.'

'I'm sure you do,' I replied. 'In this case it is true. That's my apprentice, Jason. Why are you manhandling him?'

'He was carrying prohibited weapons,' said the first police officer. 'These.'

'Yes?' I raised the eyebrow again. 'He was taking my cook's knives, in their proper covering, to Maison to have them sharpened. On my orders. If they are prohibited weapons then you had better arrest me too. Shall we go?'

'You don't know this kid,' protested the first cop.

'We used to see him around, sleeping rough. He's on the gear,' the second said to me, leaning close so that I could tell it had been a long time since he and a toothbrush had been acquainted.

'He's a bad boy. You'll wake up with a knife in your throat one night,' said the first.

And that was quite enough of that.

'Goss, just get me a pen, will you? I want to note down these officers' names and numbers. Now you have been assured that Jason has committed no offence, I am sure you will give me back my knives and leave him alone in future. Officers...thanks, Goss...Kane and Reagan. So kind of you to be concerned,' I said sweetly. 'He's off the gear. And I know my own business, as I am sure that you know yours.'

Kane, the taller and heavier of the two, stuttered for a moment on the verge of some unwise declaration. Reagan, the shorter, gave him a push and started him out of the shop. Jason sagged against the counter, his arms full of sharp knives.

'Just take the knife roll away from him, will you, Goss?' I prompted.

'Bloody jacks,' mumbled Jason. 'I wasn't doing nothing! Just coming back with the knife roll. It was all closed up and tied around. Not as if I had a shiv in me sock. But they had to stop me and make me open it and then walk me all the way down here as though I was a murderer. Saying how they were gonna lock me up with rapists.'

'Yes, they weren't nice people,' I agreed. 'It just hasn't been our day, has it, Jason?' I put a hand on his shoulder and he covered it with his own for a moment.

'They used to move me on,' he said. 'In the old days. I suppose they don't know I've changed,' he admitted, tearing the last ham roll in half and eating it in two bites.

'No, but they could have given you the benefit of the doubt. And taken a look at you. Officious, both of them, and I like my police persons at least thirty and not getting their street talk from *NYPD Blue*. Don't worry, Jason. I never doubted you for a moment.' And I hadn't, either, I realised.

'I won't mind the cops if you don't mind your mum,' said Jason, eating the second last cheese roll.

'No deal,' I told him, handing over the last cheese roll to its predetermined fate. 'Your Constables Kane and Reagan are gone. My mum is staying.'

'Fair enough,' he conceded, and we closed the shop.

Jason blended his pumpkin soup with a grating of nutmeg and it went into the big fridge. Soup is always better the day after it is made. He started mopping the bakery and I saw Goss out, locked the shop, and went upstairs to my own apartment, escorted by Horatio, who was not impressed with the excitements of the day. He is a cat of rigid values and requires harmony in his surroundings. Scenes ruffle his whiskers.

In pursuit of which I made a firm decision to leave seeing Starshine to the evening. Then I wallowed in a very foamy lush bath, dressed in my lovely blue robe made out of double quilted polar fleece, loaded the drinks into my esky, lifted Horatio, and ascended to the roof garden. This is a small piece of paradise on top of our building. It is tended by Trudi, who is Dutch. She also makes sure that the elevator works, that there are functioning globes in all the lights, that no one gets in without a key and that the garden does not send too many tendrils down the stairs in its attempts to take over the whole building. She was outside in the cold wind, planting tulips which had been in her fridge for six weeks. They would reward this care with brilliant blooms in spring, she said.

With her was a small orange cat, digging industriously. Horatio rose to his paws to greet Lucifer, Cat Most Likely To Be Found In Trouble. Until Trudi had given him an outlet for his bound-less energy, Meroe and I had feared for Lucifer's stock of lives, which had been going down rapidly. Now he works off his energy accompanying Trudi on her rounds and occasionally engaging in a brisk exchange of views with Mrs. Pemberthy's rotten little doggie, Traddles. So far the score is Lucifer sixteen, Traddles nil. When Lucifer gets bigger he will be able to beat Traddles with a brick tied to his collar. I look forward to the day.

Having greeted Horatio, Lucifer went on with his digging. Trudi sat back on her heels. The wind had whipped her cheeks pink above her blue jumper and pummelled her short white hair into punk spikes. I offered her a drink.

'I'm nearly finished,' she said, trying to find a clean bit of arm to wipe her forehead on. 'You go into the temple.'

The temple is probably the only glass-walled all-weather marble-columned Temple of Ceres, complete with statue of the mother goddess bearing a sheaf of corn, in the world. It is warm because the architect set pipes in the floor to circulate waste heat from the building, as in a Roman hypocaust. The builder may have been a tad eccentric, but he built very solidly. Thus the temple is a splendid place to sit and drink a well earned gin and tonic whatever the weather outside.

I sipped my drink and closed my eyes. It had been an awful day but, for me, it was now over. The shop was shut, the day's trading safely banked by Goss and the doors secured. The Mouse Police were on patrol, or more likely reposing on their flour sacks until night came and the vermin crept out from their holes. Horatio perched on the arm of my marble chair, watching the wind tear at the branches of Trudi's linden tree. He likes winter. He loves warmth; any sort, he is not fussy, from air blowers to the full blown actual flames in a fireplace. To this he sits so close that last year he melted his whiskers on one side and had to allow a metre's clearance on the left until they grew again. I like winter too. People buy more bread than in summer, because somehow they instinctively know they need more food to keep warm. It is not pleasant to make bread when it is hot outside, because the bakery air conditioners can only do so much, and the temperature only goes down from 'inferno' to 'possible to survive'. Winter is the season for baking.

Trudi cradled her last bulb in her hand, whispered to it, socketed it gently into the ground, covered it and tamped it down. Then she stood, stretched her back, and led Lucifer into the temple, pausing to wipe his paws with a duster as she scraped her own boots. Lucifer was attached to a harness, but seemed to have adapted to it. He clawed his way onto Trudi's shoulder and sat there as smugly as if he had just eaten the parrot.

'Ah!' she said. 'Warm in here!' I passed her the bottle. Trudi doesn't like foreign materials in her gin. She took a strengthening gulp.

'How does your garden grow?' I asked.

'Good, good. Settled down, snuggled,' she said. 'Now until spring nothing much, which is good, my bones get old. Then we fight the snails for the tulips. I win,' she said.

I believed her. She was perfectly capable of sitting up all night and shooting the invading snails with a BB gun. What had happened to BB guns? They were probably prohibited weapons too, I thought sourly. Those two cops had not improved my day.

'Horatio enjoys this weather,' I said idly.

'He likes the heat. Maybe he remembers Africa. Luce, he likes any weather, eh, Luce?' Lucifer flicked an ear and ran his hard little head under Trudi's chin. 'We go and fix the plumbing in Arachne next,' she promised him. Lucifer gave a brief purr. As long as it was dangerous and preferably wet, he would love it.

'What's wrong with it?'

'She was dyeing in the bath,' Trudi explained.

'What?' I was startled.

'Dyeing. Cloth. Too much fluff. Clogged the drain.'

'Oh, right, dyeing. I see. What do you make of Ms. Webb, Trudi?'

'What Meroe said. I can't remember the word. She's a nice woman, kind. Likes to make things for people. Likes to teach. But she trips, drops things, breaks things. She hits table corners with her hip. If a plate is next to the edge, it falls. Meroe said…'

'She's a klutz,' said a dark brown voice. My very own Daniel, putting in a word. Trudi nodded briskly.

'Klutz, that was it. So many words. Come on, Luce, we go find the unclogger,' said Trudi. She smiled at Daniel and departed, Lucifer clinging tight to her shoulder with his ears forward.

'Have a drink,' I said, emerging from a comforting embrace. Daniel smelt of spices and his own scent, infinitely dear and infinitely comforting. 'I will a tale unfold which will make Horatio's whiskers spit sparks. But first, how are you?'

'Fine. Underslept. But I got the thief and the girl who was accused has been exonerated. It was a manager, I might have known. Unreliable, the middle class in middle age.'

'Thank you very much,' I said, pouring gin.

'Ketschele,' he chuckled, 'you're too young to be middle aged and far too independent to be middle class. But you're worried. What's been happening? In such a short time, too! I only saw you at seven.'

'A lot can happen between seven and three,' I said. I took a deep breath and told him all of it. He frowned over the names of the officers who had arrested Jason.

'They're known for harassing the street kids,' he told me. 'Jason was lucky that you stood up for him so fiercely.'

'Luck didn't enter into it,' I said. 'Everything I said was perfectly true.'

'That ought to have rarity value,' he commented. 'And your mother—mothers are a problem.'

'You said it,' I agreed. 'Where is yours?'

'In Israel.'

'Lucky you.' I was feeling mistreated by fate.

'You know what the real problem is, don't you, ketschele? She's come here for your help. You'll have to give it or—to put it bluntly—she won't go home.'

'Oh, Daniel.' I put down the glass and leaned into his embrace. 'Surely...' He held me gently as I worked it out. He was, of course, right. 'So what do we do?' I asked bleakly.

'We have another drink,' he said, kissing me. 'Then we go and find Sunlight.'

The man who was not yet a murderer went into the room and closed the door against the hated voice. He put both hands over his ears to shut it out.

Chapter Three

It looked like I was going to have to interview Starshine. Well, nothing to be gained by putting it off any longer. I wasn't going to take Daniel with me—why expose him to insult? But he insisted.

'I'm going to have to do a lot of this investigation,' he told me gravely. 'You've got a business to run. Bread to bake. Therefore I need to have the news straight from the shoulder.'

'It isn't her shoulder I'm worried about,' I said. 'It's her tongue.'

'She isn't my mother,' he replied. 'I don't mind what she says about me.'

'But you won't like what she says about me,' I said. Even the frightful James, who had exploited me rotten in our far too long marriage, had taken offence at some of the things of which my biological parent had accused me.

Daniel sighed. 'Come along,' he said. 'Perhaps she won't be so poisonous if she is worried about her missing husband.'

'You're such an optimist,' I said. But I gathered up my possessions and Horatio and went down to my apartment, put on a respectable pair of trousers and a hand-knitted jumper which had been too big for Meroe. Daniel had a notebook and pen and a small tape recorder. We ascended, unspeaking, to confront Starshine in her mourning.

I hadn't got to know Therese Webb, really. All I knew about her was that she made tweed, liked hard crusted bread and preferred chocolate muffins to any other. And that she was polite to shop assistants but noticed when Kylie gave her the wrong change, something she is prone to do after a hard night on the sauce or periods of prolonged starvation. When she answered the door of Arachne, which had a large frieze depicting the Goddess Juno turning the young woman into a spider, she looked motherly and cheerful.

'Corinna! Come in! I've just persuaded Jacqui to eat some lunch. I'm sure she'll be all the better for telling you about what's worrying her,' she said. I doubted it.

I was ushered inside, Daniel following. The layout of all the apartments was identical. I knew that at the end of the narrow hall was the parlour. There sat Starshine like a heap of old garments, but before her on the polished wooden table were a cup and a plate, and the plate had not only crumbs but apple cores. This meant that she had eaten fruit which had not fallen helpless from the tree and eaten bread which might even have been mine. With yeast in it. And—did I detect the scent of cheese? Any sign that the rigid boundaries were breaking down was welcome. Inside the strictures of her code, Starshine was as armoured as a fifteenth-century knight. And as helpless, if she fell off her steed.

Daniel sat down at the table as Starshine took a breath and directed her gaze at me. It was almost as diamond-hard as it had been in her prime. But the face around it seemed to have fallen away. Long creases almost hid her mouth and eyes. Her hair was still long but it was streaked with grey and white strands and hadn't been combed in a while. Her fingernails were filthy and she smelt unwashed.

'Hello,' I said. 'Let's talk about Sunlight, and where he might have gone. This is Daniel Cohen. He's a private detective. He's going to help me.'

'Why would he help *you?*' grated Star, the emphasis on 'you' meaning 'such a valueless thing as you'.

'Because he loves me,' I told her. That set her back on her metaphorical heels and I hurried along before she could recover and start telling Daniel why he really couldn't love someone like me.

'When did he leave, Star?'

'Time,' she said, making a broad gesture, 'is immaterial.'

'No it isn't, Jacqui,' put in Therese Webb. 'You can manage it. You must have some method of telling what day it is, or what phase of the moon it is,' she added. 'You were always so interested in the moon.'

'Third day past full.' Star knew her phases all right.

I could check with Meroe.

'Where is the moon now?' asked Daniel gently.

'Two days past full,' Star answered.

'He's been gone nearly a month and you only started looking for him now?'

I observed: 'But you were so close!'

'Once,' she said gloomily. 'Once we were as close as the fruit and its stone. But since I went to the crone he has been restless. He does not desire female flesh beyond its climacteric. He yearns after young women. There are none in the collective who would accept him.'

There couldn't have been many women in the collective under fifty, anyway. Not many young women wanted to abandon *Australian Idol* and Long Island Iced Teas and hot pink hi-top sneakers in favour of dead vegetable stew, undiluted weather and mud. If you couldn't take a mobile phone and an iPod to it, I'm sure that Kylie and Goss wouldn't go. I swallowed. The thought of my own biological parent searching the city for young women was strangely unappetising. On the other hand his chances of success had to be very limited. The last time I had seen Sunlight he was growing bald, growing grey, a bit stooped, with two missing teeth. Not attractive at all.

'So you believe that he came to the city to seek for…er…' Daniel searched for a word.

'Yes, young man, I believe that "er" is what he was after,' said Star, giving Daniel her full attention for the first time. 'So you are Corinna's lover?'

'I have that honour,' said Daniel.

'And I suppose that you too are a carrion eater, a drinker of corpse broth, inflated with yeast and poisoned with alcohol, salt and sugar?' she asked in a rising tone.

'All of those things,' said Daniel equably. 'When did you begin to think that something was wrong about your husband's absence?'

'It was all wrong,' she snapped. 'He said he would be away for a week. I gave him his week. I gave him more, in case he had found some young flesh who could tolerate him once his money ran out. But after three weeks, I knew something was wrong. He had not called, he had not written.'

'So, no contact at all?' Daniel made a note.

'Someone called,' admitted Star. 'After three weeks. A man. Said that Sunlight wanted to tell me that he could not come back.'

'And that was all?'

'That was all. Not his own voice, a stranger, calling to say that Sunlight could not come back. No reason. No explanation. Just that he could not come back. So I packed my things and I came here. To find you, Corinna. To make you find your father.'

'Do you remember anything about the call? Were there pips? Was it long distance?' asked Daniel. Star shook her head violently and tried to run her dirty fingers through her dirty hair. They stuck and she pulled roughly, tearing at her scalp. Therese Webb came to her side and held her hands as she gently untangled them from the strands.

'I don't remember,' Star wailed.

'And how much money did he have when he left?'

'About three thousand dollars. We never spent much,' said Star indifferently.

'And where would he go, in the city? Where would he stay?' urged Daniel.

'We used to stay at the YMCA,' she said. 'Corinna wouldn't have us in her house,' and then she broke down completely, weeping like a child, nose running freely, tears spurting from her eyes. Therese made pushing gestures and we let ourselves out into the nice quiet hallway and then out of the flat. It wasn't until we were in the lift that either of us spoke.

'Phew,' commented Daniel.

'I should have asked her for a picture of him—oh, hang on, I've got one,' I said. The relief at not having to go back into that room full of anger and tears was considerable. 'It's a passport photo,' I added. 'But we can blow it up on the computer. They went to a conference on natural magic once. In New Guinea. Not a success, apparently.'

'Because?'

'The shamans were all male,' I said. 'No one really appreciates the Goddess-like women who have their own legal rights. Thank you for coming with me,' I added, kissing Daniel.

'It was instructive,' he said. 'Now, let's find that photo and wander down to the YMCA. Which has some advantages. One is that the Victoria Market is nearby. The other is that I can buy you a drink in the Stork Hotel, a charming hostelry unspoiled by success. By then we will probably need one,' he added.

'Deal,' I said. I was feeling wobbly. From being bigger than me and a creature in damn big with the devil, my mother had shrunk and become almost...pitiable? I thrust the thought sternly aside. That woman did not deserve pity.

After the usual hand to modem combat with the printer, the hard drive, the thingy and the widget, the printer made passable copies of a balding, unsmiling man who had the honour of being my progenitor. The day had brightened as much as it was going to, just before the sun prepared to leave. This is a Melbourne weather custom and never fails to annoy both inhabitants and visitors. Melbourne is the only city I know of where you must, at all times and in all seasons, carry an umbrella and a pair of sunglasses. A full change of clothes, a lot of coins to buy tram tickets, sunscreen, a snakebite kit and a charm to repel beggars are also useful. No, I exaggerate. You don't often need a snakebite kit.

'Bad news,' said Daniel, as if he had suddenly remembered something. I bumped into him, never an unpleasant feeling.

'What?'

'Monday. The market won't be open.'

'Drat, you're right. Never mind. Young Men's Christian Association it is. Pity neither of us qualifies. I'm not a young man and you're not a Christian.'

'They're tolerant,' he answered, and took my hand.

I am willing to walk anywhere if I am holding Daniel's hand so a mere trot down Elizabeth Street to the Y was an unexpected treat, considering what the day had delivered so far. We passed the motorcycles which congregate there and the strong people who rode them, me appreciating the beards as I went. There are some fearsome beards to be found among bikies. I always deal very politely with anyone who has long hair and a speckled white-red-grey beard, on the well-tried principle that getting my head kicked in is bad for business. Then we were up into the far end of the city, which is full of backpackers, people speaking a lot of interesting languages, and the YMCA. A very superior building, with an expensive souvenir shop and a curved and polished reception desk. I wondered how Daniel was going to approach this. Was there a special set of code words? Was he going to have to bribe someone?

The clerk was a puffy, spotty youth, no good advertisement for the health-giving properties of the spa and pool advertised on the wall above him. He looked like a pig who had just been told that he should put an apple in his mouth, lie down on a baking tray, and not make any long-range plans or start any long books.

Daniel walked up to the desk and said, 'Hi, Nige,' to the clerk and the clerk said, 'Hi, Daniel,' and his whole face lit up. Who would have thought that sullen porcine face could smile like that? He didn't look any less like a pig, but he looked like a very happy pig, a piggy to whom endless carrots and mash have been vouchsafed. I have always had a soft spot for pigs. Daniel laid down the photograph.

'Seen him?'

'You know,' said the boy, 'I reckon I have. I reckon so.'

'Staying here?'

'You know I can't tell you that,' whined Nige. He shot a glance at a woman with a thick blonde plait who was peacefully entering a column of figures into a database. She was not looking at the desk. Supervisor, I thought. I moved so that I was blocking her view of the good little piggy at the desk.

'Name of Chapman,' said Daniel persuasively. 'I know he was here, Nige, I just want to know when.'

'You'll get me into trouble,' warned Nige, flicking fingers over the computer terminal at the desk. What happened to the good old days of a nice big leather-bound book which anyone could read if they distracted the clerk?

'No, Nige, I get you out of trouble,' said Daniel jovially. That was an interesting comment. Nige flushed as red as a sunburnt Blandings White and found the entry. 'In on the second, out again the next night,' said Nige. 'Says here, asked to leave. Paid cash.'

'Who asked him to leave?' Daniel enquired. Nige nodded towards the woman with the plait and I moved over to converse with her.

She was as thin as a lath, as Grandma Chapman would have said. Certainly, I'd seen fatter laths. This might be a problem. Some thin women react to me as I once reacted to standing on a slug with a bare foot—a sort of revolted, retching, amazed disgust. It's very hurtful. I once had to have an X-ray in a clinic, and the attendant who dragged me around on the glass plate handled me as if I was half a ton of decayed elephant flesh. The blonde woman's hair was the only rounded thing about her. Her fingers were like claws, her collarbones contained not just salt cellars but coal buckets, and her cheeks were hollow, as though she had no teeth. On her bony wrist was a green rubber band. This she snapped incessantly, the elastic slapping against her reddened skin.

I took a breath. 'Hello,' I said as pleasantly as I could, holding up the picture. 'This is my father, who has…psychiatric problems. He's gone missing and I'm worried about him. I know he stayed here on the second, and someone threw him out the next day. Can you tell me why, perhaps?'

Bethany—according to the name tag on her nonexistent bosom—was a brave person. Although I stood there representing everything of which she was most afraid, she answered politely, though she never looked directly at me.

'Have you some ID?' she asked.

I handed over my driver's licence. She winced a bit at the picture on it. Then she twiddled a few keys on her computer.

'It just says *inappropriate behaviour*,' she said. 'I don't know what sort. Sorry.'

'Maybe someone made a complaint?' I suggested. Inappropriate behaviour was all too likely from someone who had spent the last thirty years in a mud-brick slum.

Bethany tapped again. 'Yes,' she said. She paused, trying to spare my feelings, which was nice of her but not helpful. My feelings weren't involved. 'She wasn't hurt, you understand, just a bit shocked, and really I think the only reason she reported it was in case he did it again to a younger girl.'

'What did he do?' I asked, resigned to some embarrassing attempt to pick up that 'young flesh' my mother spoke of so scathingly.

'Look, I really can't go into it,' said Bethany, when another voice cut in loudly: 'But I can, so what about it? Is the old deadbeat yours?'

'Yes,' I sighed. 'Who are you?'

'Allie. From California,' said the young woman.

She shone with health. Her hair was as glossy as a chestnut horse's coat, her skin was lightly tanned and she stood a good two metres high, a lot of it long, smooth, muscular leg. Most of which was revealed in her bicycle shorts.

'Come and let me buy you a drink,' I offered. 'That old deadbeat is my father and I'm looking for him.'

'Better you than me. Just wait until I change and I'll meet you back here, okay?' she said, eyes widening as she took in Daniel.

She whisked away and I smiled my thanks at Bethany, who went back to her computer, never once having looked me in the eye. Nige grinned at Daniel and I saw his trotter close over a ten dollar note which had miraculously appeared on the polished desk.

'It all goes on expenses,' he said.

'But no one's paying us for this,' I protested.

The crowd in the YMCA ebbed and flowed. Chinese students chattered past, carrying bags from McDonald's. Australians belted up the stairs bearing cartons of sushi and tempura. I heard a fascinating babble of languages—Greek, Arabic, Japanese, even French. Daniel was drawn into a sharp discourse in a harsh language, all consonants—must have been Hebrew—by four tall olive-skinned boys with number one haircuts, flourishing maps. They were accompanied by four tall, olive-skinned girls, stalwart and very pretty with their glistening black curls. The Israelis were going to St. Kilda and I idly wondered about the fate of anyone who decided that those girls were fair game...

Then Allie was back in a bright purple tracksuit and hot pink trainers. I had seen their kind before.

'Oh, they're Fair Trade hi-tops,' I commented. 'Goss just bought a pair. Are they comfortable?'

'I guess. It makes me feel better knowing that I'm not walking around in something which some little kid has gone blind making,' she told me. 'Are we going to take Mr. Wonderful?'

'As soon as he explains the tram system,' I said. Daniel handed back the map, farewelled his compatriots, and we went out of the Y.

'So that creep is your papa, eh?' Allie asked me as we crossed the road to the Stork. 'Bad luck.'

'I have always thought so,' I said, wondering a little at the candour of Americans. This was the sort of fresh faced, innocent plain speaking that started wars.

Daniel took over. 'Come along, ladies, there will be a fire,' he said, shoving open a recalcitrant door and letting out a scent of beer, cooking and wood smoke. I have always liked the Stork. The food is restaurant class and the wine list is extensive, but it is still basically a comfortable pub where anyone is welcome, even if he or she is wearing work clothes. Indeed, occupying the big table in the saloon bar was a gang of Maori women in their roadwork boots, looking amazingly sexy in their blue singlets and dungarees. They were drinking beer as though the six o'clock swill was still a reality, and picking bits of concrete debris out of each other's hair. I'd heard them working. Male road crews are quiet. The Maori women talk all the time, in a high shriek with frequent laughter, as they tunnel their way down gutters or excavate for pipes. Their comments on passing men, however, cannot be quoted in any reputable newspaper, which was, I suppose, why no one but me had noticed them.

Allie looked a bit askance at all this rampant femaleness but settled down near the fire and accepted a glass of Australian red wine, which was nice of her considering that California made good red wine of its own. I had a glass of Marlborough Sound sauvignon blanc, wine of the gods. Daniel had mineral water.

'Your papa is creepy,' said Allie.

'What did he do to you?' I asked. 'I can only apologise in advance.'

'It was weird,' she said. 'I was in the spa and it's a public spa, all right, so when he came to sit in it I didn't pay any attention. Then he started sort of sliding closer to me, you know, creeping up? And then when he was right next to me and I was about to move away, he put his hand on my leg and said, "We could be cosmic together," and when I said, "Get your hand off my leg," he said, "You're groovy, California girl," and then I got up and got out of the spa. He didn't grab for me or try to follow me. He didn't say anything else either, just looked real sad. I wouldn't have complained but he might have tried it on someone who'd be real scared. I mean, he doesn't look...'

'What does he look like?' I asked.

She sipped and thought about it. 'A deadbeat. A street person. Long grey hair and beard. Clean, though. Just...not sane.'

'I'm so sorry,' I apologised again.

'Did you get any idea of where he was going?' asked Daniel.

Allie shook her head and her chestnut hair gleamed like a shampoo commercial.

'No, but he might have stayed around here. Sorry I couldn't help more,' she said, getting up from her low seat with the grace of a heron.

'I hope this hasn't turned you off Australia,' I said.

'Got good wine, fantastic boys, good weather, terrific forests,' she said, grinning a grin which showed that absolutely every tooth in her head was buffed to the blinding whiteness of new snow. 'One creep isn't going to kill that. After all, my home town has a lot of creeps of its very own.'

'I've always meant to go to California,' mused Daniel.

Allie grinned again. 'Come in September,' she told him, pressing a card into his hand. 'Or October, for Halloween. Summer's cold and damp. Thanks for the drink. Hope you find the parent.'

Then she was gone. The door swung back with a thump. Brightness had been removed from the room. The Maori women called for more beer. The Stork settled back into being a comfortable, slightly pre-loved, pub. I liked it better that way. I was more than slightly pre-loved myself.

'Phew,' said Daniel, examining the card. 'You know that young woman is a plant biologist?' he went on, showing it to me. 'University of Southern California. Worst case of aggressive galloping health I have ever seen. Well, your dad's lucky she didn't get annoyed and belt him one, in which case he would probably still be lying stunned at the bottom of the spa.'

'And thus easy to find and no longer a problem,' I replied hard-heartedly. 'Did you hear what he said to her, Daniel? This is going to be so embarrassing. This is going to be like following Austin Powers around the town.'

Daniel laughed. People were coming into the pub from a hockey match, with sticks and shorts, screaming for warming beverages. I stared into my empty glass. Groovy. Cosmic. California girl. Lord have mercy.

'Cheer up,' said Daniel. 'Have another glass of wine. Let's get some dinner here. They do wonderful lamb shanks with maple syrup and pumpkin. Then a nice bracing walk back to your apartment, feed Horatio. Perhaps you might like…' He leaned over and whispered in my ear. His offer was so exciting that I blushed. The Maori women were giving me a thumbs-up and frankly lecherous comments about Daniel were being exchanged. I didn't begrudge them it as I went into the bistro for a delicious dinner and more wine. After all, I was the one going home to be kissed all over.

Chapter Four

Morning announced itself with a shattering alarm, followed closely by the clock hitting the floor as my flailing hand batted at it. Horatio doesn't like alarm clocks either, especially when he has chosen as his place of repose the bedside table. (With a whole soft warm bed to sleep in, I know, but who can fathom cats? They are unfathomable.) His abrupt leap in response to the alarm spilt my glass of water, and I rose quickly to mop it up before it fused the radio. I really ought to get used to a bottle of water. A plastic bottle, with a screw top. Mornings! Aargh! And no Daniel, who had faded back to his own apartment after, as promised, kissing me all over. Every finger. Every toe. Every inch of skin. And a few other attentions not relevant here.

Coffee. Daniel had left the coffee maker ready for boiling water. I boiled water. I poured. Then I soaped and rinsed myself, dressed in my trackies, brushed my teeth and reflected that no matter how I cleaned the toofy-pegs, they would never be California White. People there must be some sort of subspecies. *Homo Californiensis.* Perfectly good teeth, mine, but not white as snow. Horatio completed the grumpy, slapdash, all-over wash of the cat who has been surprised into an uncool action. He recovered his poise and gave his morning milk the devout attention it deserved. I heated some slightly failed muffins (even Jason makes mistakes sometimes) and decided that today I would complete the baking before I even began to think about where to look next for my father. And drank more coffee.

Jason was sorting orders when I came into the bakery. He was laying out the papers, fingermarking each one with what might have been blood but was probably—jam? He didn't seem to be wounded at all.

'Fruit bread,' he said to me. 'And that rye and caraway for the vampire café . Otherwise just the usual stuff. I thought I might make choccy muffins.'

'Good,' I commented, pouring out kitty dins for the Mouse Police and counting their night's work—eight mice and three rats. I disposed of them thoughtfully. 'What's that on your hands?'

He looked down and sucked at his fingers.

'The donut bloke at the Vic market was knocking off as I was passing and he sold me the last dozen half price,' said Jason. He had jam on his chin, too. 'I got three left. Want one?'

Considering how starvation is Jason's normal state, that was a kind—indeed, generous—offer. I suppressed my shudder.

'No thanks, bit early for me. All right, if you want to do your chocolate orgasm muffins, I'll start the ordinary bread and then measure for my bara brith. And wash your hands,' I added, though he had already gone to the bathroom to do just that, and put on his baker's overalls.

Silence outside, silence inside, except for the sound of flour sliding silkily from the bag, yeast bubbling gently in its bucket, Jason's cream and chocolate mixture throbbing in the microwave. The Mouse Police had absorbed their breakfast and were idly grooming each other, lying side by side on their flour sacks. If any Food Inspector ever springs me with cats in the bakery I will be in deep trouble, but they are the best hunters, clean and neat, they always bring their prey out of the nooks and crannies because they are rewarded for catching it, and they never do wicked things like walk on just rolled pastry or shed fur in the mixing tubs. Also they are entirely—so to speak—organic, and I don't like poisons anywhere near my stock. I keep remembering a terrible story about one sack of flour, carried carelessly in a truck where a pesticide had leaked, which poisoned a whole

French town. I could not bear it if I injured someone with my bread. Bread has always struck me as close to holy.

'Oh, there's another order,' Jason told me after we had been working seamlessly for more than an hour. 'Nothing serious— health bread made to their own recipe. For some monks.'

'They'll pay through the nose for that,' I said. 'Did you negotiate this, Jason?'

'Yes. You were busy. Anyway, it's made with half lentil flour, and I priced it at the wholesaler's, and added nuisance money before I gave them an amount. It's just a tryout,' he said anxiously. 'We make it for them, they see if they like it.'

My eyebrows rose at the negotiated sum. My Jason struck a very hard bargain indeed. The monks had either been very unworldly or entirely outclassed by my artful dodger. I favoured the second explanation. Jason had survived on the streets at fourteen.

'Jason, dear, that's twice the price of health bread, which has the annoyance factor built in,' I said. 'Well done! But God knows how we are going to get this muck to rise.'

'I thought the same thing,' he said eagerly, terribly relieved that he hadn't made a mistake. 'No sugar, no salt, no leaven, even if there was yeast there's nothing for it to eat.'

'It's what they call "famine bread",' I said. 'Hand me down that baking encyclopaedia and I'll see what the English peasants used to do while you get on with the fruit bread. It's all measured, just make sure that the mixer doesn't stop or all the fruit will belt down to the bottom and ruin our reputation.'

'Yeah, all right. What do you mean, famine bread?' he asked, doing as I requested.

I laid the book flat on the table. 'You can make bread out of almost anything that can be ground into a powder,' I said. 'Except plaster. And sand. You know what a famine is?'

'Like in Ethiopia. No food. Drought. No crops. Everyone dies,' summarised Jason.

'Right. So when your wheat crop fails, you use barley to make bread, or rye, even though it's heavy and reluctant to rise.

You get, in fact, black bread. Or corn, even though it's crumbly because it lacks gluten. What happens if your neighbours steal your corn, your barley gets barley weevil and your rye gets washed out in a flood?'

'Potato,' said Jason, really thinking about it. 'Carrot, parsnip, pumpkin—you can make bread out of all of them.'

'Excellent. Root vegetables. What we need is starch and they have lots of it, and though it's pretty depressing bread, it is bread. And of course there are…'

'Lentils,' he said, enlightened. 'Beans. They got starch too.'

'Exactly. In bad times, according to this, the starving peasantry have made bread out of all sorts of nuts, acorns, root vegetables and sawdust. People really need bread in poor economies. It's the starch that bulks out your stomach and makes you feel—well, full.'

'Okay. We can do the famine bread,' decided Jason. 'I got the lentil flour and I suppose we'll just use baking powder. And can I go get breakfast?' he asked, suddenly very young. 'That talk about famines has made me really, really…'

'Hungry,' I completed. 'Off you go, and bring me back a BLT. Contemplating famines makes me hungry, too.'

He vanished, I opened the alley door, the Mouse Police romped out in search of fish, and the morning came in: damp and chilly. Today we were trying Jason's soup and his herb muffins. It looked like ideal soup weather. I opened the shop door, set the big pot onto the trivet to simmer, found the sour cream and the carefully chopped chives, and counted cups. This was an experiment, so I had just bought a small stove to heat the soup. The main danger was Jason. At all costs we had to keep him away from the shop. One hungry teenager could scoff a whole pot of soup on a famine morning.

I mixed the famine bread. Lentils and rye flour. It would be heavy, almost solid, even though I was doubling the usual amount of baking powder. Mixed with water. No salt or sugar. No taste, either. Perhaps the good brothers were mortifying the flesh. I looked at their order. It was handwritten. There was a smudged letterhead. The name of the group seemed to be—the Discarnate Brotherhood? Frates Discarnarti? I couldn't read it properly. I didn't recognise them but I don't know a lot about the Catholic Church. I knew that the admirable Sister Mary was a Franciscan. Now there was a woman. Small, stout, utterly determined, intelligent, with a heart as big as Phar Lap and a will that could drive a feather through a marble tombstone. It was my turn on the soup van later this week. I always looked forward to it with a mixture of keen anticipation and serious apprehension. It was my taste of squalor and my thanks-offering to the gods who had made me healthy and sane and safe.

On with the leavenless lentil bread, and I set the clock to remind me to take it out. Usually I know when bread is cooked by the scent, but this stuff was only going to smell like old beans until it began to smell like new charcoal. No accounting for tastes, I thought as the kitchen filled with the intoxicating scent of rich Welsh fruit bread, heady with spices.

By the time Jason was back, the rye and caraway bread was in the oven and he was free to compound his chocolate muffins. When they were done I took three of them over to Meroe's shop. I needed kitchen herbs for the herb muffins, and hers were extremely good. I don't know whose organic garden she robs to get them, but she has packages of parsley and thyme with the dew of fairyland still on them.

I got to the Sibyl's Cave just as Meroe was unlocking the door. This morning's mantle was of fine, bright scarlet wool figured with white sheep. Belladonna was taking up her position on the back of Meroe's big chair, on which she has been stropping her claws since early kittenhood. She awarded me a brief purr as I stroked her, then returned grimly to her task.

'Oh, those chocolate muffins,' exclaimed Meroe, packing me a bundle of herbs. I watched carefully to see that I recognised each plant as she laid it down. Meroe also sells magic spell ingredients and I didn't have any customers who needed to be turned into toads at present. Though this could change without notice, of course. 'That boy was a find, Corinna. The Powers That Be were both merciful and on the alert the day he came into your bakery looking for a job. Of course, if you had not been receptive to their influence nothing would have happened.'

'That's me,' I replied carefully. 'Receptive.'

'I have been talking to people in Sunbury,' Meroe said. 'Since their leader left, the coven has been in disarray, with quarrels and much disharmony. In which I am afraid your mother had some part.'

'No kidding,' I said, sitting down and cradling my herbs. Belladonna extended a thoughtful paw and combed her claws through my hair. She didn't touch my scalp but it made me shiver. Or something did.

'Star seems to have favoured a very strict, very punitive form of vegetarianism,' said Meroe. 'She had followers, but not enough to put her in charge of the coven. According to my friends, she won't be welcome back if she tries to return alone.'

'But she's been there all her life,' I protested. 'She hasn't got anywhere else to go!' I swallowed down my fear that this meant she would stay near me.

'Nevertheless,' said Meroe, patting me, 'she lives in a collective and the majority opinion rules. While Sunlight was with her, she was protected from expulsion, as everyone liked him. Also, he acted as a rein on her extravagant temper. Now he is gone, she is going to be on her own.'

'Then we have to find him. We really have to find him.'

I would have jumped to my feet but Bella still had her claws in my hair. Meroe gently detached the black cat.

'I think that Therese will take care of Star for a while, at least,' she told me. 'She doesn't seem to even notice how rude Star is to her and Therese has managed to modify some of her very rigid standards. Come up this afternoon and you'll see what I mean. I'll be there. I'm teaching Therese to embroider in the Hungarian manner. It's very pretty.'

'I'll think about it,' I lied. 'Now I'd better get Jason his herbs. Come over later and there will be pumpkin soup,' I offered.

Meroe smiled. Bella waved a paw at me. I left the shop, jangling through feng shui crystals and Celtic charms.

I needed to get back to basics. Back, in fact, to bread.

The shop was opened by Kylie, who was wearing a strange little blue bolero called, she told me, a shrug. It failed to cover any salient features but that has never bothered Kylie or Goss, who live and die by Fashion. At least she had warm armpits.

The soup was bubbling, the herb muffins came out of the oven an incitement to gluttony, and the shop was suddenly full of people. Horatio sat by the cash register and received his public graciously.

We sold out of pumpkin soup by ten thirty. I yelled into the bakery to tell Jason that his experiment was a success and to go out later and buy some more pumpkins—'butternut, repeat after me, Jason'—and he gave a whoop of vindicated pleasure. As the furore died I went to count the loaves into Megan's rickshaw. The lentil bread had come out fairly well. It was a bit grey but not too crumbly. Megan looked at the address.

'I have to sting you extra for this delivery,' she said.

'All factored into the price,' I told her. 'By Jason, with whom you should not play poker any time soon. The Castle, eh. Do I know the house?'

'It's on Studley Park,' she told me. 'Near where I live. One of the big houses that are set back from the road. Been empty for ages. There was some huge argument about it—heritage against developers, as usual—and the owners got pissed off and let it lie empty. Hoping it would fall down on its own, I suppose. I did hear that someone had settled there. They aren't allowed to alter it and it must be pretty spooky by now.'

'Well, just hand in the bread and refuse all invitations to look at their etchings,' I advised. 'They're some kind of religious brotherhood. And if they eat this bread for preference, they aren't into fun of any kind.'

'Too true,' she said, and gunned her engine.

The luncheon rush came and went. The loaves were all dispatched, the coffee was poured, and I grabbed the last chocolate muffin and ate it myself. It was, as usual, wonderful. Kylie minded the shop while Jason went to get his butternut pumpkins and I considered whether we ought to have bought slightly sturdier cups. A good pumpkin soup is a solid thing. And when the customers got sick of pumpkin we would have Scotch broth. And pea and ham, my favourite. All good, solid, stick-to-the-ribs cold weather soups. Which would freeze beautifully so could be made in advance. Not that one needs much skill to make soup. They mainly require assembly and a lot of chopping, and I had a Jason for that.

Life was good. I leaned back in my chair and sipped. Heckle fell asleep on my foot. I closed my eyes. Just for a moment.

Daniel woke me with a kiss, always a nice way to be woken, and I dislodged Heckle as I got to my feet. Heckle is an ex-alley cat. He gave a broken snore and fell asleep again. Jason was back with more pumpkins and the baker's day was getting on for over.

'Butternut,' Jason declared, thumping them onto the big table.

'Great,' I responded. 'Start cutting. You can use a knife on these ones. Get the big pot and scour it clean, Jason, and put the sour cream in the fridge.'

'Yes, Master,' he said blithely. Jason is only cheeky when he's happy.

I loaded the sack for the soup van. Kylie was cashing up and the shutters had already been pulled down over the shop window. I remembered that, other than a chocolate muffin, I had had nothing to eat since the BLT at seven, and here it was nearly three. I had, of course, had two hours' extra slumber, which is not to be sneezed at in these sleep-deprived times. What with George W. Bush and the Federal Government, or Heartless Australian Hegemony, it doesn't seem safe to sleep. Unless you like really bad news on waking…I shook my head and rubbed my eyes. Daniel, I judged, also looked hungry.

'Did you lunch?' I asked him.

'No,' he said. 'I've been doing a little investigating and I didn't have time.'

'Then let's have a late lunch or early dinner of unusual extravagance,' I suggested. Daniel smiled quizzically.

'What are you suggesting?' he asked. 'Tea at the Windsor?'

'No,' I said. 'At Southbank. All of those restaurants are good, and we can have the best ice cream, sorbet or gelati in the world by way of dessert.'

'Where?'

'Limonello,' I replied. Surely he had heard of it? Even Goss and Kylie went down to Limonello for their non fat peach ice cream.

'Need to clean up and get changed,' he said. 'And so, forgive me...'

'...do I,' I agreed. 'Right. Jason, put the soup on to simmer and I'll take care of it when I get home. And here is a small bonus for your good idea, against which I fought until you defeated me.' I gave him fifty dollars and folded his fingers over it.

We had just got Jason a bank account by dint of obtaining a birth certificate and all the other things he needed, like a Medicare card. This had been hard because we couldn't contact his family, Jason absolutely forbade it. But Sister Mary knew a social worker who understood such things and we slid it in through the cracks in the system. The same ones that Jason himself had fallen through in his drug-addicted, desperate past. I no longer feared that giving him money would send him back onto the gear again. Every useful productive bread-making day put Jason further and further from heroin.

He grinned. 'Ace,' he exclaimed. 'I c'n get that CD, and go down to the Games Room and play Nude Twister tonight.'

Of course, everyone to their own...

The tram clanked along the new road, which I still hadn't really got my head around. I had known Melbourne so well for so long that when the river end of it started evolving, my mental map dissolved. I was as lost as a tourist in Sydney trying to work out which side of the Harbour Bridge they were on. I mourned the loss of that wonderful red-brick wall which had shut Victoria Dock off from the world, but I had to admire the palm trees. We descended from the tram.

A small sprint, avoiding Jaguars, through the car park and we were out onto the edge of the river. A fine cool wind was blowing. I had worn my trench coat and was glad of it. The prospect across and along a city river is always fascinating. This one still had cargo sheds on the other side, and boats, and ferries, and people in small craft. And at the foot of all those tall buildings were restaurants selling every cuisine, except possibly Martian. Delicious scents wafted out from them as we walked along.

'What's your pleasure, madame?' asked Daniel. 'Chinese? Indian? Italian?'

'Can't decide,' I said, mouth watering. 'What do you fancy?'

'This is one of those problems which arise in relationships,' he said seriously. 'Do you really mean, decide for me, or do you mean, pick something and I'll see what I think, or do you mean, have you a serious preference which I'll go along with because I love you even though that's not what I want?'

'Hmm,' I said, sorting through the possibilities. 'All right. When I was with James and he said, you choose, he meant, let's see how little you know about food so I can spend a few hours criticising you later. So when I say "what do you fancy?" I mean, state a preference and I'll see how I feel about it. I won't go along with it if I don't like it. Only teenage girls do that and it always breeds bitterness.'

He smiled his beautiful smile. 'You are very wise. Agreed. I will mean the same. If I have an absolute yearning for one or another I will say so. As it happens, I don't have a serious desire, but I do have a leaning towards steak.'

'One of my carnivorous days as well,' I said. 'Steak it is.'

The Italian restaurant Renzo's did a wonderful rare steak with mixed vegetables. We drank red wine with it. The waiter lingered, brushing off crumbs, picking up unnecessary cutlery and removing glasses. He was a plump young man, very attractive, with curly black hair and soulful eyes like a cow. Round his right wrist he had a yellow rubber band which he kept snapping at every unoccupied moment. Some kind of new fashion, apparently. I recalled that the Raskols in New Guinea used to wear rubber bands made from car tyres—who told me that? That's the trouble with arcane information. Bits of it stick in the mind like burrs in a sock, memorable beyond any use they might have had.

We finished the meal and the young man cleared away. But I could have sworn that, as soon as he was out of sight of the door and the kitchen, in the little alcove where the side wall abutted, I saw him grab a handful of leftover bread, stuff the trimmings from the steak inside it and swallow it whole. It was a furtive, frantic bolting movement, more like a stray dog's than a man's. It jolted me, but it was over before I could draw Daniel's attention to it. And it wasn't as though it was important.

Time for a heavenly gelato from Naevio, the gelati master. There were so many ice creams to choose from and they all looked so gorgeous that Limonello ought to provide a discreet gutter for their patrons to drool into. Cherry Ripple. Caramel and Honeycomb. Chocolate. Pistachio. I finally chose lemon and orange, and Daniel chose coconut and coffee. We licked them comfortably, strolling down the riverside, admiring the strange sculptures and wondering at how many people were loose on a working day. And why all those children weren't at school. Not that I cared. They weren't my children.

It was still early when we came sailing back to Hebe, full and a little soporific.

Therese Webb immediately rang the bell. She must have been watching for us to come in. I was not pleased to see her. But I opened the door. At least she wasn't my mother.

'Tea, coffee or a glass of wine?' I asked.

'A glass of wine,' she said, sitting down heavily next to Horatio.

I poured her a glass of chateau collapseau and had one for myself. Daniel sat behind me on the sofa and I leaned back into his embrace.

'How do you know my mother?' I asked. I don't for a moment believe that curiosity slew any felines.

'I knew her at school, where she was very nice to me,' said Therese. She shrugged her tweed cloak off her shoulders. A lot of it fell on Horatio. He clawed his way to the surface, unnoticed by the weaver, and then stretched out on the fabric luxuriously. 'We went to a very tough girls' school, and I was bullied badly. You know?'

I nodded. I knew. I still couldn't contemplate an upright locker with equanimity, due to having been repeatedly stuffed into one by Julie, our resident bully.

'No one bullied Jacqui!' mused Therese proudly. 'She told them where to get off! And she took me under her wing, for some reason. I've never known why. But she was always kind.'

Not my experience of her. 'So you kept in contact after she left school?' I said.

'Oh yes. She went to Nimbin, of course, met your father—they were so sweet together, like Babes in the Wood—and then they came back here to start a collective. Very strict. I couldn't go and visit her there, my health wouldn't permit me to sleep on the ground, but she sometimes came to visit me. I was always pleased to help her out with a little money or a place to sleep. Then I inherited quite a lot of money and decided that I'd leave my shop to be run by a manager and take some rest. My heart isn't very reliable. I don't know how long I'll live. So I bought Arachne in this delightful building. I still weave, of course, but I really just wanted a rest.'

'And then you got Jacqui back on your hands,' I said ruefully.

Therese twinkled. 'Well, actually, dear, I've always been busy. I've worked every day all my life. I was getting very bored and fancying myself sick when Jacqui turned up, and now I feel fine. I need to have something to do, that's clear.'

'Oh,' I said. 'And you don't mind the way she abuses you?'

'She's heartbroken about your father,' said Therese gently. 'She doesn't know what she's saying.' She sipped her wine. 'Anyway, I came down to ask if you've had any success.'

'He was at the YMCA,' I told her. 'But he was banished for trying to pick up a Californian girl.'

'He went to the backpackers' hostel across the road,' said Daniel. 'He stayed there for a week. Then he was expelled by the management for peeking into the ladies' bathroom. He paid cash. He didn't go to another backpackers' anywhere near there. I've canvassed that end of town. I'll ask more questions late tonight, when the night people emerge from the shadows. They might have seen him.'

'Oh well, at least he isn't dead,' said Therese. 'That nice policewoman searched the unknown bodies and he wasn't there, or in the hospitals.'

'Which nice policewoman?'

'Oh, didn't I mention it? I persuaded Jacqui to report her husband missing. They say there isn't much they can do, but they at least checked that he wasn't dead. Here's the young woman's card. You could call her if you like.'

'I will,' said Daniel, and wrote down the details. Therese took her leave.

'And I have to go and do the Nerds Inc accounts,' I sighed.

'Right now?' he asked, pained.

'I promised,' I said.

The problem with favours is that they are often more onerous than anything for which one would be paid, and this particularly applied to the accounts of Nerds Inc. I was checking their Business Activity Statement, or BAS for short, as a return favour for them setting up and disentangling my internet connection and talking to the nice boy on the help line. They speak fluent techno, while I barely get by with a few words. The main one of which is 'help!'. It wasn't that they didn't have the best accounting software and the most up-to-date spreadsheets. This doesn't help, as I had told them in exasperation, if you don't enter all the data. They shuffled uncomfortably. Like most extreme nerds, they don't get out much in daylight and they don't meet a lot of mundanes. I was a definitive, even extreme, mundane.

Nerds Inc consists of Taz, who is tall and has scrubby blondish hair and a face that hasn't seen sunlight in years. Rat, named for his long rat tail of hair at the back of his neck, had otherwise close cropped dark hair and is shorter than the other two. And Gully, who is the most presentable and articulate, now sports a reasonable hair cut and, I believe, he actually owns a suit. All had the rolls of fat round the waist which indicated a total lack of exercise and a diet of Twisties, tacos, nachos and their preferred drink, Arctic Death, a vodka and lemon concoction which probably sterilises newts. They are dressed alike in jeans and t-shirts. Someone's mum, I was willing to wager, appeared every week and took home a huge load of washing, returning them nice clean t-shirts on which they could spill more chili sauce. They run a fairly good business, or did. This time I was not getting good news from the figures I could estimate.

'No other way to do this,' I said, 'than that someone sits down and reads out all the receipts, and then someone else reads out all the bills and outgoings. Which will take hours. So someone else will have to make me coffee and give me a bottle of spring water.'

Their shoe box method of record keeping did have this to say for it: all the receipts were there and could be arranged by date. I set Rat to do this while Gully worked on the outgoings and Taz made the coffee.

I was sitting in their office, which was a mess. I had cleared some space for my chair and my feet amongst the piles of games, printouts, old t-shirts and pizza boxes. Though definitely squalid, it wasn't actually fetid, because they have a cleaner who comes in once a week to wash the old coffee cups and remove the uneaten food. She must be a woman of iron nerve and grim purpose. I stirred the mess with one foot and turned up a photograph. There were my three nerds, all dressed up in costume from a variety of sources: from *Babylon 5*, Gully as a Centauri in a bald wig; from *Star Wars* a storm trooper, Rat, grinning; from *Doctor Who*'s Meglos, Taz in a cactus mask. A genuine sci-fi conference experience. I smiled.

That was the last smile for the night. After hours of gruelling work, I had to tell Nerds Inc that unless they got an injection of capital, they were going broke. They nodded. They had guessed things were bad.

'But at least you get a lot of GST back,' I said. 'Put in the return just as I have written it. That ought to tide you over for a month or so. You're getting good money for research,' I added. 'Perhaps you can try for more of that sort of work. Importing so much stuff from the US, you are very vulnerable to fluctuations in exchange rates. Well, goodbye.' I extracted myself from my chair, into which I seemed to have grown. 'Sorry about that, boys.'

And I was sorry, but Daniel was waiting, my mother had arrived, and my father was missing.

Eventually Daniel and I shared a bath and, finally, a bed. It was a good ending to the day, but we still hadn't found my father.

Chapter Five

I woke, I baked, I drank coffee, I baked some more, I finished cooking Jason's soup, I tasted his herb muffins—usual sort of morning. For a Wednesday. For some reason stories about St. Theresa of Avila, my favourite saint, were running around in my head. It is nice to have something to think about when making bread and Saint Theresa falling off her horse into the mud, lying there and shouting up at God, 'If this is how You treat Your friends, it's not surprising You don't have many!' has almost reconciled me to religion several times. Though never quite.

The Professor wandered down for a loaf of pasta douro and a chat about eleven, when all the morning-tea people had gone back to their offices. Professor Monk is seventy-six, a well dressed, charming gentleman who bought into Insula and had Roman furniture made, so that his apartment looks like it was snatched from Pompeii by time machine just before their mountain did the big firework. It has lately been augmented by Nox, a small but imperious black kitten who has Dionysus Monk firmly under her tiny, soot-coloured paw. She is as perfectly black as Belladonna and employs just the same resolute but kindly management of her human. He was idly reading the top invoice in my bundle and gave a short laugh.

'What's funny?'

'Oh, sorry, Corinna. I just deciphered this letterhead. The Frates Discarnati.'

'Oh?'

'And I wondered what on earth the bodiless brothers would want with bread.'

'Bodiless?'

'Yes. The opposite of incarnate. You know—it went into English as Discarnate—no flesh. Unfleshed.'

'Euw,' commented Goss. I agreed with her. I might have said 'Erk' but the sentiment was the same.

'I suppose they mean they are very spiritual,' I ventured. 'Still, if they eat that lentil stuff they don't like the flesh, that's for sure. Never mind. Can I offer you a cup of soup and a muffin?'

'No, much as I would like to indulge, I am lunching with Mrs. Dawson at the University Club. You might consult our resident Sibyl about those unfleshed brothers. I don't like the sound of them,' said the Professor, who collected his loaf and went away.

A good idea but I had troubles of my own. The fleshless ones could wait. Still, it was a strange name. I now recalled why I had been thinking of Saint Theresa of Avila. Her nuns were discalced—shoeless—though definitely not fleshless, and somewhere in the back of my cerebral cortex my mind had been trying to make the connection. It is sometimes a little eerie to discover how much of one's thinking is going on without conscious direction from the person whom I have always thought of as 'me'. Whoever she is.

I wandered into the bakery and found someone standing at the Calico Alley door. He was tall, clothed in black robes, and was in the act of putting the hood back from his face. Two others, in brown, stood behind him. He must have been a solidly fleshed man once, but was now thin and flabby, with drooping wattles of empty flesh under his chin. He was holding one of my famine loaves.

'Well?' I asked. 'You didn't like the bread?'

He was taking deep breaths, I noticed, as though he appreciated the scent of fresh baking which flowed past him, but he said only, 'You made it too well.'

'Too well?' That was not a usual complaint. The Brother's voice was rough, as from a raw throat.

'You included some salt, I believe. A little too much baking powder.'

'And what do you want me to do in future?' His air of restrained menace was getting to me. I broke off a bit of the bread and tasted it. Pah. Dry as ashes. I could not detect any flavour at all except a fugitive taste of carbonised chickpeas.

'Make it worse,' he said.

Then, with a flick of the robes, he and the others were gone. I paused, searching for an appropriate swear word. Nothing occurred. I binned the famine bread. I would not put that into my bag for the Soup Run. Or even the destitute would be complaining.

Daniel came in with news, but it was not good news.

I could tell from the way he walked. A slow plod rather than a fast stride. I knew he had gone to talk to Constable Wellesley, the 'nice policewoman' at Missing Persons.

'Nothing,' he said. 'He was picked up by the police in St. Kilda Road exactly two weeks ago. They thought he might have been drunk or drugged but he was neither.'

'Then why did they pick him up?' I asked, pouring soup into a cup. A china mug, for special patrons. 'It's—and I acknowledge that I ought to put an exemption clause into this statement—a free country.'

'It is,' Daniel conceded. 'But even free men are not allowed to walk along the middle of the road and they are really discouraged from lying down in front of a tram.'

'He lay down in front of a tram,' I said evenly. I was proud of myself. I didn't spill one golden drop of the remarkable Jason's pumpkin soup.

'Repeatedly,' said Daniel, sipping. 'So they picked him up and stuck him in the cells until the Crisis Assessment Team arrived and they said he wasn't mad so they let him go again.'

'To go and lie down in front of another tram?'

'He promised not to do that again.'

'Damn,' I said angrily. 'Couldn't they have taken him to a nice safe loony bin so that we could find him again?'

'They were abolished,' said Daniel, breaking off a piece of herb muffin. 'There's almost nowhere to put someone if the CAT team says they're not dangerous. If I say Previous Government again will you promise not to throw anything?'

'Never did before,' I told him.

'Frying pan,' he pointed out, and I had to concede this.

'But it was only once. And I sort of dropped it, I didn't really throw it.'

The deep brown eyes considered me as he absorbed more soup. Dispassionate eyes, my Daniel's, problem-solver's, social worker's, private detective's eyes, eyes which had seen a lot of prevaricating, most of it more convincing than I was presently being. I gave up.

'Okay. Sometimes I throw things, stress of emotion, it runs in the family. My very own grandpa said that his grandfather called his wife an "argumentatious, pan-flinging female." Any idea where the man went after they let him out of the cells?'

'Last seen wandering vaguely towards the city,' said Daniel. 'That was really wonderful soup. Cheer up, my pan-flinger, it's not all bad news. I got something else. He had to give the arresting officers an address and he did, and I've got it. Interesting thing, though. He had a passport as ID.'

'No driver's licence,' I explained.

'Oh. I was wondering if he was intending to flee the country,' said Daniel.

'Possibly, though I don't know how much money he's got left. Where's the address?'

'Braybrook.'

'Where's Braybrook?'

'Ah, my inner-city darling,' said Daniel indulgently. 'Like a cockney, born within earshot of Bow Bells. The world ends at Docklands. West, to be sure, west away towards Ballarat. But not that far. Want to come and check it out?'

'Will it be disgusting?' I asked.

'Probably.'

'Then I ought to come,' I said.

'A Protestant conscience,' teased Daniel. 'I'll come back at three and get Timbo to pick us up in the car. The inhabitants ought to be getting up about then.'

Suddenly raised female voices impressed themselves on my ears. I knew them. Both of my shop assistants making enough row for a secondary school maths class or a zoo at feeding time.

'Seth!' said Kylie. 'It has to be Seth, you blind?'

'Seth's a nerd, just like Taz, and you didn't even make it with Taz,' sneered Goss. 'It's got to be Ryan. Ryan rules.'

'Ryan likes them messed up, you skanky ho,' screamed Kylie. 'So maybe he is the one after all! Not like my Seth!'

'*Your* Seth?'

'Ladies,' I said meaningfully. They paid no attention to me. Kylie was wearing pink overalls, Gossamer blue, but there the resemblance to good little children ended. They were red faced and shrieking like fishwives. Jason had retreated to a corner of the shop, cut off from escape to the street or the bakery by either a furious girl or the end wall. I raised an eyebrow at him.

'Dunno,' he said, shaking his head. 'They were talking about this TV show and then they just went postal.'

'Daniel?' I asked for a diagnosis from the most streetwise amongst us. 'Drugs?'

'No idea,' he said. 'They remind me of maenads, but I suppose they haven't been drinking. And neither of them even takes E, or so they have assured me.'

'Seth!' shrieked Kylie and swung a clawed hand at her friend. I knew that those talons could open tins and felt that I must intervene. WorkCover would sniff if I asked them to pay for fingernail wounds amongst the shop staff and my premiums were high enough as it was.

'You take Kylie into the bakery,' I said to Daniel. 'I'll keep Goss here. Jason, nick down to Café Delicious and ask Del for two of his banana creams, will you? If we can't get a rise out of them with a banana cream, then we might have to call that

Crisis Assessment Team who said my father wasn't insane. Then tell Meroe I need her at once. Run!'

Jason, freed, ran for his life. I saw him vanish out the door and into a street which so far did not contain a lot of curious customers. I put both arms around Goss and dragged her out of range of Kylie's claws. Daniel lifted Kylie off her feet and carried her, still screaming, into the bakery. I held Goss as tightly as I would a child who'd just had a bad dream and said, 'Calm, Gossamer, calm. Take a nice deep breath now. It's all right.'

She was shaking as though she was very cold and straining against my arms. But baking makes a baker as strong as a wrestler when it comes to underweight teenage girls. I sighted a magazine open on the counter and two names caught my eye. Goss was trying to breathe deeply but was gasping. Her hair was wet with sweat. I leaned her against the counter and read about two actors in a show called *The OC*, which I had never seen. Adam and Ben were their real names. But they played characters called Seth and Ryan. Both good-looking boys, if you like them quiet and brooding. Which, of course, I did. But Kylie and Goss had got into this state over an article in *Girlfriend?* I had seen them disagree before but never like this.

I could feel Gossamer's heart pounding like a drum and see the pulse in her throat. But at least she had stopped screaming. Now she started to cry, which was a good sign, if you call that progress. I sat her down behind the counter and applied a handful of tissues to her eyes, which were running with black tears. She sobbed as though her heart was broken. I really didn't feel I could leave her, though I was wondering what on earth was happening in the bakery. I could hear Daniel's soft, honey-sweet voice murmuring and then Kylie started to cry as well. Poor girls! They sounded like children whose dog had just died and whose whole world was crumbling around them. What had brought this on? Teenage emotions were vehement, of course, but not usually so destructive out of a clear sky.

'Blessed be,' said a voice from the door. My resident sibyl had arrived. 'Jason told me what happened so I have brought some herbs. We shall make a tisane. Meanwhile, we shall take Gossamer into the bakery and Jason can look after the shop. He is coming up the street with two of the Pandamus banana creams, which ought to be useful. Nothing like the shock of sweetness to break a hysterical thread.'

'I'll just see how Daniel is getting on,' I said, and slipped through the bakery door. Kylie was weeping into Daniel's shoulder. He was clasping her lightly.

'Safe to bring Goss in here?' I asked quietly. He shrugged, which is hard to do with a weeping maiden in your arms.

'I suppose,' he said. 'I've never seen anything like this. What were they arguing about?'

'The respective merits of Seth and Ryan,' I said.

'And they are?'

'Really, Daniel, haven't you heard of Seth and Ryan?'

I asked scornfully, and returned in a moment with Goss, who sat in the baker's other chair and wept and wept. She did not react to Kylie, which was good. The kettle was nearly boiling, and Meroe produced a glass teapot and began measuring herbs into it. As the level of weeping did not diminish, she shook fully a handful into the pot and poured boiling water over it. In the shop I heard Jason draw a long breath of relief. Then he slid inside the bakery, stuck the banana creams in the fridge, and removed himself with alacrity from this scene of woe. I would have been glad to do the same. But it was my shop, my bakery, and they were my girls.

Meroe asked me what had happened and I reported it as well as I could.

'Odd,' she remarked. 'Daniel, what about drugs?'

'I've been around the drug scene for a longish while,' he answered, patting Kylie gently between her shoulderblades. 'I've seen speed-fuelled rages and narcanned kids coming out of a death trance to scream with outrage. I've seen the Ice jitters and heard the cocaine raves and the Mogadon mumbles, even met a few bad acid casualties left over from the sixties. But I've never seen anything like this,' he admitted. 'They went from being angry to being sad, and that doesn't usually happen with drugs, even when they wear off. And while neither of them is a genius, I know they know about the risks of E and the party drugs. Meroe?'

'I can think of some herbs which might do this,' she said, her lips pursing in disapproval. 'Some combinations of herbs. They would have to have been taking them for a while,' she added. 'And they are not herbs which I would ordinarily combine.'

'Poison?' I asked, wondering if this was some strange double suicide over Seth and Ryan.

'Of course,' said Meroe. 'All the best poisons are organic. Cyanide. Ricin. From an ordinary garden I could make you a distilled water which would kill a horse.'

'The strongest poison ever known came from Caesar's laurel crown,' murmured Daniel, and Meroe nodded at him as might a teacher to an intelligent pupil.

'Precisely. Laurel water could knock out a hundred horses. This is ready. Do you have honey, Corinna? It will taste fairly foul.'

'I have honey,' I said, producing the jar. 'And how are you going to get them to drink it?'

'Like this,' said Meroe. It was very clever and very touching. She mixed the brew to her liking, then approached Goss and wrapped her in her long shawl so that the girl's head lay on Meroe's shoulder. Then with her little finger dipped in honey she touched Goss' lower lip. The sweetness must have penetrated the crying, because a little red tongue slipped out and licked up the honey. Then gradually Meroe substituted her brew for the honey, and though there was a small grimace it went down like magic. Goss drank the whole cupful and by the time she had finished it, she was no longer crying. Her breathing had eased.

'You will now eat what Corinna gives you,' she told her patient, 'while I attend to your friend.'

I sat down on the table and handed Goss a spoon and a Café Delicious banana cream, a speciality. It was a small pie containing custard, fruit and cream and topped with meringue. I rationed myself to one a week and I knew that they melted in the mouth. I was expecting a struggle with Goss, who dieted even more strenuously than Kylie, but she took the dish and ate the pie in little mouse-like nibbles. Tears, for some reason, pricked my eyes and I looked over to see how Daniel was managing.

Meroe had just finished with Kylie, who had also stopped crying. At last. Daniel released her and fetched the pie, and she, too, ate as biddably as a lamb. She even put the plate down on the floor for Heckle, who had indicated that his diet lacked cream. They both looked as bedraggled as if they had been fighting in a gutter. Goss' hair hung down in strings. Kylie's face was still flushed.

'Now, ladies, we are taking you home to your apartment,' said Meroe evenly. She seldom sounded severe, but when she said that something was going to happen, there was never any sense that it could be evaded. 'You need to sleep. Come along now. Who can stand up?'

Goss managed it, leaning on my shoulder. Kylie collapsed and Daniel carried her.

We got them into the lift and conveyed the two poor little waifs to their apartment and Goss managed to open the door before she fell on the couch. Daniel was excused and returned to help Jason with the real world of bread and deliveries. Meroe and I did a little elementary housework—making two beds, for instance, clearing a path through the underwear and shoes to the said beds, trying to find some food in their kitchen. We were not conspicuously successful. They had a lot of dried soups and so on, all guaranteed 150% fat free (and how much sugar?). They did have real coffee and tea, and a lot of herbal teas in pretty packets featuring dragons and unicorns. And a whole box of hangover remedies. I put on the kettle to make Meroe and me some coffee. There were plenty of cups but the dishes had not been done recently. I loaded the dishwasher and switched it on.

I spent some minutes reassuring Tori, their kitten, who clearly hadn't been fed yet this morning and was sitting on my foot telling me all about it. As an apology, she was about to get a tin of that very expensive cat food which makes a human, on reading the contents, think that a diet of cat food might not be so bad at that. My mouth watered as I dished up Seafood Symphony, with selected prawns and salmon in a lobster bisque aspic. So did Tori's, for she mewed the plaintive mew of a fluffy and charmingly blonde kitten to whom nothing had previously been denied. I put down the plate and found that her water dish was empty. Dry and empty. The girls loved Tori with a passion. How could they leave her thirsty?

I left the kitchen—which was, of course, otherwise clean, being hardly ever used—to find Meroe very gently washing Goss' face with a make-up removing wipe. Goss seemed to be asleep now. Her pulse was good. Her eyes were shut. She murmured a little as Meroe tended her like a mother cat. I did not trust my touch so I allowed Meroe to remove both of those panda-faces while I browsed through the bathroom cabinet. I did not think that my shop assistants had gone mad together just by coincidence. They had taken something. But Daniel didn't think it was drugs. And he didn't recognise the reaction. Was there something new on the street? Or was this something altogether more sinister than just a new recreational drug?

Those girls had more make-up than a theatre company. It was everywhere, stuffed into every corner of the bathroom. I did find some soluble aspirin, some contraceptives, something called bikini line wax, that made me shudder, and a lot of miscellaneous instruments which I did not recognise. Eyelash curlers? Hair crimpers? They looked remarkably like something that the Inquisition might have found useful in extracting confessions from one of Meroe's forebears. Most of them fell clattering into the bath when I opened the towel cupboard. Which contained one towel and more make-up. Lipsticks of every hue from bone white to black, through avocado and berry and sunset and Malibu and desert and tangerine and portulaca and True Red. Foundations enough to build a small Greek temple, eye shadows in little pots, and little boxes, and little palettes, and wands of mascara and eye pencils to supply Ancient Egypt for a dynasty.

And most of it in the bath. I went looking for a plastic shopping bag and stuffed them all in. The girls could have hours of fun sorting it all out and none of it had broken. Fortunately. I had seen the labels and I could not afford to replace this stuff without taking out a mortgage on Earthly Delights. But I had not found anything out of place. Tons of make-up, dried soups, cat food, shoes enough to make the late President Marcos' widow cry with envy—yes, expected. The same went for clothes in various degrees of fashion and disarray, some still in their drycleaner bags. I began to feel like a burglar and wondered how burglars did it. This wasn't my house and I had no right to be here.

'Meroe, I'm feeling like an intruder. Shouldn't we call a doctor for them and get out of here?'

'No,' she said. 'Not yet, at least. We do not know what they have taken—you agree it must have been something, Corinna—and if we call a doctor and they test the girls for some illegal substance, they might easily be charged by the police. And I happen to know that their fathers said it was back home with them if they ever got involved with drugs. They are resting comfortably,' added Meroe.

'We could wait until they wake up,' I suggested.

'I need to find it now,' said Meroe. 'Because if it has other ingredients, we may need to call an ambulance and get them to hospital before liver failure sets in. Actually, there isn't much anyone can do for liver failure. Look for a packet, Corinna, probably of dried herbs, and we must pray to the Goddess that there is no loose white powder in the mix.'

'Loose white powder?' I thought, not liking the sound of this at all. I returned to the kitchen and lay out on the bench all the pretty boxes of herbal teas. They contained exactly what they said they contained, which was herbal tea in tea bags: fruity, peppery, and one smelling just like hair conditioner.

I stacked them back into their basket.

'It's that serious, this white stuff?'

'Yes,' she said. 'It's paracetamol. Perfectly safe painkiller when used as prescribed. An excellent liver killer when the dose is exceeded, and it doesn't have to be exceeded by much. The trouble with a lot of drugs is that the toxic dose is very close to the effective dose. And anyone can call themselves a herbalist. Some benighted idiot was selling his own home-picked soothing tea with paracetamol in it and nearly killed two young women. It was in the herbalists' magazine. I sell herbs: I do not like to think of them being so misused. Nothing in the teas? I'll try the fridge.'

Tori, who had finished her breakfast, padded off to sit next to the fridge, posing prettily. Meroe was not moved.

'You have been fed, young daughter of Basht,' she told Tori. Tori, recognising an iron will, yawned (also prettily) and strolled off to find a suitable background for her wash. Meroe exclaimed at the number of pre-packaged meals in the freezer. All of them in the original wrapping. A tub of Double Death by Chocolate ice cream, half full. Much as expected.

I had gone back to examine the built-in kitchen cupboards, which were almost empty. Up on the top shelf of the highest I found a set of those stubby canisters which were so popular in the fifties, about the same time as there had last been any sugar in this flat. They were made of dark brown plastic with orange highlights and I took them down one by one as Meroe swore and slammed the fridge door. They were all empty but one, the flour canister.

'You said it would be a packet of herbs?' I asked from my perch on the kitchen chair.

'Yes?' she said curtly.

'But it might be loose leaves?' She flew at me and grabbed the canister and set it on the table. She combed through it with a wet finger and tasted. Gingerly.

'Are we out of the woods?' I wanted to know.

'Not even strolling on a path yet,' she replied, spilling some of the leaves onto a clean piece of kitchen paper. She smoothed them out then put them in piles. Even I could see that some of this tea was mint. It had a strange, musty smell which seemed familiar. I couldn't remember. Nothing to do with tea, though. Meroe was paying special attention to some shrivelled berries which ranged in size from peppercorns to what looked like lilly pilly berries. But, it appeared, weren't.

Meroe stood up and massaged her temples. 'Not too bad,' she said. 'No sign of chemical contamination. Most of the herbs are benign, even though the combination makes no sense. There are hot herbs and cold herbs here, and herbs for bile and herbs for blood, and —'

'So it wouldn't actually do anything?' I asked. 'With all the remedies acting against each other?'

'There are some that are meant to act together. Powerful laxatives, powerful diuretics, in strong enough concentrations they deplete the body of water and strip it of potassium. That can kill a weakened person. Though I've never heard of our girls' hysteria before, it is probably a strange conjunction between the ingredients. No one has heard of it because no herbalist in their right mind would use these together.'

'So, what do we do?' I asked. I was still feeling very uncomfortable.

'You wait with them while I arrange a watcher,' she said, wrapping her shawl around her shoulders decisively. 'We have businesses to run and they will sleep for a long time yet.'

'Not Mrs. Dawson or the Prof,' I told her. 'They're at lunch in the University Club by now. And I do not think Mrs. Pemberthy would be a wise choice.'

We thought about our very own vindictive, blue-haired, aggressively frail Mrs. Pemberthy and her rotten little doggie, Traddles, and shook our heads.

'Trudi will be busy,' said Meroe.

'Nerds Inc and the Pandamuses have their own businesses,' I went on, dreading what she was going to say.

'Andy Holliday and Cherie are at the zoo,' she said. 'It will have to be Ms. Webb.'

'Therese would be perfect,' I said, not knowing or caring how this was going to sound, 'but I'm not letting my mother anywhere near Kylie and Goss.'

I looked down, ashamed, but Meroe was agreeing with me. 'Certainly not. In her jangle of hatred and sorrow, she could do them incalculable damage in their present state. Let me call Therese—surely Star can be left for a little while—and you find the wrapper for that tea.'

I found it, in the almost empty rubbish bin, between a copy of TV Week with all the articles torn out and one sad little packet of instant soup. It was a modest wrapper for such dangerous contents. I patted it out flat on the table.

Meroe and I examined it. A nonprofessional packing job, I considered, with raw edges on the bottom. It was also not entirely square; the edges did not meet perfectly at the top. On the beige background a slightly blurry black stamp proclaimed 'Weight Loss Tea' and underneath 'Melb. Pkng Cy'.

'And a fat lot of use that is,' I said on my released breath. 'No manufacturer, no instructions even. Oh no, here they are. Inside the packet.'

I laid out a piece of common typing paper and read out the words printed in black Gothic type: 'Infuse contents in one litre of water. Strain. One wineglass on rising and on going to bed. Keep infusion in a cool place.'

'And that's it?' asked Meroe. I searched the packet.

'That's it,' I told her, taken aback. Meroe was gradually going pale. Her hands had fastened on the front of her shawl and her knuckles were standing out. Sometimes Meroe looks like a young woman, especially when she laughs. She wasn't laughing. She was aging. In front of my eyes something like the Wicked Witch of the West was evolving. I stepped back a pace. I was glad I was on her side, whichever side it was.

'Therese has left your mother asleep and will be here directly,' she said. 'Tell her to call me if anything happens. If the girls wake she should let them drink as much water or tea—not coffee—as they like and eat as much ice cream as they desire, and tell them I said so.'

I fought down an urge to salute. 'Yes,' I said. 'What are you going to do?'

'I will get onto the net,' said Meroe. 'I will talk to all my customers. I will report this to all reputable herbalists. And we will find out who is selling this poison, and we will make the seller really, really sorry.'

Then she did laugh, briefly, but it did not make her look young. She left without slamming the door. I might have felt better if she had slammed it. All that anger had to go somewhere.

In all it was a relief to hand the invalids over to Therese, who came in bearing an embroidery bag and a thermos. She clucked over the sleeping girls and settled herself next to Tori on the couch, where she could see into both rooms. Tori approved of the embroidery bag and tried to climb into it, but was gently dissuaded.

'I'll just sit here in this splendid light and get on with my Lady and the Unicorn,' she told me. 'No, dear, not into the bag,' she said, closing it firmly. 'Too many spiky things. Now, here's a nice cotton reel, see if you can catch it.'

Tori indulged the kind lady by springing down and batting the cotton reel across the rug. I conveyed Meroe's instructions and Therese repeated them without fault. She opened the thermos and I smelt coffee.

'I'll be fine,' Therese assured me. 'Jacqui can't stand the smell of coffee so it's a chance to have a nice cup in peace.'

She seemed perfectly at home and in charge, so I went back to the shop, where Daniel and Jason were managing the morning-tea rush creditably. So beautifully were they impressing the customers and giving change that I had time to go to Café Delicious and devour a whole serving of moussaka. I was starving. Daniel followed me, and then Jason, and then it was time to pull down the shutters. Jason had asked after the girls and been reassured. He went off to buy his CD with a spring in his step.

Timbo pulled up in his car. Braybrook might be squalid, perhaps, but I would prefer a little honest squalor to this careless poisoning of two young girls.

◇◇◇

The man who was not yet a murderer contemplated the work before him and picked up his large knife. He sat, perhaps, a little too long, cleaning the blade, listening to the whetting stone glide grittily over the iron.

Chapter Six

I told Daniel all about it on the way. I was still furious when I had got to the end. Daniel had more experience than me with human stupidity and cruelty, but even he was shaking his head. 'Appalling,' he said. 'But what amazes me is that they would just gulp down any stew of weeds—no proper packaging, even.'

'You've underestimated the lengths to which the girls will go to avoid being fat. It is similar to the lengths to which people went to avoid catching the Black Death. It's turning into an obsession in the twenty-first century and frankly I can't see that I am going to enjoy the next few years.'

'Not even with me and the cats?' he asked, his mouth quirking at the corner. This required a kiss, so I kissed it.

'It's like footbinding or infibulation or wasp waists that needed the removal of a few unimportant ribs. Star always said that the female sex was fatally flawed. The Goddess cursed us with vanity and so we could never rule the world while we were willing to spend half our energy worrying about how we looked.'

'It does seem like a waste of energy,' Daniel commented. 'As to whether it was the Goddess, there I defer to Meroe. Though nothing else but some sort of curse could explain platform shoes.'

'True,' I agreed. I leaned back into his shoulder.

Timbo, a large, cuddly young man who drove for Daniel when he needed a car, eased the vehicle around a corner with tender care. I understand that the robbers who employed Timbo in the bad old days all went to jail on their own merits, not through any fault of his getaway car driving. Daniel had helped him get his licence back and in consequence he worshipped Daniel and the road he drove on. One could not imagine Timbo without a car. It would be like imagining him without feet. He was a great help, as I hate driving and Daniel has no licence through some sort of principle (which I will get to the bottom of eventually). Also, though a sweet, gentle soul, Timbo was a large-framed lad and most of the local villains knew him as an acceptably loyal offsider. Or so Daniel said.

We were rolling along Ballarat Road. I had only ever noticed Braybrook as a place which had a rather huge old pub with two statues of footballers outside, on the way to Ballarat. Daniel made a gesture of respect at the statues.

'Ted Whitten and Dougie,' he said.

'Who?'

'That is Dougie Hawkins,' he said, as Timbo hung a left hand turn down a side street. 'And I don't want to hear a disparaging word about football in this conversation should the subject arise. Football really matters to you if you don't have anything else,' he added. 'These places have lost their industries, their reason for existing. Sunshine was called Sunshine after the Sunshine Harvesters.'

'The Harvester Judgment,' I said, taken right back to my law lectures. 'Equal pay for equal work...that was just up the road?'

'Yes, but all the factories are gone now,' Daniel told me. 'These places were built to house the workers in those factories and now there is no work. Braybrook was mainly Housing Commission, inhabited by English migrants, with the overflow from slum clearance in Richmond and Collingwood. None of them had any stake in the area.'

'Not an auspicious beginning,' I commented.

'Most of Braybrook is perfectly decent and ladies speak very well of Spotlight as a place to buy sewing materials,' said Daniel. 'In fact, Therese Webb has given us a commission for the way home.'

'I must have mentioned that I was coming here,' I said, though I didn't recall doing so.

'But every suburb has its bad streets,' continued Daniel. 'Giving one of those streets as your address is tantamount to a plea of guilty.'

'And that's where we are going?'

'Yes,' he said. 'Sorry about this, ketschele, but you get to do the traditional female thing on this visit.'

'Keep quiet?'

'Talk to the women and children,' he told me, smiling. 'Now, before we get there, take most of the money out of your purse, and leave your phone and any other valuables in the car. Timbo will mind the car.'

'They're going to rob us?' I asked uneasily, doing as he said and leaving only a folded twenty dollar note and a handful of change in my purse.

'Not directly,' he said. 'But the kids tend to rifle visitors. Here we are. All right to be left, Timbo?'

'All right,' said Timbo in his soft voice. 'You give me a yell, Corinna, and I'll come running,' he added, which was nice of him.

The house had originally been smart. In its time. About 1950, perhaps. It had a bright red roof and the walls had been white; it would have had the jaunty charm of a toadstool. It was made, however, of concrete sheeting, which cannot be repaired if it gets damaged. There were multiple holes, covered with tacked-on plyboard which had been painted over and was now curling and peeling. One window was broken. The other had a sheet of cardboard Blu-Tacked on the inside. It was already sodden and folding. Next to a dead geranium was a disembowelled lawnmower, an engine block, a couple of leaking black garbage bags and a deflated paddling pool.

There was a soul-chilling snarl. Out from a hidden corner a dog erupted. I jumped. The animal strained at its chain, its matted fur cloaking its insane eyes as it bayed and pawed and choked. It seemed to be made of flashing teeth. I do not like dogs.

Daniel threw something in an underarm toss which would have been the pride of Trevor Chappell and the raging fury vanished as if it had never been there. All I heard was the dragging of its chain and a wolfing noise. I raised an eyebrow.

'They call it housebreaker's sausage,' he said, grinning. 'Oatmeal and chopped offal cooked with Valium. The Valium was a later idea. I believe that the original recipe included opium, which isn't easy to get in these parlous times. Won't hurt the poor hound. Looks like it could do with a decent meal. Hello! Anyone home?'

'Who wants to know?' asked a voice from behind a small crack of opening door.

'It's me,' said Daniel. 'Daniel from the Soup Run. Sister Mary wants to know how Sharelle is. I brought a lady to see her.'

'She from Human Services?' growled the voice. I hoped I wasn't from Human Services.

'No, have a heart, what do you think?' said Daniel. 'Now either let us in or I'll have to go back to Sister Mary and tell her it was a wasted visit. No pressure. I've just got Timbo waiting.'

'Okay, okay,' grumbled the voice.

When the door opened, screaming on its hinges, I saw that the house was of a simple design. Four rooms off a central hall and a large kitchen and bathroom at the back. The gaping back door revealed a yard with one withered sapling, three dogs on chains, several children and a pram with a wailing baby. No grass. No flowers. Nothing but discoloured washing flapping in never-drying festoons.

I was overcome with a strange mixture of annoyance and pity and shook myself. I needed to find my father. That was why I was here. And this was the address he had given the police when they arrested him for lying down in front of a tram. These people knew something and I was required to treat them with respect. If only they didn't reek of poverty and dirt and hopelessness and dog shit and pot smoke. If only someone would change that baby and feed those dogs and fix this door.

'She's in there,' said the man. He was not prepossessing. He might have been attractive once, before the hamburgers, pizza and beer diet had distorted his waist and added all those chins to his unshaven face. Then again, who had just been railing against the view that fat equalled ugly?

The three young men lying half asleep on the remains of two sofas and a car seat in the living room were thin as gutter rats. Their loose homie clothes let me see corded arms gloved in tattoos which made them look as though they were netted in dirty green lace. Their eyes were flat and ravenous and they stared in a way that made me feel like the meat course at a butchers' picnic. Luckily the TV was on and they went back to watching it. I slipped past to a room where I could hear a baby crying, leaving Daniel to his fate.

The room had contained more furniture once. There were faded patches on the wall. Now it had a hospital bed and a pram and a pile of cardboard boxes. There was nowhere to sit. A woman opened her eyes when I came in.

'Sister sent you?' she croaked.

Sharelle's mouth was as dry as a mummy's. Her scalp bore only a faint fuzz. She was stick thin, her eyes glazed. The room smelt of mortality, though it was clean enough.

'Nurse comes in every morning,' she told me. 'Jog the pram a bit, will you? Nyrie'll be back soon. I sent her to the shop for her dad's fags. I'll have to leave Breehanna with her. I dunno how she'll manage.'

'How old is Nyrie?' I asked.

Sharelle thought about it. 'Must be ten, maybe eleven.

I was real healthy when I had her. Anyway, tell Sister Mary I'm doing good. Blokes leave me alone now I'm so thin. Nurse reckons she'll be able to get me into palliative soon. Have to be soon,' she said, shifting in her bed. None of her bones had any covering at all. She must have been in constant pain.

I shelved my outrage at the implications of 'blokes leave me alone now I'm so thin' for later.

'Can I get you anything?' I asked conventionally.

The young/old face wrinkled. 'Don't you go into that kitchen,' she said. 'Nurse says you'll get cholera. She's funny, that nurse. Open the top carton and there's a thermos. She leaves it for me. I like things hot, now,' she said. I poured out thin chicken broth and helped her sit up enough to drink it. The baby had settled down into a low, unhappy murmur.

I had no idea what to do about it.

'I'm with Daniel,' I told Sharelle. 'I'm looking for a man who gave this address as his own.'

'To the jacks?' asked the sick woman, interest fading.

'Yeah. He's my father and I am trying to find him.'

'Fuck, you want to find your father? I spent years running away from mine,' she told me. 'Might have been anyone through here lately, love. I been stuck in here. Not even a TV. I asked Nurse for one and she said she'd see.'

'They wouldn't let you have the one in the living room?' I asked.

Sharelle grunted a dry laugh.

The baby stopped whimpering. I looked around. A small girl had whisked her out of her pram and was rocking her expertly in her arms. She was coltish, with skinned knees under a too short school skirt, and she was glaring at me with bright, intelligent eyes. This had to be Nyrie.

'Hello, Ny,' murmured Sharelle. 'Lady wants to know about her father…'

She drifted off. Nyrie kept glaring at me over the baby's bald head. That heavy child seemed to be half her size. I hadn't seen anyone like her since Doré did his engravings of London by night.

'She's dying,' Nyrie told me abruptly.

There didn't seem any point in denying it. 'Yes,' I said. 'Sister Mary sent me to ask about her.'

'We're all right on our own,' Nyrie declared. Her voice was flat and unemotional. Only her eyes were as hot as little coals with fear and love and defiance. 'Me and her and Bree.'

'Yes,' I agreed. 'But I also have a question and I can pay for an answer.' This child was like Jason—she did not need, and would not trust, any attempts at guile or persuasion.

'How much?' The small face shrank into calculation. She had plaited her dark hair into such tight plaits that they drew her eyebrows out straight at the edges, like wings.

'Twenty is all I have on me except for some change.'

'Make it twenty and a dollar coin. He'll take the dollar off me as soon as you go but I can hide the twenty.'

'Deal. This man was called Chapman and he was here maybe two weeks ago. Do you remember him?'

I showed her the picture. Her nose wrinkled. She nodded.

'Gyp brought him in off the street. Said he was mental. Stayed here until he had no more money. Then they threw him out.'

'Threw him where? When?'

'School night. I was doing my homework.' She nodded to a cardboard carton in the corner under the window. Schoolbooks lay on it, and a set of pencils. 'Wednesday. Yeah, last Wednesday night. He didn't want to go and they bashed him and Darryl drove him away. Never saw him again.'

We were getting closer to finding that disturbed man, my father. I fished out the folded twenty. The note vanished like a fly in a fish's mouth. I gave her the dollar coin and she held it loosely in her hand. Such a small, red, hardworking hand. The child was indomitable, durable, and knew no other life. How could such as Nyrie survive in such a place as this?

Perhaps only such as Nyrie could survive in such a place as this. I heard sounds of laughter from the living room. Daniel was making a good impression. I wondered how long I should wait. I didn't want to go out into that pool full of young sharks prematurely.

'Pretty soon they'll have shaken Danny down for all he's got to give,' Nyrie told me, reading my mind. 'Then they'll get nasty. You can hear the voices change. They get rough. We're all right in here. Sister Mary said she'd skin anyone who came in here. And she will. She's all right, that Sister Mary. They're scared of

her. I reckon you ought to go—now. I'll take you,' she offered.
She put the baby back into the pram, gave her mother a glance
of cool pity, and took my hand.

Her timing was perfect. All the young men were on their feet,
Daniel in the middle. He was backing away so slowly that they
might not even have noticed that the door was getting closer.
He had a piece of paper and a plastic bag in one hand.

'Sister Mary's lady's going now,' announced Nyrie abruptly.
The men parted and we slid through them, down the corridor
and into the yard. As we left, I saw Nyrie surrender her dollar
coin to the big man, handing it over with no complaint, but a
look of total contempt which stuck and should have stung like
a bikini line wax.

Timbo was leaning on the car, smoking a cigarette. We got
in and shut the doors, feeling suddenly safer. Timbo started his
engine.

'I was giving you another ten,' he said to Daniel.

'We managed,' said Daniel. 'Besides, I had Corinna with me.'

'Daniel in the lions' den,' I said.

'Was visited by an angel,' he riposted, and kissed me. It was
very nice, having a lover who could riposte. We were drunk with
relief at getting out of the Braybrook Den.

'We need a drink, Timbo,' said Daniel.

'I know just the place,' said Timbo.

Thus we soon found ourselves in the plush parlour of the
Royal Hotel, a watering place from the old days, with a gin
and tonic and a whisky on the table, and a feeling that we had
escaped doom by a mere whisker. Daniel put the plastic bag on
the polished wood and folded his hands over it.

'How do you feel?' he asked, concerned, as I sucked down
the g-and-t and signalled for another.

'If I think about it I shall have post-traumatic stress disorder,'
I told him. 'That was a terrible place.'

'So it was,' he agreed, as he swallowed his whisky.

'How is that child going to survive with that baby when
her mother dies?' I asked, shaken and horrified and somehow

drained. I hadn't known there were houses like that one in what I had thought of as a prosperous state and a passably compassionate nation.

'Sister Mary says that faith manages.' Daniel tossed off his drink. 'When she is on the case it mostly does. Nyrie will be all right. Men like Darryl and Gyp are essentially weak.'

'And blessedly short lived,' I snarled.

'That, too,' said Daniel, and ordered another drink. The first one hadn't touched the sides. Timbo, who did not drink while he was driving, had wandered off to play the pokies with all my remaining coins.

'What's in the plastic bag?' I asked when I could bear the suspense no longer.

'Stuff that Sun left. Or that they scammed from him,' said Daniel, opening it. The contents bore that same unwashed smell, most unpleasant in this clean environment. There was a stained t-shirt and a pair of yellowed Y-fronts. I handled them gingerly. The stain on the cloth might have been tomato sauce but it looked like blood. Wrapped in the shirt was a wallet.

I had last seen it when I had handed over a hundred dollars eight years ago, in order to get them to go away. It was old and soft and had a half-effaced crest on the front. Inside was a passport, a Medicare card, some bits of cigarette paper and a little pencil.

'I remember the tiny pencil,' I exclaimed. 'It came off a dance card. He always had it in his wallet in case he needed to write something down.'

'He has made some notes,' said Daniel. 'But too faint to read in this light. We'll do better under UV, perhaps. Some leaves, maybe a four-leaf clover? Nothing immediately useful. No money, of course.'

'Of course. What's the book?'

'Looks like a bible,' said Daniel.

'Surely not.' I opened it carefully. It was small and damp and the suede cover was limp. It was written in Latin. I saw no signs that it was a bible. Even I can pick out the names of the Christian deities. 'Have to ask the Professor,' I said, disappointed. I shook out the bag, harvesting a worn black sock. That appeared to be it for Sun's belongings. I put them away again.

'What's this?' I asked, pointing to the piece of paper Daniel had been carrying.

'Darryl gave me the number of a mobile phone they sold to another mate of theirs. Sun had it on him when they found him.'

'Sun had a mobile phone? Impossible,' I objected. Daniel left a pause while I added two to two and came up with an ineluctable four. 'As far as I knew him,' I conceded. 'And I don't really know him at all, as you are carefully not saying. So when they bled Sun dry, where did they dump the body?'

'Down by the river,' said Daniel. 'But he isn't dead, or Constable Wellesley would have known.'

'Maybe they just haven't found the body yet. Daniel, I am so sorry about getting you involved in this affair. It's awful, and it's probably going to get awfuller.'

He took my hand and patted it. 'Now, now, you're my client, and I can't allow you to withdraw when the going's getting interesting. Drink up and I'll buy you a packet of bacon crisps. Then we can collect Timbo and go for a little walk. That is, we'll go for a little walk, and he'll sit in the car. Timbo isn't built for hiking.'

I allowed myself to be comforted. I nibbled my crisps.

I drank my drink. Timbo came back beaming with handfuls of gold coins. He insisted on paying me back double for my initial investment. At least someone was showing a profit on the day.

The river was surprisingly beautiful. It was just after clean-up day so I assumed that someone had removed all the rubbish. A cycle path followed the bank, the water foamed and the wind in the tall eucalypts made a sound like the sea. The place was empty apart from a few worn-out ducks, who were staying right against the bank to avoid being swept out into Bass Strait. They were making plans to fly somewhere else as soon as there was a break in the weather, I could tell. I saw their point.

'Here,' said Daniel. The wind caught his leather coat and blew it out on either side, like wings. The ducks rose as though he had given them a signal and rocketed up, forming a clumsy skein which pointed due north, and struggled into the face of the gale. I saw a flattened set of blackberry canes and a lot of tyre marks, and in the middle a lump of something. Cloth. Shoes.

My heart dropped. Hearts do not rise into mouths, I find, they drop. Mine had turned into a plummet and landed with a thud in my lower intestines. It was such an immediate physical sensation that I coughed.

'Is it him?' I asked, wading into the prickles. I got one hand to the edge of the bundle—it was a sheet, I saw, twin of the one hanging at Sharelle's window—and pulled as hard as I could. The bundle was heavy and resisted me. I hauled. Daniel joined me. We dragged and stamped and thorns raked our hands.

Then the sheet unrolled, and we could haul it out onto the grass. Thank the Goddess, no body, no corpse. It was a heavy wet blanket and a pair of shoes and an unravelling green woollen sweater. It was just junk. But it was my father's junk. The blanket was handwoven and had covered the swag he always carried when he went anywhere. The shoes were Uncle Ho sandals soled with car tyres, as made in Sunbury. And I had repaired that green jumper every time I had seen my father, catching up the threads of thin wool and patching it because he refused to buy another one. I vividly remembered the last time I had done so, perhaps three or four years earlier, listening to Star assassinate my character as I stitched and ravelled.

My father had been here. And the fact that he was here no longer meant that, probably—unless he had flung himself into the river—he was not dead even after the beating Darryl and the sharks had inflicted on him. So the quest had to go on. Suddenly I found myself very, very tired.

We had to bribe Timbo with a packet of salt and vinegar crisps before he would allow me to put the stinking wet remains of Sun's luggage in his lovely car. Even when stuffed into a black rubbish bag. Even in the boot.

Halfway home Daniel remembered his Spotlight task and we had to turn back. The day wasn't going to get any lighter or more pleasant and Therese was doing us a favour by looking after the girls. That was another problem. I wondered if Meroe and I had done the right thing, not calling a doctor. I sat, nervously sucking blackberry prickles out of my wrist and wishing that the week had begun in some other way, or I had been born in some other universe. Except that universe might not have had Daniel in it, and that would never have done.

Spotlight, on the other hand, was a pleasure. We had to buy tapestry wool, some fabric paint and some new crewel needles, all of which were somewhere in a place roughly the size of an aircraft hangar stuffed to bursting with fascinating…well, stuff. I left Timbo and Daniel in the car, listening to the news, and dived into the shop with a delight which I had not expected to feel after a day containing what my day had contained. I am clearly a superficial person after all.

Beautiful materials lay casually unrolled around me. Satins, embroidered silk, taffeta in every possible colour, gaudy as the wings of butterflies created by an artist on good acid. Intoxicating combinations of hues as varied as a cottage garden—hot pinks, strong pinks, pale pinks, apricot pinks, barely there at all pinks—presented themselves to my distracted eyes. Sky blue, teal blue, jade blue, baby blue, cornflower blue. It was only when I was telling myself very firmly that I did not—really did not—need a length of fine double damask in bright crimson with phoenixes woven through it that I recalled the two men waiting and busied myself about my errand. Never a good idea to keep men waiting, Grandma Chapman had always said.

Then again, sending me into this shop was like instructing a hungry mouse to go into a granary and not eat anything.

I found the needles, matched the wool, bought the paints, and then added three metres of the double damask to my basket. There are days when one needs to be restrained in one's purchases. This was not one of them.

The nice thing was that when I did finally emerge, Timbo grinned and said, 'You broke the record. My mum's always more than an hour in there. You were only thirty minutes.'

So everyone was pleased, and we all went home. The girls were still asleep. Meroe was with them. Daniel went out to talk to the night people, in pursuit of the mobile phone. I scrubbed myself clean of the day. I heated myself a strengthening bowl of goulash and ate it with my own bread. But even though I was exhausted and aching I could not sleep, and lay awake, hugging Horatio and sorrowing for the cruelties of the world until the alarm went off and it was Thursday.

Chapter Seven

Jason had started the mix as I came down the stairs with coffee and toast (coffee for me, toast for him) and he kept a respectful morning silence as we set all the baking on its way. There was nothing unusual in the orders except more famine bread, and we knew how to make that now. I sat down to chop the ginger for the ginger muffins and before I knew it my cheek was on the cold metal table and Jason was shaking my shoulder.

'You fell asleep,' said Jason severely. 'What have you been doing, Corinna?'

I realised that my apprentice was accusing me of taking drugs. I delved for outrage but it was out to breakfast.

'I've been visiting Braybrook with Daniel,' I told Jason. 'Then I thought I'd found my father's body on the river bank. Then I couldn't sleep. The only drug I've taken is a gin and tonic or two.'

He ruffled his hair and put his cap back on. 'You look like shit,' he said kindly. ' I can do all this. Get back upstairs and get some more sleep.'

'I can't,' I said. Jason bristled. I dredged up an explanation. 'Not that I don't trust you. But if we don't have the girls, who's going to run the shop? You can't do that on your own. Even the amazing Jason can't be in two places at once.'

'That dude shouldn't have taken you out to a dump like that,' he grumbled. 'Nice lady like you. You don't need to see shit like that. I know that Darryl. He's an evil dude and Gyp is a stone-mad animal.'

'How shall I make amends?' asked a soft voice at the alley door. Daniel had returned from the night.

'You want to help me in the shop?' asked Jason promptly, before I could speak. 'She didn't get no sleep and that's down to you, dude.'

'So it is.' Daniel looked worried. 'Come along, ketschele, we'll get you back to bed. Then I'll come down and Jason can tell me what to do, which will make him feel better.'

'No shit,' grinned Jason.

I allowed myself to be persuaded. I re-donned my soft nightdress. I drank hot milk and brandy. I fell asleep on the last mouthful. Sometimes I am not as strong as I think I am.

When I woke it was to a solid sense of comfort and peace. Horatio was curled up beside me, purring gently. The light through the blind was bright. It must have been afternoon. I snuggled down for another few minutes of quality cat-appreciating time and then got up. Two o'clock already. I had slept away my working hours. Not much point in hurrying, I thought. If disaster was going to land on the bakery it would have done so by now, and all seemed peaceful downstairs. No one was shrieking at anyone else, which was a blessing.

So I took a nice leisurely shower and carried my nice leisurely cup of coffee onto my balcony, where there is always something to look at in Calico Alley below. People crossed Flinders Lane and dived into my alley, intent on Kiko's Japanese food or Babka's Russian doughnuts or perhaps to buy stamps or coins or find the back way to Centreway Arcade. Or maybe to get in out of the rain. A fine, soft sleet had begun to fall, or rather float past. I appreciated my fleecy tracksuit and my furry boots and the heat of my drink. I finished the coffee and was just wondering whether I should go down to the shop when there was a ring at my bell and who should be at my door but Mrs. Sylvia Dawson.

Mrs. Dawson had been a famous society hostess, known for her good works and generous nature. Then her husband died.

She got sick of being a public person and decided to come and be a private one in Insula, where she improves our education by wearing the most beautiful clothes. She was wearing a gorgeous bitter-chocolate cashmere sweater and ochre trousers over her signature Russian leather boots. She is a small, upright, elegant lady and I still find it hard to call her Sylvia.

'Ah, Corinna. I have an invitation from Jon and Kepler for drinks this evening at six,' she said. 'They seem to have a problem which they want to share with us.'

'Who us?' I asked.

'Meroe, Dion, Daniel, you and me,' she replied crisply. 'How are you, my dear? Jason said you were feeling…unwell.'

I hoped that Jason hadn't told Mrs. Dawson that I looked like shit. Not that she would have turned a hair if he had.

'I'm fine now. I just had an overdose of other people's misery and couldn't sleep.'

'Ah yes, it can take you like that sometimes,' she said. 'See you tonight, then.'

I made a note on the hall table diary, in case I did forget, and then I let myself out of my apartment and went down the stairs. Insula has a very impressive entry hall, called an atrium. It has Pompeiian red tiles and copies of wall paintings and a fishpond (an impluvium) with a rather artfully censored statue of Priapus. I sat down on the garden seat and watched the fish. Horatio likes doing this too, when he can slip out of my front door. He hasn't managed to catch one yet but both he and the fish know that once he gets his paw in they are going to be entrees, and it makes them anxious.

I sat there until Trudi found me. She was on her lawful occasions, coming down to feed the fish. Lucifer was riding on her shoulder. He sighted a fish, leapt down, and slid sideways into the pond in a skilled and seamless piece of klutzery which Mack Sennet's Keystone Cops could not have bettered. The waters closed over his furry little head, but in an instant he was up and cat-paddling after the fish, which, after a moment of astonishment, had decided that elsewhere was a good place to be. I was laughing so hard that my sides were beginning to ache. There was something so earnest about Lucifer. Whatever insane thing he did, he did with his whole heart and right now he was bent on being the first aquatic fishing feline in Australia. Even though he had to keep stopping to sneeze importunate water out of his delicate nostrils. When he stopped paddling, he started to sink, then paddled twice as hard to catch those fleeing, golden, impertinent tails always just out of claw-reach.

'You think he could catch one?' asked Trudi, grabbing for the end of the leash and preparing to drag, in the manner of a Japanese fisherperson and tame cormorant.

'I really couldn't say,' I temporised.

The fish had worked out that this predator was confined to the surface and had dived, but who could say what Lucifer might take it into his head to do? Trudi hauled and Lucifer left the briny deep to hang dripping in the air, still swiping with both front paws. She put him down on the edge to drain. It's amazing how much water even a small kitten's coat can hold. Lucifer shook his head, sneezed an absurdly shrill sneeze, wiped at his bedraggled whiskers, then spun around to stare down into the water at the fish, who had risen to sneer at him.

'No you don't, my boy,' said Trudi, restraining him before he dived in again. 'You are wet enough for two cats. You hold him, I'll get a towel.'

Trudi's cart, a groaning wagon loaded with whatever might be needed in a building this old, was parked near the goods lift, which only she understood. Ever since Lucifer's advent she had stocked her wagon with salad oil, for removing paint, chewing gum and tar from fur, betadine for scratches when Lucifer became overexcited, bandaids ditto, disinfectant and kitchen towels in case he forgot himself in a corner, towels and soft cloths and a cat cage for when she couldn't secure him to anything solid and she had to do something dangerous—climbing a ladder with a Lucifer free to roam under the feet, she told me, gave a whole new meaning to the word 'perilous'.

I wound the leash around my hand, for although Lucifer was a lightly built animal, he had a lot of torque when he threw himself into things. He had given up on the fish and was beginning a rather ineffectual wash when Trudi wrapped him in a coarse towel and began to rough-dry him. He took this as an invitation to play a few rounds of shred the towel. Just watching him was re-energising. I got up. Somehow I felt fine. I could remember the events of the day before but they no longer had that deadly weight which had borne me down. Look out, world, I thought, Corinna's herself again.

Such was my faith in the Daniel and Jason partnership that I did not look into the bakery—well, I peeped around the corner and saw that people were going in and out, loaded with bags. The boys had obviously managed famously and I wasn't going to bustle in at the last moment and take away their triumph. So I decided to visit the girls, who might, by now, have recovered from their collapse.

But first I had to do something about the pitiful relics we had found by the waterside. They were too revolting to take to a drycleaner in their present state. They were presently sulking in a black garbage bag in Calico Alley, where at any moment they might cause me to be summonsed for polluting the environment. I had an outside tap, didn't I? In that very same alley.

I went around the building, emptied the garbage bag and rinsed it, then laid the handmade garments and blanket down in my gully-trap and rinsed them and soaped them with the stuff I use on the floor. The initial effluvium wasn't pleasant but soon the cloth began to smell less like sewerage and more like wet wool. I wrung them out as best I could and went into the bakery through the unlocked alley door. I stuffed the waterlogged refuse into the washer without being noticed, added a large amount of wool wash and set the machine going.

I was pleased. That job had seemed just too hard before I was sent back to sleep off my attack of the horrors. Now I had done it without a hitch. Reminding myself not to be cross with the boys about the unlocked door, I let myself out again and went along the lane to see Meroe. Perhaps the girls ought not to be disturbed.

Belladonna waved a languid paw as I went into the Sibyl's Cave. She was lying in the window, perfectly black, perfectly supine, batting at the Celtic charm for longevity which hung over her nose. I greeted her politely. It is never a good idea to treat a witch's cat disrespectfully.

Meroe's shop is very small and completely stuffed with occult paraphernalia. If, for your divination, you want a sheep's shoulderblade or yarrow stalks or tarot cards or runes (three different types), beautifully bound copies of the I Ching, a computer program to cast horoscopes or a nib-tipped pelican feather to write spells to Poseidon in aquamarine ink, you will find it at the Sibyl's Cave. At the sort of prices which make me feel that I am in the wrong business, I might add. Though this is justified by the expert advice you get along with the goods. Meroe would never let anyone use the wrong fern seed for their love potion. She was talking to a thin young man in a Metallica t-shirt.

'Never heard of it,' he was saying, in the the voice of someone who was scared enough to be punctilious with the truth. 'Makes no sense, Lady Meroe. Look at the combinations.'

'I know,' said Meroe. 'But it's not entirely random. Not as though someone just grabbed a handful of herbs. There is the diuretic dandelion, the purgative cascara.'

' And the croton and the wormwood. Not to mention the aloes and the valerian.'

'And the belladonna and the bearberry,' concluded Meroe.

'With just a touch of juniper berry. I never heard of the combination before,' he said again. 'But if I find out anything, you will be the first to know. Blessed part,' he said. He took up a bag of herbs and passed me on the way out. He was just managing not to run.

'No one has ever seen anything like it,' said Meroe, blowing out a frustrated breath. 'Hello, Corinna, you do feel better.' Meroe always knows.

'Yes, I do. One thing you know about this recipe, Meroe.'

'And what is that?'

'The girls will have taken an overdose of it. Their motto is if one drink is nice, two will be nicer. Ergo, if one pill is good, two must be better. How much is a wineglassful, anyway?'

'Half a cup,' said Meroe absently. 'You are right. And that does date the recipe. After the Second World War people started analysing herbal medicine on a scientific basis. Standardising doses is a sensible thing to do if you want to test whether something works. So Europe went into teaspoon, tablespoon and cup measures or ounces, and America too. And now it is all in mls or mgs. Someone's mother's recipe, perhaps, badly copied from a grandmother's handwriting, possibly translated from another language and some of the herbs misidentified.' She fiddled with a tray of shining crystals, polishing them with the end of today's bright yellow shawl. 'That happens a lot, even now. And it's worse if you are trying to use an ancient recipe. The Hippocrates school tended to say "everyone knows what this herb looks like" or if they were being really accurate, fine it down to "tall green marshland version of this herb which everyone knows." It drives reconstructive archaeologists up the wall.' Amethyst crystals cast tiny purple lights on her hands, green lights on the shawl.

'And would they have taken an overdose?' I asked, wanting my point accepted.

'Is the Goddess powerful?' asked Meroe.

Fortunately I didn't have to answer that question. If she was, how could she defend her treatment of dying Sharelle, Nyrie and the baby?

Meroe went on. 'Those two could believe that a wineglass was the size of one of those brandy balloons they have in their apartment. Blonde to the brainstem,' she added. 'Sadly.'

'I was about to visit,' I said. 'Are they fit for callers?'

'Yes. Take them some more ice cream. I've told them to stay in bed today and eat cool things. They have mint tea and Yai Yai Pandamus made them lettuce and pine nut eggplant rolls for lunch. All cooling things. They should be back at work tomorrow. Luckily it's such a foul day that no one would want to be going out. Are you dining in?'

'I thought of taking Daniel and Jason out to the Japanese place as a reward for all their hard work.'

'A good idea. But we have drinks with Jon and Kepler at six, remember? You can take your helpers out tomorrow night. Have these salad leaves—you know they don't taste as good the second day after they are picked.'

'Thanks,' I said. Meroe's salad leaves are rushed into the city by express broom from some fairy garden. One day I must ask her where they come from. As I left the Sibyl's Cave I noticed that Bella had turned over in her glass case and was now a perfect round cushion of black fur, with only a delicate thread of black whiskers to differentiate her from a construct, puppet or pyjama-case. Unless, of course, one was unwise enough to sit on her...

Goss answered the door, squeaked at the sight of a tub of double chocolate marshmallow fudge ice cream and led me into their parlour, where they were watching re-runs of Buffy.

They were a touching sight. They had shed their surface sophistication. On the huge white sofa Kylie reposed, teddy bear at her side, Tori on her lap, both the teddy and Kylie wearing pink flannelette pyjamas patterned with little red hearts. Goss, returning from the kitchen with three bowls and spoons, an ice cream scoop and the tub of ice cream on a tray, boasted identical jammies, though her teddy bear was clad in a frilly pinafore. Goss gave me the tray and laid herself down again. Tori stretched, got off Kylie's lap and moved to Goss'. The two girls were lying with their feet into the middle of the sofa, so that each of them had an arm to lean on. The coffee table in front of them was littered with DVDs, CDs, and a tea tray. I could smell the bracing scent of mint.

'Tori is having a lovely day,' I commented, digging out ice cream with the scoop and distributing it with a generous hand.

'She sits on me for an hour,' replied Kylie, 'then she moves to Goss for an hour. She shares herself out equally and she really gets cross if one of us upsets her timetable. I tried to hang on to her last night and she scratched me and came out here and slept on the couch until it was Goss' turn.'

'You can't compel cats,' I agreed, handing over the ice cream. 'How do you feel?'

'All right,' said Kylie. 'Meroe says the poison is out of our systems and we just have to stay cool and we'll be all right. She says that poison is hot.'

I thought about food poisoning I had contracted, about a mouthful of wasabi which had once unexpectedly infected my sushi, about how sea-sickness feels. Yes. All hot. Hot and nauseating. I nodded.

'Meroe knows everything,' said Goss dotingly.

'Except where you got those herbs,' I said. The two of them looked at each other and plied their spoons busily. They looked so delightful, little red tongues coming out to lick up the frozen treat, that I almost forgot about my question. But not quite.

'Come on, ladies, this stuff is dangerous. People might die. You need to tell someone, so why not me?'

'I s'pose…' Kylie said, as though the words were being tortured out of her.

Goss was putting a spot of ice cream on Tori's nose to see if she liked double chocolate marshmallow fudge. A lightning lick informed them that she did. I had to step in before Tori filled herself up with forbidden substances.

'You mustn't feed cats chocolate, it makes them sick. We'll give her some cream in a moment. Where did you get the herbs, Kylie? Were you together?' That was a silly question.

Goss raised her eyebrows and decided to answer. 'Oh, all right. We were in the new goth site. Café …what's the name, Kyl?'

'Vlad,' replied Kylie. 'Vlad something.'

'Tepes?' I asked, pronouncing it correctly as Tepesh.

Goss swallowed her mouthful with voluptuous enjoyment which did the heart good to see. 'That's it. It's a nice straight café by day and by night it goes all goth and dark and creepy and we like it because there are new people there. Gay boys. Lesbians. We make bread for them. Remember that weird little guy who came into the shop and wanted to check that you were...er...?'

'Fat,' I said. They might mouth obscenities but nothing was going to make either of them say the forbidden word.

'I remember. So you were at Café Vlad Tepes and someone was selling this weight loss tea?'

'Sort of like that,' said Kylie. 'Except not really.'

Well, that made everything crystal clear.

'What happened, then?' I asked, unwisely settling back into the white chair. It racheted backwards and a footrest came up and collected my ankles. Within moments I was reposing with the ice cream tray on my bosom.

I struggled upright to deposit the tray on the table, but then sank down into the octopus-like embrace of the chair again. I'd tried to hurry the story along and the girls had got confused. Better put it on track like a toy train and just lie back and wait for some facts to chunter past. Tori snuggled down between Goss and her teddy, which looked almost unbearably cute.

'We were dancing,' she said. 'Me and Kyl. With a couple of gay boys. They were gorgeous, eh, Kyl? Gorgeous. Cut. Like they spent every day in the gym. Then I realised that we knew one of them.'

'Went to school with my brother,' affirmed Kylie. 'Aaron. My brother is called Aaron, I mean. The gay guy was Tobias. Real slim. We got talking about ways to lose weight, and they said exercise every time, it wasn't weight it was body mass, and we said we didn't want to look like those body-building girls, and then Toby said he stayed thin with this weight loss tea, but you couldn't buy it anywhere. So we said, how did you get it then, and he said you had to know a witch.'

'Spooky,' said Gossamer. 'You'd think he was talking about drugs. So we asked a bit more, you know, and he wouldn't tell us, and then he got cranky and went away. But his mate Bo was still dancing with us and he said he'd get us a packet and we could try it. But it was going to cost us.'

'And the next night we were there and I handed over my fifty and he gave us the packet,' said Goss. 'Simple as that. We made up the infusion like it said and took it like the instructions said and it nearly killed us. Just wait till I see that Bo again! Or that Toby!'

'Hang on,' I said, soothingly. 'How much of it did you take?'

They shifted uneasily. Tori looked from one girl to the other. They seemed to wither under her regard, or mine. Or maybe both.

'Didn't know how much a wineglassful was,' confessed Goss, 'so we just drank a cup each. A big cup. Or maybe two,' she said shamefacedly.

'So it might have been safe enough if you hadn't OD'd on it,' I said. 'No need to go looking for Bo or Tobias. Meroe's on their track and they'll be really, really sorry when she lays hold of them. And she will. If it's about herbs, she knows everyone in this town. They must be getting their ingredients somewhere and some of them are quite hard to find, she says. Well —' I levered the controls so the chair let me sit up again—'it's been fun. Stay warm and I'll see you tomorrow.'

'After you give Tori her cream,' Kylie reminded me. Tori had already sprung to the floor and was posing by the kitchen door, looking fluffy. She seemed to be able to do fluffy on demand. She was a cat of many talents, all photogenic. I fed Tori her cream and departed.

When I came downstairs again Earthly Delights was shut. My own apartment was empty. Missing also was the esky and Horatio. I gathered up the gin bottle and an extra glass and ascended to the roof garden where, in the Temple of Ceres, I saw two exhausted labourers recruiting their strength with beer, pickled onions and doorstop cheese sandwiches. Daniel was more than a touch floury round the edges of what must have been my big apron, and Jason was scrubbing one hand through his hair, recently freed from its cap. They were both slumped on the padded marble bench as though they had been stonecutting since dawn. Beer flowed down their parched throats.

One not at all exhausted cat rose politely to his paws and greeted me, his welcoming mew somewhat damped by his mouthful of cheese.

'Corinna, I don't know how you survive a day's work,' said Daniel, moving over on the bench. 'Jason works like a slave but it is still a good day's work for a wharfie or a moderately overloaded water buffalo.'

'Thank you,' I said, putting down the gin, finding some ice and tonic and pouring myself a drink. 'You must have done very well—when I looked in the place was full of people.'

'It was a good day, and I am extremely pleased that you are going to be doing it tomorrow. How are the girls?'

'Sitting up and taking nourishment in the form of ice cream by the oodle,' I replied, sipping my drink. It hit the spot. 'They will be back tomorrow. Anything unusual happen?' I asked Jason, trying not to sound like I was nagging him.

'Nothing,' he said, suppressing a yawn. He put the yawn in its place with a huge bite which comprised two pieces of bread, a chunk of cheese and a whole onion. 'All the orders went out, the flavour of muffin was that peach one I've been working on—I added some almond essence and it tasted ace. I kept one for you. Daniel made me,' he said, disarmingly. 'The famine bread blokes came and collected the stuff. Two of them. In brown robes, hoodies, weird. Never saw their faces. They don't like paying extra for delivery. You'll see 'em tomorrow. Daniel didn't take to them either.'

'No, I didn't,' said my beloved, crunching a pickled onion. 'Good onions, Corinna. Made or bought?'

'Made. I have a pickled onion binge every autumn. Autumn just seems to say "pickles!." Great-grandma Chapman's recipe. Thank you for today, gentlemen. You did very well.'

'Our pleasure,' said Daniel. 'Since it was my fault. And, as I say, it is probably just as well that I understand how hard you work.'

'I was going to invite you out to dinner, Jason,' I told my munching apprentice. 'But we've been invited for drinks at Jon and Kepler's. So how about a small donation so that you don't have to cook tonight?' I pressed a twenty into the hand which wasn't full of sandwich.

Jason grinned. 'Ace. I'll go to that all-you-can-eat buffet, the Violet House. Last time they let me take a doggy bag home,' he said.

I caught Daniel's eye and laughed. The only way that an all-you-can-eat buffet could break even with my Jason in the dining room would be to send him home while there was still some food for the others. Cooks had been known to sob in the face of Jason's appetite.

He finished his beer, put the bottle back into the esky, shook crumbs off himself and slapped Daniel on the shoulder. 'We make a great team, dude,' he said, and went out, fingering his twenty and envisioning just how many garlic prawns he could manage before either the supply gave out or the management begged for mercy.

I snuggled into Daniel's side and pinched a piece of bread, cheese and pickle. Daniel hugged me. He smelt pleasantly of almond essence and honest toil, as well as his signature spicy scent. Horatio leaned against him from the other side. We were being kept balanced on that bench by harmonious forces alone. I bit into the pickle. Perfect. I must make some more next autumn.

'I'm so sorry about that Braybrook house, Corinna,' he said, his big voice rumbling against my ear, which was pressed to his chest.

'You couldn't know I'd react like that,' I reassured him.

'I didn't know. Nothing to forgive. And very educational for me. Let's change the subject. I've been talking to the girls, and they said they got the herbal tea from a man called Bo, who is the bosom friend of a man called Tobias, in Café Vlad Tepes. This is, as you will recall, a polite Rumanian café by day and a hangout of goths and vampires by night.'

I explained how the girls had obtained the tea. 'And, of course, they took octuple doses, so maybe the stuff isn't actually that toxic if you take it by the wineglassful,' I added, listening to the odd gulp of Daniel finishing his beer, heard from chest level. 'Meroe still thinks it's an abomination and is trying to find out whose old family recipe it is. She suggests that it was inadequately translated from (possibly) Aramaic, using herbs which are (probably) now extinct.'

Daniel laughed gently. Then he stretched. So did Horatio, first front legs, then back legs, then curving tail. By pure emulation so did I. Much less gracefully.

'We need a shower and a nap if we are to get to drinks with Jon and Kepler in our right minds,' he suggested.

'Nix on the shower, but I'll join you in the nap,' I said brazenly, running a hand up under the back of his baker's sweater and against his matchless skin. He jumped in a gratifying fashion.

'I'll take the esky,' he said.

'And I'll take the cat,' I said, picking up Horatio so that he sat, paws over my arm, able to observe his surroundings.

'And I'll be in bed before you,' he said.

But he wasn't. Horatio and I had been lying in the soft gloom of our boudoir for quite ten minutes waiting for him to get the flour out of his hair. Then he came in and threw himself down beside me, and Horatio withdrew courteously. And my world was full of spicy scents and strong hands and deep kisses. No one could ask for more.

The man who was not yet a murderer slapped the elastic band against his wrist and it broke. It was the third one he had broken today.

Chapter Eight

We made it to Jon and Kepler's door with seconds to spare. Suspiciously breathless, a little flushed, anyone would have known what we had been doing, but did I care? If I had met my mother on the stairs I might have found out how much I still cared for her opinion. But I took the lift and missed the chance and I was content enough to miss it. Meroe smiled, the Professor beamed, and Jon and Kepler welcomed us in.

I had always liked this apartment, which was draped, hung, painted and knick-knacked with fascinating things from Foreign, as I used to call it when I was a child. Wherever his strict conscience and donated money had taken him—landslides, earthquakes, collapsed bridges, civil wars, religious conflicts—Jon and his indefatigable workers had brought clean water, new livestock, seedlings, language lessons, kindness, compassion and understanding. And they had come home with trade agreements, garments woven in traditional patterns with traditional dyes, pots made of clay or wire or iron and intricate baskets to sell to the discriminating buyer. And on one such trip, Jon had encountered Kepler, a beautiful, elegant, willowy Chinese man who adored him, and was adored, on sight. Seldom does virtue get such a prompt and impressive reward.

They were so charming together that they even softened Mrs. Pemberthy, who had looked sad, hauled in Traddles and gone away when she saw them sitting in the Temple of Ceres, holding hands and drinking tea from tiny little cups. No one had ever had that effect on her before and she had to conduct a shrill ten-minute argument with Trudi about where to plant her tulips to recover from it.

Professor Dion was already holding a glass of his favourite Côtes du Rhône wine, and Daniel and I hastened to join him. Mrs. Dawson, in her chocolate coloured cashmere, was drinking sherry and Meroe was tarnishing her chakras with Marlborough Sound sauvignon blanc, nectar of the New Zealand gods.

I almost regretted my Côtes du Rhône when I saw that bottle. Kepler was drinking something colourless in a small glass and Jon was in agreement with us on the value of red wine as an antioxidant. The table was covered with a turquoise, silver and black batik of butterflies and bore little dishes of cocktail munchies in mixed Asian and Mediterranean style.

Daniel and I rather hoed in to the treats. We had been exercising hard and making love always makes me hungry.

Mrs. Dawson took a curry puff and bit it precisely in two without showering herself with crumbs, something which I would have put good money on as impossible. The old school of society hostesses learned hard lessons. I bet that she could get out of a sports car gracefully, too. And with her stockings intact. She was listening to Professor Dion, who was talking about Nox, his kitten.

'What's remarkable about cats,' he said, 'is how very flattered one must feel by their freely given affection. If they are not in the mood for a caress, they slide out from under it. If they don't feel like being polite, they won't be. I am always honoured when Nox decides that she wants to sleep on my lap, because she has a whole apartment to sleep in and perfect freedom of choice.'

I finished my spanakopita and told them about Tori refusing to allow Kylie any fraudulent extra cat time. Everyone laughed.

'And they are so different from each other,' marvelled Daniel, allowing Kepler to refill his glass. 'I mean, there is Nox, as dignified a creature as would ever have graced a Roman household and sat on a senator's shoulder. There is Tori, who makes a profession out of…well, l don't want to be unkind…'

'Being fluffy,' I suggested. 'A perfect match for Kylie and Gossamer.'

He accepted my amendment with a smile. 'Exactly, ketschele. And then—there's Lucifer. It's hard to believe they are all from the same litter.'

'Do you know, that kitten managed—somehow—to get himself shut into a locked wardrobe when Trudi was fixing my kitchen tap,' said Mrs. Dawson. 'We only found him because he leapt up and got tangled in about a thousand empty coathangers. I had to find the key to get him out.'

'A Shrödinger cat,' said the Professor, a Terry Pratchett aficionado. He began to explain that cats, on discovering they were going to be used in thought experiments in which nine times out of ten they might be dead before someone lifted the lid, found a short way through time and space and emerged later, when the physicists had gone off for a drink, in an upstairs closet. Incomplete Shrödingers, he explained, didn't quite make it back to the real world again and could be found inside locked wardrobes and curtain walls.

'I think Mr. Pratchett has it,' said Meroe. 'He's very good on cats. And magic.'

'And since that is my second glass of wine,' I observed as Jon filled it again, 'I think we might try to find out what we can do for our friends in return for this rather lavish entertainment.'

Mrs. Dawson tapped the stem of her glass and called the meeting to order. She had remarkable presence, considering that she must have weighed six stone in a soaking wet army greatcoat.

'Jon?' she asked. 'Kepler? Your advisory committee is ready to advise you.'

Jon seemed to find it hard to begin. He cleared away the cocktail food then signalled to Kepler, who brought a small heavy wooden crate into the room and put it, on a sheet of newspaper, on the table.

'You know that we import things from all over the world. This has its problems. Some of the countries have nasty governments—in fact a lot of them do. Some of them have customs regulations, some of them have customs bribery of the brown envelope school, some of them just require us to sneak the stuff out while no one is looking.' He was stumbling in his speech. Kepler took his hand. 'We have always been utterly vigilant in case someone decided to use our goods, our packaging, to smuggle drugs. It's only really a problem for our sort of organisation. We try to change people's futures by giving them an opportunity to trade, to work. Most agencies just relieve the immediate threat. We try to insulate the population against future threats. Do you know what I mean?'

This was serious. Jon was flushed and pale by turns. He loved his charity dearly and something was clearly threatening its very existence.

We nodded. We knew what he meant. It was an old saying. Give a man a fish and he'll eat for the day. Teach him to fish and he'll feed his family. Perfectly true nonetheless, though teaching girls to read was a main mission, because that was the best indicator of societal health. Or something like that. So I was told. I looked around. Everyone was worried. We all had the highest respect for Jon and his dedication.

'Then someone at the depot dropped one of these crates. They come from India. Kep, can you open it again?' Kepler produced a case-iron and levered. The lid screeched against the nails. Whatever it was it had been well sealed. Jon reached in though a fluff of wood wool and took out a remarkably ugly bronze pot. It was bulbous, with a horrible demon's mask on it, talons for feet, and a matching lid which fitted snugly. Jon wrenched it off and turned the pot on its side. Dried leaves poured out onto the newspaper. My heart sank. Just like some smarmy little drug-dealing hooligan, I thought, spoiling it for everyone, dragging the name of all these admirable people into the mud. I caught Mrs. Dawson's eye. She was thinking the same. Daniel took a leaf, rolled it between his fingers, and sniffed.

'Hang on,' he said. 'This isn't…'

'Yes,' said Jon. 'That's the strange thing. We instantly leapt to the conclusion that it was cannabis. But it isn't cannabis. We don't know what it is. We sent a lot off to the analyst but they say it will be months before we can get an answer. I thought I'd see if I could find one quicker than that.'

'You want to ask Trudi as well,' I said. I examined the leaves. They were long and dark green, a little like tobacco, smelling faintly of mould.

'Not well preserved,' commented Mrs. Dawson. 'You don't think this might be some sort of Indian potpourri?'

'No, because it doesn't smell nice,' said Kepler. 'And it doesn't seem to have ever smelt nice.'

I sniffed at a leaf. This was true. I had flirted with making my own perfumes for a while, and I knew most of the herbs which were used. This musty, old straw smell was not a fixative, like orris root, or a scent, like mint.

'They just look like dead leaves to me,' confessed Daniel.

'Someone wants them,' Jon told us. 'We searched all the other bronzes from this maker and found two had already been stolen from the depot before we discovered that they had contraband inside them. We went through the rest of the container and nothing else was found. Just these demon pots. Five of them had leaves inside. Seven with the two missing ones. Which we later found, empty, in the car park.'

'All the same leaves?' asked Meroe, who had taken a napkin, damped several leaves with wine and was now unfolding it.

'As far as I could tell, yes.'

'This is a mixture,' Meroe pronounced. 'This is wolfsbane. This is nightshade. And those long leaves are thorn apple, also known as datura.'

'Those names, Meroe…' said the Professor uneasily. 'They don't sound auspicious.'

'They shouldn't,' said Meroe, her mouth twisted in distaste. 'They're all deadly poisons. Come along. We've got to wash our hands right now.'

After we had put the leaves away and washed our hands, Jon leaned back in his chair and said helplessly, 'This is insane! Why should anyone import poisonous herbs into Australia? Haven't we got enough of our own?'

'Certainly, though those ones don't grow terribly well here. They would also be considered noxious weeds. And some poisons do have therapeutic effects, in small doses or for external application only. Think about digitalin, which regulates the heart.'

'I take it myself,' said the Professor.

Mrs. Dawson agreed. 'As you say, Dion, but thorn apple—if it's the same thing I am thinking of—used to grow in the lanes in Kew when I was a child. I was always told particularly not to touch it. It had huge, long, faintly repellent trumpet flowers. White ones.'

'Perhaps the Indian version is more potent,' suggested Daniel.

'Very probably,' agreed Meroe. 'Jon, I have a tale to tell about Corinna's girls. Perhaps, in fact, Corinna ought to begin it.'

I gave the company a potted version of the maenad scene over the respective merits of Seth and whoever else it was, which had added such a lot of interest to Wednesday. Meroe described the girls' subsequent collapse and our search, which had turned up dubious leaves packed in beige paper. I added the story of how the girls had obtained their supply.

Daniel grunted. 'I've seen boys lying at death's door while the nurses frantically try to find out what they've poisoned themselves with, and they say, "I bought a handful of pills from a bloke in a pub and took them all." This must be the female equivalent.'

'They really would rather die than gain weight?' marvelled Mrs. Dawson.

'Much rather,' I said. All right for her. She was born to be thin.

She picked up my tone. 'All I ever wanted was a bust,' she said. 'Never got one.' She looked meaningfully at my breasts. I conceded the point.

'You are having the next pick-up watched?' Daniel asked Jon and Kepler. It is his profession, after all.

Jon nodded. 'Watched and filmed,' he said. 'Everyone is being investigated, but what do we investigate them for? Thank you so much,' he said, standing up. 'Kepler and I are very fortunate in our friends.'

We filed out. The Professor and Mrs. Dawson were going out to dinner. Meroe vanished with several of the poisonous leaves for further tests. And I suspect I was even giggling as we tumbled down the steps, arm in arm, and ran straight into Starshine.

She had been standing perfectly still. Perhaps she was intending to call on me. Both of her hands were tangled in the fall of her grey-streaked hair and her eyes were hot, as though she had been weeping. But she was not weeping now and the glare she fixed on Daniel and me would have skewered an ox.

'You...dare...' she managed to say through her set teeth. I had recoiled into Daniel's embrace in sheer shock. Now I stood up, drawing myself away from him.

'Dare what?' I asked loudly. My voice wasn't altogether under my control but I suddenly felt stronger.

'He is missing and you...dare...to laugh!' she snarled.

'Yes,' I told her defiantly, 'I dare. And I'll keep looking for him, but you aren't going to destroy this relationship, Jacqui. Go back to Therese now. I'll call you when we find him.'

And she fled. She turned with a whisk of skirts and actually fled. No dog was ever so heartened as I when a bigger dog bought its bluff. I laughed again as she ran up the stairs.

'See?' said Daniel into my neck. 'It's true. Love conquers all.'

'Or something,' I agreed, took a deep breath, and went inside.

Daniel and I fed Horatio and settled amicably down to cook a couple of steaks, concoct a salad with the fairy leaves and make mashed potatoes. We had sworn off watching the news for the duration of the present prime minister, and listened instead to cheerful dance music which had kept a cold medieval hall rocking in the days when someone's selection of leaves was all the medicine there was. We even stepped a few paces of the Known World Pavanne. Uniquely, Daniel does not get in my way in the kitchen—and I don't get in his. These may be our most intimate moments. Lovemaking improves with practice, but this seamless dance we were weaving between fridge and sink and table and oven, that was grace.

We dined well. Daniel went to keep one of his shadowy appointments in the night world, and I put myself to bed. My own world had come back together, and I was pleased with it. But tomorrow, I realised, I would have to try to find my father again. The trouble with the real world, I thought as I fell asleep, is that it never just gives you one problem and lets you get on with solving it. There's always something else. In my case, several something elses. Like juggling, I thought, and didn't remember anything else until the alarm clock went off at four am and Friday announced that it was here.

Coffee, toast, feed Horatio, trackies, tray, down steps. Usual things. But pleasant because they were usual. Jason was working on a new muffin and the kitchen smelt of cooking fruit. Today's soup was minestrone and the herbs were waiting to be snipped for the accompanying muffins. Good, strong, real smells, enough to banish night and hazard. An hour's work and more coffee and everything was in preparation.

'So how was dinner?' I asked Jason.

He grinned. 'Sweet!' he exclaimed. 'I was only there for an hour and a half and they were offering to send me home with a truckload of food.'

The management of the Violet House had seen Jason before, of course. I thought their offer was a wise one.

'Jason,' I asked tentatively—I didn't want to arouse any bad memories—'if you were found naked and wet and half frozen, just crawled out of the river, where would the cops take you?'

'Hospital,' he said, snipping chives with scissors that moved faster than the speed of light.

'And when the hospital let you go?'

'Salvos,' he said judiciously, measuring his handful of herbs. 'The Salvos take anyone. Might not be able to find him a room, but they'd get him some clothes, a meal. This your dad we're talking about?'

'Yes,' I answered. 'The hospital must have kept a record of him.'

'Aren't the cops looking for him?'

'Possibly. He wouldn't be a very high priority, you know. Grown man and all.'

'And maybe he don't want to be found.'

'Maybe,' I had to agree. My aged parent's walk on the wild side was becoming a little extreme.

'Daniel'll know who to ask. Sister Mary too. They all know each other. They all swap clients. When they can't find any place for them. There, that's the famine bread done,' he said, hauling the trays out of the oven and deftly avoiding the flat bar which seems designed to scorch the baker's knuckles. 'Wish I knew why it smells like sawdust.'

'It does, doesn't it? You sure you didn't add any?'

He gave me a glare which mutated into a grin when he realised I was joking. 'Nah,' he drawled. 'Must be the lentil flour. Now for something nice. Today's other muffins are—ta da!—apricot delight. I've had the dried fruit soaking all night.'

'Wonderful. I'll get on with my rye bread,' I said.

The Mouse Police, after their foray into the alley, had sidled back inside to lick their fur dry and contemplate a nice day's rest before a vigorous evening's mousing. The vats burbled and the dough hooks clicked. Peace.

Never lasts, though. The day dawned. The rain stopped. People arrived. Mrs. Dawson, returning from one of her early morning walks, bought some pasta douro and a Jason apricot muffin. (He topped them with slivered almonds and they were gorgeous.) I asked her why she insisted on walking when the dawn was just breaking and whatever weather was around was at its worst.

'I inherited a puritan conscience, dear,' she told me, sniffing the steam from the bakery with surprising voluptuousness for a puritan. 'So I go out for a mile walk, a mile at the minimum no matter the weather, and that assuages it for the rest of the day.

I am then free to lounge, eat chocolate, go back to bed, read a stack of detective stories and lunch and dine in luxury. Not a peep out of it as long as I have performed my penitential walk. And it is a very good time to see the city unbuttoned, as it were—without its covers.'

'But there are some very nasty things under those covers,' I objected, thinking of some of the mentally afflicted homeless who might find Mrs. Dawson a good target for begging or assault. She was tiny! And very noticeable indeed in her scarlet slicker and bright red boots. Even the most bleary sleeper-out would be able to see Mrs. Dawson striding briskly across his path.

'They never worry me,' she said with blithe unconcern, 'because I never worry them.'

I didn't recognise it as a principle, but it certainly worked for Sylvia Dawson. She called out a thank you to Jason for his muffins and walked serenely on, perfectly self-possessed, on her way to a luxurious breakfast with her conscience. I really ought to persuade her to adopt a cat. Once you have a cat, you don't need a conscience.

On cue, Horatio appeared at the inner door, ready to sit on the counter and amuse the customers. I hurried through to open the shop door and take down the shutters and there was Goss on the doorstep, freezing in her pink coatee and short skirt, but otherwise looking very healthy.

'How do you feel?' I asked, examining her carefully. Her eyes were bright, but not too bright, and she seemed to be much as usual. That is, underdressed and blue of knee.

'I'm fine,' she said dismissively, handing me her mobile phone. I am not an unreasonable woman. I don't ask that she does something unthinkable like leave the phone in her apartment. I just ask that it be switched to voicemail and stored on a high shelf in the shop. 'Can I smell apricots? I love apricots. Jason? Gimme a muffin?'

I heard Jason's slightly shocked, 'Sure,' as he handed one over, still warm from the oven.

'All right if I have a cup of coffee?' Goss asked, picking up a staff china cup in one hand and the coffee pot in the other.

I nodded, amazed. Usually those two eschewed the bakery's produce as though it was carefully spiked with strychnine before it left the oven. Goss sipped her (admittedly black with no sugar) coffee and nibbled her muffin with evident enjoyment while Jason and I watched. Even Horatio seemed a little taken aback. He leapt up on the counter and began a complex operation which seemed to involve polishing each whisker separately. Goss finished the muffin and put down the empty cup.

'We've been talking, Kyl and me,' she explained. 'We could have killed ourselves with those leaves, Meroe says. And we took too much. We really felt horrible. We're used to feeling hungry but that was something else, it was gross. We were really sick. And so we thought, we'll just follow the CSIRO diet. That says I can have a muffin if I want one. And I wanted one. And it was really nice,' she added, a little defiantly. 'The almonds taste real good with the apricots.'

'Thanks,' said Jason, sensing female emotions about to erupt and fading in to the bakery to do the orders. I heard Megan's rickshaw bell in Calico Alley. I had to handle this very carefully. Any strong reaction might drive Goss right back onto the famine diet. Equally I was delighted that they had seen sense and the sight of Goss nibbling her way through that muffin had done my heart good. So I settled for a one-armed hug, which she accepted, and a 'Well done, Goss!', which didn't seem to arouse any adverse response. People complain about the difficulty of taming bears and tigers. They should try adolescents. All a bear can do is bite off your arm in a friendly way. Adolescents can harrow your soul.

The soup steamed, the bread piled up on the shelves, the public arrived out of the chill street. It was one of those odd Melbourne days when early morning is bright and sunny, so that you need sunglasses for the glare. Late morning would bring clouds and by afternoon it would either be (1) raining or (2) freezing or (3) both. That's why the sunnies and the mac are essential on any day in our great city, where there are four seasons in one day. If there were six seasons, there'd be six. It's what makes Melburnians so quick on the uptake and resilient, able to adapt to change.

Though it still doesn't explain or forgive Federation Square, the covering tiles of which are the exact same colour as the faded kitchen lino that Grandma Chapman kept thinking of replacing…years after year. And what sort of idiot would make such a space without any shelter from rain or shine, in a climate like ours? But I have never understood city planning, and I still haven't recovered from what happened to the Paris end of Collins Street. I just know Mr. Hoddle wouldn't have stood for it.

People loved the apricot muffins, though there were demands for the chocolate orgasm ones, which were Jason's masterpiece. I called in to the bakery and he promised them for Monday. Jason's art is ever-expanding. I am in awe of his talent. Who would have thought that a genius for concocting new muffins lay under that scruffy ex-heroin addict exterior? While he was still having counselling every Saturday I knew that it was cooking that had salvaged Jason from the scrapheap. That and his own strong will.

I could hear Megan's engine as she hauled the rickshaw round into Flinders Lane. There went the orders, the rye bread for Café Vlad Tepes and Le Gourmet, the pasta douro for Ristorante Spoleto and Bistrot Provence and Taverna Prasima Ble. It was satisfying, imagining my bread being moved all over the city, supplying luncheons and dinners, mopping up every delicious sauce from squid ink to rich tomato to Greek lemon. However good the food, the restaurant must have good bread. In a pinch, one can do without the wine, but never without the bread.

I had been dreaming, I think, standing at the bakery door, when Jason backed abruptly into me and stood on my tenderest corn. This has been known to break a dream state and I shoved him off my foot.

'What?' I asked a little harshly, favouring the throbbing toe.

'It's them creepy dudes,' he whispered.

'All right, I'll do the creepy dudes and you help Goss,' I said. He was really disconcerted, I could see. I went to the alley door and saw his point.

Two people stood there. I could not tell if they were male or female, partly because they were so thin and draped in black robes but mostly because they had hoods over what I believed were shaved heads.

'Yes?' I asked briskly. I was not going to be outfaced by a costume. A rag, a bone, and as Kipling didn't say, no hank of hair. So to speak.

The first person spoke in a low voice, neither masculine nor feminine. 'Our order,' it said.

'Of course.' I took out the seven loaves of famine bread and began to pack them in an Earthly Delights cardboard box. The two stood perfectly still, waiting. They were uncanny and I somehow did not want to turn my back on them, though I did. I packed carefully. If I hurry I get clumsy and I did not want to extend this visit by having to start again.

In a shiny window in front of me, I caught sight of the first robed person's face. He had lifted his head, now my back was safely turned, and the hood had slid back. It was an arresting face. My hands faltered on the greaseproof paper as I looked at him. The face of an ascetic or a saint, I thought. Pale skin, not very lined. Dark brown eyes, impossible to read.

A suave cheek and jaw, closely shaved. And the red mouth of a voluptuary, aching to be kissed. Dark shadows under the eyes. A compelling, beautiful, somehow tragic face. Then he caught me looking. The eyes flashed, the hood was pulled back into place, and I made my final knot and turned around to put the box into his hands.

If I still blushed I would have blushed, but I don't so I didn't, which was a mercy. The hoods inclined a little towards me, in what might have been a bow, and they went away down Calico

Alley. From behind, the robes looked archaic and threatening. I don't know why. I had seen monks' robes before. I fanned myself with the order book and made another cup of coffee and sat down. Jason looked in from the shop.

'You see what I mean?' he asked. I nodded, still fanning.

'Real creepy dudes,' I agreed. What a face! What a tormented, tragic face! And what, yes, what had that Savonarola countenance to do with an order of monks?

The man who was not yet a murderer leaned against the wall and bit into his knuckle. It was too much. They couldn't ask him to do it. No human could bear this. No one.

Chapter Nine

I had just recovered by the time Daniel arrived. He dead-heated two policemen. Well, well, what could they want? It was Kane and Reagan, slouching into the shop and ogling Goss. Who, admittedly, was ogling them back.

'You keep bad company,' one commented to me, glaring straight at Daniel.

'A druggie and Daniel,' said the other.

'Yes, aren't I lucky?' I said cheerfully, aiming to annoy. Nothing drives a bully up the wall like not noticing that you are being bullied. 'What can I do for you, gentlemen? Offer you a muffin?'

'Nah,' said Reagan. He was chewing a massive wad of gum like a cud. 'Not going to eat anything made by a druggie. You been asking about a bloke called Chapman,' he said to Daniel.

'Yes,' he agreed.

'Why?'

'He's missing,' said Daniel.

'And he's my father,' I concluded.

They seemed a little taken aback.

'Oh. Right. Well, he was in the Royal Melbourne overnight a while ago,' said Kane, carefully not telling me the date. 'Exposure and shock. From immersion. Know anything about that?'

'Only that he was thrown in the river by some bad acquaintances,' said Daniel.

They had not yet taken their eyes off each other. This was one of those coded conversations in which both sides knew and meant a great deal more than they were saying. Now was not a good time to ask for a decode.

'Any chance of evidence?' asked Kane.

'Not a chance,' said Daniel.

The cops shrugged. 'Too bad.'

'Yeah. Where did Chapman go when the hospital discharged him?' asked Daniel.

'Where d'you think?' asked Reagan, giving his chewing gum an extra chomp.

'If I knew, I wouldn't have to ask,' Daniel replied patiently.

'I'd quite like to know as well,' I put in. I had no patience with this *High Noon* dialogue. Unless Clint Eastwood walked in to continue it, of course. That would have been different. Both sides of the conversation, having forgotten I was there, jumped.

'Oh, yeah, well,' said Kane, the younger and more sensible. 'The Salvos. Haven't been able to trace him from there. Is he a nutcase, your old man?' he asked me, not meaning any offence.

'Oh yes,' I said with resignation, 'by now he almost certainly is.'

'We'll keep on it,' Kane assured me. 'When we got the time. So long,' he added to Daniel. 'Don't get in our way.'

'I'll try not to,' said Daniel politely.

Kane and Reagan left the shop, which immediately seemed larger. I was expecting Daniel to be angry but he only laughed. 'Idiots,' he said. 'They'd be good investigators if they lost some of the attitude. Still, there it is. He who lives may learn. I just came in to remind you that we are going to that club tonight and Mistress Dread has your new dress.'

'Oh, yes.' I had forgotten. But nothing was going to make me miss a chance of wearing one of Mistress Dread's dominance dresses. Every fat woman ought, once in her life, to wear one.

I had worn the borrowed blood-red taffeta number to a vampire club and several times after, and it was remarkable. But

I wanted a dress of my own and Mistress Dread had had her 'little man' make one for me. Oh, goody.

I was so cheered by this prospect that I decided to go and see how my mother and the admirable Therese were getting on, as soon as the shop closed, before the dress fitting and an afternoon potation and little nap. But when I rang the doorbell, it appeared that no one was at home. I wondered what Therese had done with Starshine, and decided that I didn't care. Now for Mistress Dread and the dress.

For fat women, clothes are a constant pain and a constant reproach. Not for us the luxury of taking an armload of garments and working out which one flatters our figure or emphasises our broad beam. Not for us the plaintive 'does my bum look big in this?', a silly question because our bums look big in everything, because they are big. We are confined to the chain stores plus sizes, which tend to the blue crimplene in which, I have instructed, I am not even to be buried. Or the specialists, whose clothes are lovely but expensive. It would be so nice to join the crowds ferreting through the Dimmey's sales and getting two dollar trousers. But it is not to be. A good general rule for fat women is, if you like it, it will be too small. Therefore, having a dress made expressly to one's own measurements is a wonderful thing.

I gave Goss back her mobile phone, saw Jason off with a large goody bag to stave off night-time starvation, let Horatio into the apartment and went out into the lane, to the front door of Mistress Dread's shop, which sells leather goods for the discerning customer.

The salon is hung with ivory and gold and looks like a very upmarket dressmaker's. There are large books on the coffee table, the contents of which are rather R rated. There is a scent of leather in the air. Mistress Dread is fully six feet high, and her usual working attire consists of fishnets, spike heels, a red or black leather corset, spiked collar and whip. Oddly enough, she has never been robbed. Jason says that some of his erstwhile druggie friends broke in one night and all Mistress Dread had to do to utterly undo them was smile. They broke the land-speed record in the direction of Flinders Street and retired into private life, swearing to be good. But she is a firm friend to me and Daniel and I won't hear a word against her. Today's corset, I saw, was red, and her cascading wig was fire-engine red to match.

'Corinna! Off with the tat, dear, you're going to love this dress. Oleg's outdone himself,' she remarked, locking the shop door and beckoning me into an alcove lined with mirrors. Undressing in front of a phalanx of mirrors is a severe test for any person, but I did it. And I didn't look too bad. Very Rubens, of course, but not saggy or blemished. Mistress Dread gave me an approving pat on a buttock and threw over my head a confection of black silk and lace that slid down my body and fitted exactly to my curves.

'He's thinking of a Spanish dress in a portrait by Goya,' Mistress Dread informed me, tweaking the wide neckline into place. Oh, it was lovely. The black silk made my skin look white as milk. The dress was frilled heavily from the hips downwards, and upwards clung like a second skin. The silk was heavy, soot-black and looked almost wet.

'And then over it,' said Mistress Dread, smiling, 'we have the corset.' She lifted my breasts into a thin leather shell, such as Zena might have worn, and began to lace me in. Up rose my ordinarily unremarkable breasts into perfect twin globes that might have given a Restoration poet wet dreams. I had seen this transformation before and it never failed to enchant. My long sleeves were heavily beaded at the hem, which made them agreeably heavy. I raised my hands and crossed them on my beautiful bosom. Oh, Corinna.

'And then we put up your hair,' continued Mistress Dread, dragging handfuls of my hair into a scant ponytail on top of my head and securing it with several very sharp hairpins and a comb stuck straight into the scalp. Then she draped over this prominence a fine black mantilla that framed my face in dark, delicate folds. I was beautiful. I turned this way and that, intoxicated by my own reflection.

'Say something,' Mistress Dread ordered. She still had her whip on a thong at her wrist and I had been unduly silent.

'It's utterly wonderful,' I said in a hushed tone.

'I thought so,' she said, pleased. 'You couldn't wear this if you were thin, you know. It needs bulk to fill out the curves. Oh, indeed. Walk a little. You need your boots, of course. Then the hem won't drag. Turn. Oh, yes.'

She clasped her hands on her armoured breast like the proud mother of the bride. I was overwhelmed by her kindness.

'This was so nice of you,' I started. She tapped me with her whip.

'Don't thank me. Does Oleg good to make something different. You can pay me for the dress,' she added, 'but this is a present.'

She handed me a large, brightly painted fan. Due to a school production of *The King and I*, I knew how to flick it open and shut. I did so, picking up my skirt with the other hand. The dress moved like a cloud or a dream.

Mistress Dread giggled. 'Lovely,' she said. 'You really will be the belle of the ball. Now, dear, let's sit down and have a drink and a gossip. It's been ages since I saw anyone,' she said. 'Not since that party for Mrs. Dawson's son. What happened to him, after all that?'

'He's gone back to his nice family and he's got another job,' I told her, sinking onto the ivory couch. The dress settled around me without creasing or stiffness. 'The police case is complete and he's going to testify against the people who ripped that money off from his old company. So that's all right. But we've been having troubles,' I said, accepting a White Lady from Mistress Dread's ever-available supply. 'First of all, my mother turned up...'

Mistress Dread listened through two White Ladies as I told her all about my appalling parents, the dangerous herbs which had poisoned Kylie and Goss, and the smuggling of poisons in the Fair Trade goods. Several times her eyebrows rose over her pale blue eyes. To complete the tale I threw in a description of the real creepy dudes who had unnerved Jason.

'See what happens when I don't pay attention?' asked Mistress Dread. 'All that going on and I missed it. Still, I'd like to know about that weight loss tea. If anyone is selling it in my dungeon they'll be strung up before they know what's hit them. And then they'll know what is hitting them, because it will be me. I've fought too hard to keep the drug dealers out of the club—I know they're in the street outside but they aren't in my club—to allow some swine peddling poisonous weeds to infest the place. I shall speak to my Igors. They're supposed to let me know if they see anything iffy.'

'There might not be anything,' I said, hoping that she wouldn't be too hard on the Igors. They were the dungeon's servitors, and it was a hard job, keeping the alcohol supply up while wearing a papier-mâché hump and remembering to speak with a lisp. Jason moonlighted as an Igor most Saturday nights. He said it kept him out of trouble. 'They might just be selling at Café Vlad.'

'I've heard that it isn't a well conducted place,' she said, primming up her lips like a governess of the old school confronted with a green-haired punk. 'You're going there with Daniel? Keep your hand on your money. Several people have been robbed there—well, not robbed, pickpocketed. It's not a very good location, either—street's not all that safe. But you'll be all right,' she said, patting me on my bare shoulder. 'Now, do me a cheque for Oleg and off you go. I've got a client coming at three thirty.'

I reluctantly removed the dress, corset and mantilla, packed them into a box, paid for it all, and took my leave of Mistress Dread. Though I yield to no one in my admiration of her character, she is a threatening presence and I always exit her shop with a small, slightly shameful feeling of relief.

Now for Daniel, Horatio, another drink and a nice afternoon snooze to prepare me for the evening. Since I had been potating freely (one does not refuse a drink from Mistress Dread), I made a very small gin and tonic for myself when Daniel and I were settled on the marble bench in the Temple of Ceres. Horatio, who was feeling clingy, sat down rather markedly on Daniel's lap, curling his tail around his paws. I leaned on Daniel's shoulder.

He bore up very well under this, managing his glass with his one free hand. Black clouds loomed outside, riding the top of the buildings. Suddenly I loved Daniel so much that it literally hurt my heart. I put a hand on my breast. Dark eyes looked down at me with perfect understanding.

'Me too,' he said. 'Never thought I'd find you. Couldn't bear to lose you.'

I hugged him closer. We watched the fine rain slant across the glass. I had never been so happy.

Before we sank into complete blissful immobility, however, Horatio rose and decided it was time to return to the apartment for a suitable nap. He emphasised this by driving a selection of claws into Daniel's thigh, which awoke us with an 'ouch'. I finished my drink and got up. Daniel allowed Horatio to ascend to his shoulder, and we went down in the lift, still not speaking, and put ourselves to bed.

Where instead of making love we fell asleep as though stunned, and didn't wake for four hours. And when we did our relationship had changed to something which felt solid and enduring and very, very comfortable. I'm new at this love thing. Perhaps this is normal. But it felt fantastic.

We dined lightly on grilled cheese sandwiches and soup left over from the shop, a good solid minestrone with a lot of vegetables. It was no use going to a vampire club until eleven at the earliest, so despite our self-imposed ban we sat down to watch the news. A bad mistake. Internationally, things were terrible. Assassinations, wars, and did I really need to see (1) the bodies from an Indian flood and (2) the remains from a huge chemical explosion and (3) a sniper on a Palestinian roof? Why show me these terrible images? In the interests of more nightmares? Our domestic news included murders, rapes, suspicious deaths and a few merry car crashes. Who defines disasters as news? Who, indeed, actually wants to see these things? Did anyone ask us? I don't remember anyone asking me.

Sickened, we slotted in a *Buffy* DVD. These are contained disasters and known horrors. And good, mostly, wins in the end. This restored our humour. At least there was still Buffy in the world.

The night wore on. We got dressed. I donned the black dress and Daniel laced me up. I had a black cloak to go over it to hide my glorious attributes from the uninitiated. Daniel had decided against the half-naked slave, largely on account of the weather. He was wearing impeccable eighteenth century evening costume and he looked gorgeous. His hair had grown out from its severe cut and was brushed forward, en brosse. His suit coat was of an inky blackness and his cravat of towering whiteness. He carried a gold-topped stick and a perfumed handkerchief, which he flourished in the hand which wore the big emerald ring. Sir Percy Blakeney, in fact. I curtsied. He bowed elaborately over my hand.

'Oh yes, I think I shall like this game,' I observed.

'Od's bodkin, ma'am,' he said ironically. 'What is not to like?'

'Careful,' I said. 'You're slipping into Captain Hook.'

He shrugged on a swagged coat and tricorne and I put on my cloak. We were going to walk through a not very savoury bit of the city, and having a good stout stick might be of more uses than one. Nothing unseemly met our eye as we paced soberly up Flinders Lane but the occasional passing cat, the occasional scurrying rat (which doubtless occasioned the cat) and a few gentlemen who had dined well and who catcalled a little as they passed. The important thing with catcalling gentlemen is that they keep passing, and these did with barely an extra jeer. I was having to hurry to keep up with Daniel's long stride, and put out a hand to detain him at the exact same moment that he slowed down of his own accord.

'Sorry. I forget that my legs are longer than yours,' he apologised.

'Don't mention it,' I said, taking his left hand in mine. We were in tune now. It was a strange feeling. In my high heeled boots I was taller, almost as tall as Daniel. I liked the way the world looked from higher up. On the other hand no one designs those come-fuck-me boots for stability on wet pavements. I was planting my feet carefully, scared of slipping. A thin woman falling over is sad and conjures immediate help. A fat woman falling over is funny and produces immediate laughter. Unfair, but there it is. Luckily, I had a Daniel to lean on.

'You nervous?' he asked me as we crossed a main street.

'Yes, a little. I've never been good at making a superb entrance.'

'Me neither,' he said gravely. 'Goes against the grain. Detectives are meant to be unobtrusive. I've worked on not being noticed for years. Never mind. I've been asking around about this place.'

'Me too. Mistress Dread says it is not well run and we should avoid pickpockets.'

'And I've heard that it's a very formal Georgian levee, with appropriate music and a lot of gay clients. Well, we shall see.'

'Is that why you got the Scarlet Pimpernel gear?' I asked. 'Which suits you amazingly well, I have to say.'

'Yes,' he replied. 'And no Sir Percy ever had such a beautiful woman on his arm. Mistress Dread's little man did a good job.'

'I'm prostrated by your lordship's approval,' I said, snapping my fan, and we arrived at the front entrance of what, during the day, was Café Simisoa, and now proclaimed itself to be Café Vlad Tepes.

The door bitch was a woman with legs, I swear, two metres long, sleek in blue silk stockings. She was otherwise clad in a footman's costume, with a short grey wig. Behind her stood two large young men with that 'you're not interesting unless you make a fuss and I can pound you into a fine paste such as is used to fill the cracks between floorboards' look I have often noticed on bouncers' faces. The door bitch scanned Daniel and smiled. I opened my cloak and she flapped a hand up and down. This must have been the 'open the door' signal because the bullies let us in and closed the heavy door behind us. Not a word had been exchanged.

We were in a hot narrow hall. On one side was a cloakroom with an attendant in a footman's costume. On the other were the sanitary facilities. Not promising, but we had a mission. We checked my cloak and Daniel's coat and hat and went into the main room, where I could hear sweet music playing. A string quartet. I knew the piece. I had often played the tape. What was it?

We stopped at the door and gasped. The management of Café Vlad Tepes had solved the problem of transforming a nice civilised daytime Café Simisoa into a vampire's haunt by hiring a very good artist to paint four stage-set sized trompes l'oeil of a Georgian house and garden. It was hard to gauge how large the real room was, because on one side it led into an enchanting garden with a gazebo and sheep; on the adjoining one it led into a sumptuous kitchen, on another a ballroom, on another into a salon where men were playing cards.

'Kylie didn't mention the paintings,' I said weakly.

'She probably didn't even notice them,' said Daniel. 'Let's get a drink.'

We paraded across the ballroom to the servery, which was set up in front of the painted kitchen door. The young woman in standard wench costume sold us red wine and dimpled when Daniel gave her a tip. They were a set of good dimples so I did not begrudge her them.

'Quiet tonight,' he observed.

'It'll get busy after midnight,' she answered. 'When the night people wake and come to feed. If you are looking for dance or techno music, gentle sir, you need to find another club. The most modern we get here is the saraband.'

'What's the attraction, then?' asked Daniel.

'Calm,' she said. 'Formality. Manners. Not a lot of them about in the club scene. Later we'll darken the room and play soft music to murmur sweet things by. You'll see. There'll be supper at one and then it all gets cosy. There's our historian,' she said. 'My lord D'Urbanville! Favour us with your wisdom.'

An elderly man in the impeccable knee breeches, plain waistcoat and blue coat of Beau Brummel himself crossed the room and made an elaborate bow, which we returned civilly.

'You are interested in my club?' he asked in a sharp, decided voice. 'Come, drink a glass with me and I will expound. Abigail, bring the bottle.'

'If you please,' I said, curtsying again for the pleasure of feeling the flow of my beautiful dress. I snapped my fan open. My lord D'Urbanville offered me his arm and we were conducted to a set of chairs and tables where some young men were playing cards. Coins were piled up to perilous heights.

'Deep play was a Georgian prerogative,' observed the elderly man. 'As a practitioner of the love which, once upon a time, dared not speak its name and now appears to shout it incessantly, I was appalled by the noise of the clubs in this city and the unbridled behaviour of the patrons.'

'Noisy indeed,' I agreed.

'Definitely unbridled,' said Daniel, sipping his wine.

'So when I inherited this building and was minded to set up a club for my co-amorists, I thought—what is missing from my sex's world? Quiet, that is absent, and so is civility. In the eighteenth century there were places of homosexual resort called Mollyhouses. I decided that I should have a Mollyhouse. Then I thought, it is unfair to the heterosexual to deprive them of this, so both genders are encouraged to enjoy our facilities. When my dear friend wanted to have a café which reflected his own Rumanian homeland, nothing could have been easier. During the day he has his café . During the night I have my Mollyhouse. Who is most likely to find this attractive? The goths, who value historical accuracy, good food and music. Here they can sup well, dance sedately and conduct their amours where they can see their partners, and perhaps choose more wisely than those who go home with someone they met in flaring red light and a daze of exhaustion and sweat.'

'What a very good idea,' Daniel commented.

'And your artist has done a wonderful job with the *trompes l'oeil*,' I said. 'It looks like Vauxhall or Ranelegh.'

'Do I speak to a fellow historian?' he asked, eyeing me narrowly.

'No, I just read a lot of Georgette Heyer,' I admitted.

His sharp face softened. He patted my hand and poured me another drink. 'Who did not?' he asked rhetorically, and we began to discuss his favourite Heyer, *The Grand Sophy*.

I argued passionately for *These Old Shades*. Daniel, unable to contribute to this feast of reason and flow of soul, watched the people.

The room was filling up. Pretty youths drifted by in sketchy eighteenth century attire. Pretty maidens in various garments wandered up to the bar and bought drinks. My lord D'Urbanville was forced to half rise and greet several people as they passed and bowed. Finally he pleaded a further engagement, ordered Abigail to bring us another bottle, and left us.

Daniel grinned at me. 'What an amazing old person! And what a good impression you made! Should we tell him about someone selling weeds in his precious club?'

'Not if we can avoid it, he'd be terribly upset. How do we go about finding Kylie's friend Bo?'

'I suppose we could ask around,' he answered. I always thought detectives had secret means for doing things, but it looked like Daniel was in the same class as the rest of us. He smiled and poured some more wine.

'Never mind, ketschele,' he said. 'Have another drink.'

I had another drink. After all, it was free. And the sweet music played on my ear, tantalising me. I began to watch the string quartet. They were worth looking at. Very handsome people, those musicians.

The violin was played by a young woman with a thick plait of blonde hair down her back. The second violin by another, so similar that they might have been sisters. The viola by a thin dark young man with both whiskers and spectacles, and the cello by a blonde girl with the face of a Botticelli Madonna. They were all dressed in tidy dark blue and looked competent and sane.

And I had the work, at last, it was the Propitia Sidera by Muffat, the concerto grosso XII. Oh, such music. And they were playing it very well, with the effortless unison only achieved through endless muscle-racking rehearsal. Daniel got up and held out a hand.

'If madame will favour me with this dance?' he asked.

I put my hand in his. I didn't know what the dance was called, but neither did most of the people who now filled the room. All I had to do, following the old Noël Coward advice, was to say the lines and not trip over the furniture. I thought I could probably do that. And I did. I paced carefully beside Daniel through what I thought might be a modified pavane, a dance which cannot be bungled provided that the aspirant can reliably walk.

I surveyed the crowd. It was mixed. Several trannies in immaculate eighteenth century costume—though one had strayed into Elizabethan and was having trouble with his ruff. Several straights in costume, differentiated by their chest hair and wigs. Dancing in front of me was a gay boy in buckskins into which he must have been poured, twitching his buttocks insolently. They were, however, very pretty buttocks indeed. Beside him was a slouching, bored girl in a bedraggled gown which her mother might have given her for dress-ups.

Daniel was suppressing a giggle. If the display was for him it was wasted. We turned and reversed. Now in front of me was a tall young man in an extensive collar and blue coat with a sprightly elderly lady, who was skipping to keep up with him.

'I think it's going to be a strange night,' I said to Daniel. He squeezed my hand. But we had barely begun to ask around—I had received only two proposals and Daniel three, all utterly indecent—when a plump young man sat down next to me and said, 'I'm Bo. I think you are looking for me. Though I can't imagine why.'

The man who was becoming a murderer found that if he thought very hard about blood and death, he could shut out the voice. His dreams dripped with gore. Blood from the wounds of the crucified man streamed down the cross.

Chapter Ten

'Have a drink,' I said, pouring out more of my lord D'Urbanville's wine. 'I'm Corinna and this is Daniel. You are not in any trouble. We just want some information.'

'If it's about who's screwing who,' he said, flushing all over his very fair skin, 'then I won't tell you.'

'We don't care who is screwing whom,' I said, getting it grammatically right as well. 'We want to know who sold Kylie those weight loss herbs.'

'Didn't they work?' he asked, dismayed.

'Er...' I began. Did we want to tell him they were poisonous? This was a nice boy. He had 'nice boy' written all through him, like Brighton Rock. I hated to hurt his feelings. Daniel smiled at Bo and inspired fresh revelations.

'You see, we have to be thin,' he said, tossing off the wine and refilling his glass. 'The beautiful boys won't look at you unless you're slim. Muscular, of course, with perfect abs and all, but slim. My friend Tobias...' His voice trailed off.

'Tell us about your friend Tobias,' I prompted gently.

'Took it all to heart,' said Bo. 'Stopped eating. Didn't take anything but the herbs. Now I don't know where he is. I'm worried about him,' he stated, suddenly sounding mature.

'Where did he get the tea?' asked Daniel.

Bo looked frightened. 'I don't want to tell you,' he said.

I laid a hand on his. 'But you are going to,' I told him.

He looked down at the table as though he had never seen a hand before. I felt his fingers flex. His hand was soft, as though he had never done any manual work. Poor, sweet, soft, buttery boy.

'The apothecary,' he whispered. 'He comes around most every night. With the witch. She can sell you a maigre doll to witch away your fat. He can sell you a tea to melt it away. At a price,' he added bitterly. 'But only to special customers.'

Daniel palmed fifty dollar notes. Four of them.

'Buy us some?' he asked. Bo paused. 'Please?' asked Daniel and smiled his melting smile.

'All right,' said Bo. 'But he isn't here yet.'

'Then we shall wait for him,' I said. 'And we won't tell him you told us. How will we know him?'

'Hat,' whispered Bo. 'He wears a tall hat.'

Then he got up and scuttled away amongst the dancers. Daniel and I looked at each other.

'A maigre doll,' I said.

'A tea of herbs,' he answered.

'Charlatan,' I decided.

'Poisoner,' Daniel added.

The quartet started playing the fireworks music. The polite gathering danced. Daniel and I danced, too. We awaited the arrival of the apothecary and the witch and listened to the music of a sprightly minuet.

The night people had woken, as Abigail had said, and were filing into the formal drawing room. Vampires. Not for these the wild antics of the crypt; these were genteel. Only a flash of fang or an unwary glance at dilated eyes showed that Daniel and I were in the presence of the undead. They paced a pretty measure, presumably learnt in Prague in the old days, before the defenestration.

Daniel was cut out and I was whirled away in the arms of a black clad gentleman of substantial girth. He smiled, showing sharp teeth.

'You have such beautiful, white, plump flesh,' he drooled. 'It demands to be bitten.'

'Not all gentlemen appreciate plump flesh,' I rejoined.

He grunted a laugh. 'Fools. A thin woman is a bed full of bones. You can bruise yourself on her hips. Now you—you could take my weight…'

'But I'm not going to,' I told him. He whirled me round again and contrived to shrug. Not easy to do while dancing.

'No harm in asking,' he commented. He danced very well and was affable so I agreed.

'No one minds being asked,' I said.

Over my vampire's shoulder I could see Daniel dancing with a skeletal blonde dressed in wispy grave clothes. Her face was painted pale green with charcoal highlights and she looked ghastly—which was the idea, of course.

My boots were beginning to hurt my feet so I had my cavalier leave me at the little table. He tripped off to find another plump lady and I dropped back into my chair to survey the crowd. They were very good looking. It was hard to tell how much of the nerd-pale complexions were real or produced by cosmetics. Against them the bright eyes and pink cheeks of the musicians and wenches seemed over-coloured, almost vulgar. How delightful to be a vampire, to wake when the world slept, to haunt the dark lanes, to fly the unfriendly skies and never, never to die. One could see the attraction.

The lights were getting low. The music was becoming, as Abigail had said, more cosy. One thing about the eighteenth century, there was always Handel, who had written so many operas and oratorios and songs that there was a Handel for every possible mood. Amorous Handel was charming.

But it was late and I was getting sleepy. I had, after all, arisen at four this morning—no, yesterday morning—and I was no longer at the Kylie and Goss age where I could stay up all night and never notice. I poured myself a glass of orange crush, which Daniel had bought, because more wine would just have made me sleepier.

Lord D'Urbanville alighted like a bird and I offered him some orange drink. He shuddered lightly.

'No, I thank you. I will take wine, if you please. Are you enjoying my club, Mistress Corinna?'

'Very much,' I said, truthfully. I poured a glass of wine for the elderly man.

'And yet you are not here entirely in pursuit of pleasure,' he observed.

'No?' I asked. I retreated behind my fan, snapping it open.

'Your escort has been recognised,' he told me. 'A private detective. A very toothsome one, I admit,' he added. 'What are you seeking here?'

I had to make an instant decision. After all, it was his club. He seemed honest and concerned.

'The apothecary and the witch,' I said. His old hand closed on my wrist with surprising force. His blue eyes were flinty under his white wig. His face had grown more lines. His voice hardly rose above a whisper.

'You suspect them of selling...drugs?'

'Not exactly. We are trying to trace some weight loss tea which made two girls very sick.'

The grip slackened a little. 'Nostrums,' he said. 'I agreed to allow those two to visit the club because they added some very convincing period colour. But they assured me that everything they sold was harmless. And accurate. Well, I will let you deal with them,' he added, getting up. He was now leaning on his cane for support. Poor man. His club was dear to him.

Vampires swirled past wearing very decorative opera cloaks and long skirts. One slim young man was dressed in every possible texture of black: silk, satin, velvet, lace. His hair was white and his eyes red; an albino. Only here, perhaps, could he be seen as a beauty. The Mollies were quarrelling over who got to dance with him next, and he was smiling a little smile.

As Abigail had promised, a supper was being laid out in the corner next to the kitchen *trompe l'oeil*. I wandered over to look. Pure Georgette Heyer: jugs marked 'orgeat', 'lemonade' and 'ratafia', little pies marked 'game' and 'pate', small dishes of artfully crafted vegetables for those vampires who had sworn off a carnivorous diet (perhaps they were teetotallers, like Terry Pratchett's black ribboners who don't use the b-vord), small dishes of sorbet, plates of almond biscuits, little sandwiches of roast chicken and roast beef with watercress. Daniel returned as I picked up a plate.

'Allow me,' he said. I curtsied and returned to our table. There Daniel brought me a selection of dainties and we picked at them as we surveyed the room.

'That girl I was dancing with, she uses the weight loss tea,' he said quietly. 'And I could feel every rib, every knob on her spine. If she isn't anorexic, I'm Pontius Pilate.'

'And you're not him,' I said. 'My lord D'Urbanville said that the apothecary and the witch swore that their potions were harmless.'

'Well, they would, wouldn't they? And maybe they are, if you don't take quadruple doses. Have one of these little pies, they're fantastic.'

They were. We dined amiably. So did the rest of the crowd. The lights were getting lower. The strings were getting sweeter. Then, with a bang and a cloud of greenish smoke, the apothecary and the witch arrived.

As the smoke cleared I saw the witch in the classic fairytale garb, ragged black dress and tall pointy hat. She also had a nose like a carrot and a profusion of stick-on warts from the Magic Shop. She might have been pretty under all that, but who could tell? She might not even have been female. Green skin, ragged garments and a funny nose are very disguising.

Daniel and I waited until the crowd had surrounded them before we lounged over to inspect their wares. The witch had a couple of baskets which contained such things as red toffee apples (for poisoning Snow White), packets of coloured sweets (for enticing children into the oven), gingerbread shingles from a gingerbread house, and small dolls and the packet of pins that went with them. They were labelled with instructions for linking the doll with the victim. Meroe had always refused to sell voodoo dolls and now I could see why; they were such ugly, obvious things, evidence of raw emotions like fear and lust and greed.

The witch's voice was also disguised; it was a throaty cackle. She threw out her arms in a broad gesture and revealed that she was festooned with charms. They were cheap pot-metal hearts, phalluses, heads, other miscellaneous body parts and skulls, hung from coloured ribbons. The crowd purchased freely and moved away. We were pushed to the front. Daniel bought a toffee apple at a ruinous price. The witch leaned close to me and offered me a wax doll.

'Tired of the flesh, lady?' she insinuated. 'Maigre can melt your fat away.'

I was about to hotly deny any desire to be thin when I remembered my role. I simpered and bought the doll, trying not to gasp at the amount she was asking for it. At these prices for a scrap of wax, the witch must be coining money hand over broomstick. Then we moved to face the apothecary.

He was wearing a tall hat with price tickets around it.

I searched my memory. Aha! The Mad Hatter from Alice in Wonderland. He was wearing a gentleman's evening costume which had seen better years; the lapels were threadbare and the material was shiny. Someone's op shop purchase, I guessed. His shirt lacked a collar. His hands were gloved in pale kid. But his face was alarming. It was a mask, of course, I realised a moment later. A shiny, bland, young man's face with all the personality of a shop mannequin. The voice which came from behind it was epicene and more than a little eerie.

'Well, master, are you the cunning man?' I asked, recalling my role in *The Recruiting Officer* at university.

He did not answer but swept a hand over the goods displayed on his folding table. Interesting. There were bottles labelled 'water of green pineapples' and 'Gregory's cordial'. There was 'Walter Raleigh's Elixir'. There were soaps and bath powders, crudely scented. I could smell the cheap perfumes even through the packaging. I could not see the badly made beige paper wrapping of the weight loss tea. I took up a bottle of Gregory's cordial. As I recalled from my careful reading of the immortal Heyer, Gregory's cordial had been made with mercury. We had better get this tested. The apothecary extorted a shocking sum from me, and Daniel and I drifted away.

It was getting on for three in the morning and I was tired. Daniel felt the same.

'Let's wander along to bed, eh?' he said, allowing me to take his arm. 'Want a bite of my toffee apple, princess?'

'Zounds, no,' I replied. 'I do not wish to sleep for a hundred years.'

We claimed our cloaks and went out into the street. Daniel's pocket contained a packet of tea. Bo had come through. All was silent and shiny. It had been raining. Our footsteps rang in the cold air. Daniel's stick tapped a rhythm. It was very quiet. Not even a car passed us.

The attack came without any warning. Two men jumped out of an alley and they both grabbed for Daniel. That was a mistake, because it left me free to kick. I had spike-heeled boots on and I kicked hard. I got one behind the knee and he fell. I jumped on him, pinning him to the ground under my knees. Daniel had his attacker with an arm twisted up behind his back. It all happened so fast I didn't have time to be afraid, which was lucky. Now it was all over it seemed silly to be afraid, so I wasn't. Besides, we had won. That always warms the cockles.

The man under my knees was squirming. He was a young man in a blue t-shirt with Folsom Prison on it, which reminded me vividly of Jason as I had first seen him. He had that same heroin pallor and pinprick pupils. But that didn't mean he got to attack innocent passers-by. I glared my best dominatrix glare at him and he subsided.

'Lemme go,' said the first assailant to Daniel.

'Now why should I do that?' he said, sounding amused. 'After I went to all that trouble to catch you? And your friend is making a nice cushion for my lady. However, I will think about letting you go if you tell me what you were after.'

'Just money,' mumbled Daniel's thug. The only difference I could see between our two attackers was that Daniel's prisoner had a bone t-shirt with 'condemned' printed on it.

'Why don't I believe you?' Daniel mused. 'Corinna, do you believe him?'

'No,' I said. 'This attack was far too pat. You —' I joggled the man I was kneeling on—'who sent you?'

'You weigh a ton, you know that?' he groaned.

'Yep,' I said. 'I know that.'

'All right,' said the crushed one. 'You'll let us go?'

'Probably,' said Daniel.

'It was the dude in the Vlad club,' he said. 'The one in the mask. Told us to get the tea back. Said we could keep your money and your watch.'

'All right,' I said. 'Do you know the dude's name?'

'Nah,' said Daniel's prisoner.

'Not only will we let you go,' said Daniel, releasing his prisoner and holding him at stick's length. 'But I will give you this splendid toffee apple to comfort you for missing out on my wallet and my watch.'

I clambered off my cushion and he arose, groaning and rubbing his knee.

'Off you go,' I said. 'If I see you again, I'll sit on you.'

They took the toffee apple and I saw the first one bite it as they scurried off down their alley. I shook myself into order. Daniel brushed his hands together as if wiping off a contaminating touch.

'The crime rate,' he commented as I took his arm again, 'really is climbing.'

'Fortunately the apothecary hired a couple of idiots,' I said.

'You just can't get good help these days,' he agreed.

We walked home without further incident. I expected to feel some emotion after all that excitement, but all I felt was a little elevated. We let ourselves into the apartment, were greeted with sober pleasure by Horatio, and put ourselves gently and slowly to bed. Gently and slowly we made love and then we fell asleep, gently and slowly. It had been an action packed night.

Chapter Eleven

Saturday is my favourite day. I do not have to get up, and I do not have to go to bed early. Bliss. Daniel brought me croissants from the French baker and we breakfasted in bed. Horatio joined us for his statutory dab of butter. He is a dairy cat descended from a long line since humans began to domesticate the cow. When the first woman sat down to milk the first cow, Horatio the First would have been there with his head in the pail and his whiskers covered in cream.

Then we drifted back to sleep until suddenly it was lunchtime and time to be up and doing. Neither Daniel nor I felt like doing much so we compromised with lunch at Café Delicious. Del Pandamus was minding the shop. He supplied us with moussaka made by his grandmother, than which no better moussaka has ever been compounded, and all the latest gossip.

Del is a big, cheerful, moustachioed Greek man with a deceptively guileless expression. People tend to assume that his thoughts go no higher than ouzo and soccer and that is a major error. His moustache is in loving memory of Eleutherios Venizelos the Great Patriot and his expression results from contemplating the fact that he comes from the same island as Odysseus of the swift word, who bluffed his way though long years of war and travel and still got home to his wife at the end.

'Them nerds,' he began, polishing a glass. 'They been shut for two days.'

'Really?' I asked. That was unusual. Nerds Inc, otherwise known as the Lone Gunmen, might be erratic in the morning hours, since they mostly stayed up all night playing computer games, but they stayed open late to compensate. At least one of Taz, Rat or Gully could mostly be found either drowsing at the desk or engaged in furious debate with some other gamer. Had their cash flow slumped so low that they had closed the shop? But they had enough to trade for another month at least, provided they had sent in that BAS form.

'Did they mention going away?' asked Daniel. 'Is there a sci-fi convention anywhere?'

'There's always a sci-fi convention somewhere,' I told him. 'No, I saw them a few days ago when I went to do their accounts and they didn't say anything about going away. Then again, they mightn't want to disclose such things to a mundane.'

'Maybe their diet of tacos and Twisties has finally done for them,' said Daniel, taking up another forkful of eggplant and lamb mince, unctuous and rich.

'Chili sauce finally penetrated the brain, you reckon?' I asked idly. 'Did they say anything to you, Del?'

'They don't like my food,' he grunted. 'We don't talk much. Anyway, their door's been shut for two days.'

'Maybe we'd better enquire,' I said to Daniel. 'If they are in there, suffering from chili sauce poisoning, we could take them an antidote.'

'All right,' he said agreeably. 'After lunch.'

'We can talk to Trudi. She always feeds Helob for them when they're away.'

'I almost don't want to know the answer to this,' said Daniel, raising his glass of water, 'but what is Helob?'

'Their bird-eating spider,' I told him.

'And what does it eat?'

I had never thought about this. 'Birds, I expect. No, I can't imagine Trudi countenancing that. Let us leave the subject. I'm sorry I mentioned it.'

Café Delicious is a small room, with only three tables. Most of the trade is takeaway. Del has hung the walls with pictures of Ithaca, all blue sea and blue sky and olive groves. And water cisterns, the emptiness of which was the reason his family left the island. The tables are blonde wood and the chairs hard-wearing cane and wide enough for the broad-beamed to sit on without discomfort. We were just dividing a piece of baklava to eat with our Greek coffee when the Professor pottered in, seeking a Pandamus roast lamb and tatziki wrap. I recalled that I had a question to ask him about the book we had found in my father's possessions.

'I'm always delighted to offer advice on the classics,' he said affably when I had explained. 'Bring it up to my apartment after lunch and we shall see.'

He paid for his food and departed. Daniel and I sipped Del's coffee, which would guarantee that we stayed awake for the foreseeable future. If we ever find zombies lurching along Flinders Lane, like in *Night of the Living Dead*, it will be because someone has injudiciously allowed some of Del's café hellenico to spill on a corpse.

After lunch, I collected the book and we rode the elevator to the Professor's apartment, Dionysus. His Roman furniture, specially made for the space, is so comfortable that I revised my views on Romans as strong-jawed soldiers to luxury loving couch potatoes, except that they didn't have potatoes then, of course. Couch turnips? Couch mangold wurzels?

We were greeted by Professor Dion with Nox, his black kitten, riding on his shoulder. Nox means night and she is as black as Belladonna. She was originally called Soot and spent her early kittenhood trapped in the ducting, but this has not soured her essentially kind nature. She rules the Professor with a firm paw, and he loves it.

'Do come in,' he invited. 'Nox and I have enjoyed our roast lamb. She left me the tatziki, which she does not care for. Have a seat. A glass of wine?'

We accepted. Nox roved over our laps, stuck her cold little nose in Daniel's ear, dipped a paw in my wine, and then settled on the Professor's shoulder again. When she grew up she was going to look like Guy Boothby's Dr. Nikola (retd).

We exchanged the usual pleasantries. It does not do to hurry the Professor, who was brought up in a time when people had manners. We admired how much Nox had grown and how shiny her fur was now that she was not living on condensation and mice in the air conditioning. We commented on the weather, which was cold but agreeably wet. We agreed that Del Pandamus' business was entirely dependent on the health of his seemingly indestructible eighty year old Yai Yai. Then Professor Dion held out his hand for the book and smiled as he opened it.

'Ah, yes,' he said. 'A rather waterstained copy of the Meditations of Marcus Aurelius Antonius.'

'Who was he?'

'A sad man,' said the Professor. 'He was emperor of Rome but he really ought to have been a philosopher or a scholar, or perhaps a farmer. He was a Stoic. He hated the spectacles at the circus but he had to attend. He got a very bad press in the past for persecuting Christians, and he certainly didn't like them, but there is no evidence that he sent anyone to the lions. We don't have any good history of his time, unfortunately.'

'Who would find Marcus a good companion, Professor?'

I asked. His blue eyes twinkled. Nox yawned elaborately. Evidently, Marcus Aurelius bored her.

'The world weary, the oppressed, those saddened by life,' he replied. 'I find him a bit of a trial, to be truthful. Let's see...yes, listen to this. "Every moment think steadily as a Roman and a man, to do what thou hast in hand with simple dignity, laying aside all carelessness and passionate aversion from the commands of reason, and all hypocrisy, and self love, and discontent with the portion which hath been given to thee." That's about standard Marcus Aurelius.'

'Right,' said Daniel.

'Nice book,' added the Professor as we got up. 'Would have been expensive. By the way, have you made any progress with the herbs smuggled in the Fair Trade goods?'

'No,' said Daniel. 'Not yet. I've told Jon what to do next time a shipment comes in. We'll have to wait until then.'

'A trap?'

'Sort of,' said Daniel. 'Thanks, Professor.'

'My pleasure,' he said. 'Say goodbye, Nox.'

Nox blinked as we went out. That cat had fallen squarely on her paws. I wondered if she was a reincarnation of someone. Karmically, she was doing well.

I shook off the occult nonsense. A note from Therese Webb under my door had asked me to call on her. Now was as good a time as any. I left Daniel at my apartment and went up to Arachne, bearing the relics of my father and expecting unpleasantness. I was not to be disappointed.

Both of them were engaged in stitching a huge tapestry.

I have always thought that those who do tapestries are to be commended. The same stitch, all over a metre of canvas, varied only by colour. To me it spells hard work. This one depicted a rather smug unicorn touching noses with a winged horse. Definitely not to my taste, but difficult to make, in very fine pastel shades. Starshine was plonking her needle in and out with a martyred expression. Therese was stitching almost without looking, and talking over the music: a sugary collection of crooners. I'm sure I heard Perry Como. As long as he wasn't singing 'White Christmas'—one reason I did my Christmas shopping in July—I had no objection to Perry.

'We'll just finish this little bit, dear,' said Therese. 'Have a look around, and put the kettle on when you pass the kitchen. Jasmine tea, please, no milk or sugar.'

The apartment was laid out just as the Prof's was: two bedrooms, a dining room and parlour behind them, and a kitchen and bathroom at the back. Arachne had a front balcony, presently devoid of the plants and furniture which made mine such a nice place to sit in the evening. I was sure that fairly soon Trudi would be knocking on the door with some of her indestructible green frondy things and a choice of pots.

Therese had set up her looms in the dining room, pushing the furniture back against the walls. A wide stripe of very strong purple was wound around the end of the loom, and piled everywhere were fascinating things: rainbow coloured wool, boxes of threads, packets of needles, scissors, shears, knitting needles of every calibre, stacks of stretched canvas pictures and strange wooden things for measuring the length of a skein which looked like they would be valuable in some form of needlework martial art. And everywhere was hung or draped or placed the fruits of Therese Webb's hands: embroidery of every form, hardanger, candlewick, crewel, latchhook, point, both petit and gros, bobbin lace, pillow lace, crochet, tatting, knitting…it was overwhelming.

I dragged my eyes away from a wonderful poncho in blue and silver, made of some feathery acrylic thread, and got to the kitchen. I found the kettle and put it on, located the teapot under a tea-cosy with little dancing teacups on it, and then had the oddest feeling I was being watched.

I looked around. Being a cat owner, I first examined the floor then looked at the high shelves, to where cats have been known to ascend in order to give people early morning heart attacks. Nothing but the usual things found on high shelves in kitchens: old gadgets of unknown utility, the juicer which seemed like a good investment until you tried to clean all the bits, the blender which you never quite managed to reassemble despite the clear instructions translated from Finnish into Japanese and then into English by a Guatemalan monoglot. Three unmatched canisters, five cake tins, and eleven pretty jars which you can't bear to throw away—besides, you might make jam someday.

No eyes. I found the jasmine tea, made the brew and assembled three cups on a decoupage tray depicting Brueghel peasants at play. Still that strong feeling of being observed.

I swung around and found that a small dog, sitting on a tasselled silk cushion in the dumb waiter, was examining me critically.

Insula was originally a fully serviced apartment house, which meant that it provided meals and drinks from the kitchen in the basement. These were sent up by dumb waiter. I didn't use mine for anything. Therese's dog had found it a perfect observation point. Therese had set a chair under the dumb waiter and the animal now demonstrated how his ladder worked by hopping down with perfect aplomb.

I am sure that my views on small dogs have been made clear, but this creature was as far removed from Mrs. Pemberthy's rotten little doggie Traddles as George Bush is from the truth, justice, mercy and democracy. He was the sort of dog an embroiderer ought to have, all soft fur and rich colours. He came to my feet, sniffed pointedly, then sat down. I knelt. He accepted my hand, lowered his silky head to allow me to scratch behind his ears, then led the way into the parlour, where the stitchers were coming to the end of their row.

'Oh, you've met Carolus,' said Therese. 'He's a King Charles spaniel, of course, isn't he beautiful? I've got a rush order on that unicorn tapestry. Have to keep up with the orders, someone's undercutting us. Time was I could get two hundred dollars for a finished work that size, but someone's doing them at one fifty and I have to match the prices. If I knew who it was I'd put one of Meroe's curses on them. They must be using slave labour! Just clear some of those books off that little table, Corinna, and I think we all deserve a biscuit. And Carolus will have a dog choc,' she said, taking the big tapestry off their laps and stowing it behind the couch. She came back with a packet of oatmeal biscuits for the humans and a dog treat for Carolus. He inclined his head a little and accepted it with royal condescension.

'Don't you sometimes feel that you have to live up to him?' I asked, fascinated.

'Oh yes, dear,' said Therese. 'He has very high standards.'

'Nonsense,' said my mother.

I had been avoiding even looking at her, which was silly.

I looked. She had improved. Her hair was washed, combed and plaited. She was clean and clothed in a very superior form of tracksuit, embroidered with Jacobean designs. She seemed to have gained a little weight and some of the crazed lines had smoothed out of her face.

'Now, Jacqui,' soothed Therese, 'we've talked about this. What I want to believe about my dog is my business, yes?'

'Yes,' muttered my mother. I looked at Carolus. He was far too well bred to snarl but the royal lip lifted a little, showing a flash of white canine tooth. I might have to revise my views on the canine race on deeper acquaintance with Carolus.

'Have some tea,' said Therese. 'I'll be mother, shall I?'

I sipped from the small handpainted cup. It had gold fish on it. The tea was very good.

'Well?' asked my mother sharply. 'Have you found him?'

'Still looking,' I said. 'He's moving fast. He encountered some nasty people who threw him in the river, but he survived after a night in hospital and then I believe he went to the Salvos. I'll find out more from Sister Mary tonight. She knows everyone. I've brought everything we found,' I said, handing over the bundle of cleaned and dried blankets and clothes and the personal papers. Starshine clawed them out of my hands and examined them frantically, ripping the bundle apart.

'They're his,' she told me fiercely. 'I must have him back. You don't know what it's like. We were two halves of the one fruit, close around the stone. Even when we…parted over the matter of the flesh, we were still mind to mind, heart to heart. He's half of me, more than half of me, the better half, the calm half, the half that laughs and knows joy. Without him I am all hag, black dark, weeping alone, snarling, scratching, hurting. I need him. *I need him.*'

'I know,' I said, moved by her words. She at least partly knew how corrosive her presence was, how unsociable she was.

'Why haven't you found him?' she cried.

'He doesn't want to be found,' I explained.

'You aren't trying!' she shrieked. 'You never forgave us for bearing you!'

'No,' I said, stung. 'I never regretted being alive. And Grandma rescued me before you could kill me by neglect.

I don't even really remember being with you, except that I was always cold.'

'Lies!' screamed Starshine.

Carolus jumped down from the couch and removed himself into the kitchen. He did not like emotional scenes. I wished I could go with him. Oddly enough—perhaps because I was older, perhaps because for the first time in my life I was happy—I wasn't angry with my mother anymore. She struck me as sad and pathetic and annoying, but I wasn't angry. I was so surprised by my reaction that I sat there with my mouth open while she screamed at me.

Then I put both hands on hers and leaned forward.

'No,' I said firmly. 'No, I'm not lying. Calm down, Jacqui. I'm not angry with you anymore. I used to be but now I'm not. I'm trying to find Sunlight for you. Calm,' I suggested. 'Drink some more tea and have a biscuit and I'll have one too.'

'Desperate to stay fat?' she sneered, shaking off my touch. This had always worked in the past. Now it wasn't going to. It meant precisely as much to me as those bumper stickers which said No Fat Chicks. Less, in fact, because I always thought fleetingly of smashing the windscreen of a car bearing that sort of sticker. 'You'll die young, you know,' she continued. 'You'll get high blood pressure and diabetes.'

'No, I won't,' I said, taking a biscuit and crunching it. 'Latest research says the big risk factor is stress. And going on fad diets. I don't do fad diets. I'm horribly healthy. I can get through a day's work that would cripple a cart horse. Give it up, Jacqui. Let's be acquaintances, if we can't be friends,' I said, stretching out a hand. 'We might even begin to like each other.'

For a moment I almost thought it was going to work. But she dropped the cup and started to cry that I was cruel and everyone hated her, and I finished my biscuit and got up to leave.

'You did well,' said Therese over Jacqui's bent head. 'Give it a couple of days and try again,' she advised. I nodded and let myself out on a long drawn breath. Well.

I had had the confrontation and I had come through it almost unscathed.

Elated, I ran down the stairs to Daniel. Half of me. The best half of me? No. Sweet man, dear lover, close as a garment or a skin, but still distant enough to surprise. And waiting for me just downstairs. I was a very fortunate woman.

The man who was becoming a murderer had lost his ability to switch off the dreams. They began to print themselves over his waking eyes. Even white sunlight was tinged with red and a sunset looked like a massacre.

Chapter Twelve

Daniel and I stayed in bed so long after my elated descent from Arachne that we just had time to make a very hasty dinner of garlic, tomato and cheese bruschetta and soup before it was time to pick up the Soup Run.

'Try not to breathe on anyone,' I said to Daniel as we dressed for the night; jeans, boots, jumpers, and the wadded silk jacket that Jon had bought me in Shanghai. It is the warmest thing I own, and the lightest.

'I only want to breathe on you,' he responded, kissing me with such fervour that my knees became unreliable. I was magnetically attracted to his body; it took all my willpower not to tear the clothes off him again. He felt the same and pushed me gently away.

'Oof,' he said. I agreed.

'For God's sake put that jacket on and let's go or I won't be able to restrain myself,' I told him.

He removed his hand from the nape of my neck, which felt instantly cold without his warmth. 'Grab the bread. Did we feed the cat?'

'Yes,' I told him as we edged ourselves out of the door and down the stairs. 'Is this sort of thing usual?'

'Outbreaks of sustained, unbridled passion?' he asked.

'I don't know. Never happened to me before. Hope it happens again,' he added. 'Let me take the bread.'

I surrendered the sack. Just along the lane we came upon the Soup Run bus, with a diminutive nun hopping down from the driver's seat.

'You'll have to put the seat back, Daniel dear,' she said to him. 'I was practically standing on the pedals. Hello, Corinna, God bless you! Gina's our legal advice tonight. I think you've met before.'

Gina grinned. She had run a free legal service all on her own for years, and then gravitated to private practice. The Soup Run kept her social conscience in check. She had iron grey hair and a stout, restrained figure. And a cheeky grin like a small, bad schoolboy. I liked her very much.

'This is our nurse for tonight, Doctor Damien,' Sister Mary said, introducing us. 'He's just back from a stint with Médecins Sans Frontières in the Sudan.'

'Nice and quiet here,' he told me, a thin young man with haunted brown eyes. 'No shooting. I've been invalided back but I like to keep my hand in, so Sister Mary lets me ride along one night a week.'

'What was the problem?' I asked, handing up the bag of bread to Suzanna, the other kitchen hand. She is vivacious and Spanish and has the sort of smile Velasquez used to paint. And the most beautiful dark blue eyes—one of those Irish soldiers, I suspected, during the Peninsular war, successfully applied the blarney to one of Suzanna's ancestors.

'Oh, just everything,' he said vaguely. Offhand I could not imagine a better place to incubate a good solid nervous breakdown than the Sudan. And Sister Mary was right to allow Dr. Damien this one night of social service which would not involve firearms or blast injuries. Compassion has to go somewhere or it turns into self-pity. As Marcus Aurelius might have said, perhaps.

I loaded myself aboard the bus. Suzanna stowed the bread. Gina, Sister Mary and Dr. Damien sat down. Daniel started the bus. The Soup Run aims to cover most of the points where people sleep out in the city of Melbourne. Our route is well known. There are three shifts in a night. People sleeping rough cannot lie still all night in freezing weather or they will die, so most of them try to sleep during the day and walk about all night to stay warm. Melbourne, even at its coldest, will not actually freeze anyone, but some die from lying face down in flooded gutters and some contract that robust viral pneumonia that the medical profession used to call Old Man's Blessing, because it carried off the aged with almost no pain. Now it carries off the twenty-somethings and Sister Mary will not have it. Nothing depresses an immune system like sleeping in the cold with insufficient food and coverings. We had blankets and soup and advice and we were off to combat the forces of neglect, madness, misery and unconcern which bedevil every city. The bigger it is, the more people will walk past a fallen man on the street, serenely positive that he is someone else's problem.

Tonight the 'someone else' is us.

Sister Mary looked back at me and smiled. Everyone knows that, as one of our clients put it, 'She in damn big with God.' She is a devoted, plump nun of some seventy summers, who looks about forty with her rosy, unlined face. She also has the saint's strength of will which, in St. Therese of Avila, made bishops hide under their desks when they saw her coming.

By sheer force of personality she has kept the soup bus running despite council objections and residents' complaints. She knows she is doing God's work and nothing human is ever going to stop or deflect her. If she wasn't so funny, she would be very frightening.

First stop. Some people were waiting for us, even though it was just after eleven and the night was—for the homeless— young. Or to put it another way, it was a long, bleak, cruel time until dawn. This group was mainly aged, the old drunks whom I had come to know. They had a totally illegal camp down by the river and some shelter in the old rowing sheds. They hung together in a sort of comradeship. Not that they wouldn't have beaten each other to death for possession of a bottle. But old Jock pushed even older Ian towards the bus.

'Ian's leg's gorn bad,' he said to Dr. Damien.

Ian was batting feebly at his friend with both hands. 'Don't want to go to hospital,' he moaned. 'They die there, people die there, go there to die, not goin', you can't make me...'

'Just sit down in here,' said Dr. Damien in a voice so concerned and kind that no one could have resisted it. 'I won't take you anywhere, Ian.'

Ian gave up fighting and went to the back of the bus, where Damien had first aid supplies. I looked away from proceedings to supply the outstretched hands with soup and sandwiches. Nourishing thick Scotch broth tonight, with barley and vegetables. Sandwiches of cheese or ham on good bread. Suzanna was handing out tea or coffee and muffins from the other counter. Business was brisk.

The night was very cold. The rain had dried up, the clouds had rolled away, and the stars were twinkling. The sky promised frost. We had a lot of freshly laundered blankets, sleeping bags and even doonas, extorted from the well-to-do and the manufacturers by Sister Mary's minions. Each one came with a stout canvas bag to carry it in. I had seen a pile of those bags in Arachne. I had not realised that Sister Mary had got to Therese Webb as well. Then again, she had acquaintances everywhere. Hardened criminals and harder police sergeants quailed before the bright lance of her certainty.

She was out among the crowd, distributing blessings and admonitions. Sister Mary is so small that one can only see where she is by the respectful gap which forms around her in a mob of people. I got Daniel to lift up a big catering pack of soup to refill one of my urns and managed to decode the buttons enough to heat it. Gina was explaining a summons to an old man who had last been to the Magistrates' Court when it was in Russell Street. Dr. Damien was assisting Ian down the steps.

'You come along tomorrow night and the nurse'll dress it again,' he said. 'Here's a nice new blanket for you in this bag. Now you have a seat and Daniel will get you some soup and a sandwich.'

I supplied Daniel with the old man's food and gave Dr. Damien a hand up into the bus again.

'What's wrong with his leg?' I asked.

'Oh, a gangrenous ulcer,' he said. 'I could drag him to hospital against his will and they'd have that leg off, but where would he go then? He's not going to live long. Let him live as he wishes, with his mates.'

'Too right,' said a whiskery old man, grabbing for another sandwich. 'Good grub, this, missus. Ta,' he added, shoving a further sandwich into his pocket and winking at me.

Trade was falling off. Daniel helped Suzanna refill her tea urn. The old men always preferred tea. With lots of sugar, which kept them warm. We picked up Sister Mary, secured the urns and trundled off to our next destination, Flagstaff. This is a park in the highest part of the city (which is why it had a flagstaff on it in the first place) and is largely inhabited by what, in ordinary society, would be called the middle class. People with children who are sleeping in cars. Lost single women of a certain age. Families in which the children are related to each other in bewildering complexities of uncles and cousins, and no one can recall when they last had a job. People who, whichever way you look at it, have come down in the world. Some have come down so fast they have the societal version of the bends, and believe that they still have the right to be the first in any queue. This can lead to violence. Daniel is always in evidence at Flagstaff.

We stopped the bus at our usual place. A large crowd was waiting under the stark trees, leafless for winter. The people would have surged forward but Daniel was in front of the serving windows, fending them gently back.

'Plenty for everyone,' he said. 'And tonight we have chocolate for the kids. Everyone into line,' he said. 'You know the drill. Sir, if you please?'

They knew the drill. Those who didn't were scolded into place. And the chocolates would be very good tonight, I knew. Sister Mary had put the hard word on Juliette and Vivienne, the sisters who ran Heavenly Pleasures, our neighbouring chocolate shop. They had made two huge trays of milk chocolate animal shapes. With sultanas. I had already reserved a large wombat for myself and another for Daniel.

But for now it was soup and sandwiches for all comers. Some of the hands reaching up were so small they could hardly cradle the cup. My heart was wrung but I did not stop serving. Suzanna stopped at one point and turned her back, and Gina jumped in to hand out the coffee. Dr. Damien borrowed Suzanna to undress a wailing baby and I just gave people soup. And sandwiches. Until everything started to blur. I blinked. In front of me was a raddled woman wearing what had once been a ball gown, then several dresses and additional skirts, topped off with a man's overcoat and one of Sister Mary's new blankets.

'Look sharp, dear,' she said to me, 'or Sister Mary'll tell God on yer!'

I laughed, handed over the soup and the sandwich, and went on.

We ran out of customers for the food before Dr. Damien had completed his clinic, or Gina had finished her family payments advice, so Daniel and I took a romantic stroll around the park with a romantic garbage bag, picking up rubbish. The Soup Run was already in such bad favour with the local inhabitants that we couldn't afford to make it worse by littering.

Everywhere our clients were settling down, soothed by warmth and attention. But for the occasional belch or burst of swearing they would have been like birds in their little nests. Flagstaff didn't have a lot of drunks and they were congregated in one corner over their dreadful bottle of God knew what. By the scent, it was methylated spirits and port. Chocolate-smeared children slumped into the backs of cars or into parental arms and wrappings, augmented by our blankets. Sleep was descending on Flagstaff for a couple of hours, before the cold woke everyone at three am.

When we got back, Sister Mary had handed out the last pack of nappies and it was time to move on. We boarded, Daniel took the driver's seat and we chuntered on through the night.

It was at the next stop that the crowd, pressing forward eagerly, suddenly quailed and backed away. Some actually ran. I looked out. Was it something I had said? But it was only two patrolling policemen. They approached and who should they be but my old pals, Kane and Reagan. Sister Mary popped up beside me.

'Cold night,' I greeted them. 'Want some coffee and a muffin? You can't complain about my company tonight.'

'H'lo, Sister,' muttered Reagan. I could tell that he had had a Catholic school upbringing. Even the most atheistic of the lapsed feel abashed in the presence of a nun.

'And hello to you, Reagan, may God amend you,' snapped Sister Mary. 'And you too, Kane. What can we do for you? Speak fast, you are scaring our children away.'

'Some children,' sneered Kane.

'God's children,' countered Sister Mary. 'What do you want?'

'We've seen her father,' said Reagan quickly. 'At the Sunnies.'

'Thank you,' said Sister Mary, who seemed to understand this. 'Now I am sure that you have criminals to apprehend on this cold night, am I right? Goodnight to you, and may God bless you both.'

They were off before they quite realised what had happened, I am sure. Kane looked back, possibly wondering where the long conversation he'd expected had gone. But they kept walking, which was wise of them. Sister Mary was quite cross and she had divine protection. They might have been struck by lightning. One could hope, at least.

The crowd came back, nervously. They did not like cops. They especially did not like those cops. But they were safely gone and we had food and warmth. This pitch mainly catered to young boys. It was the haunt of paedophiles from all over and even Sister Mary hadn't anything good to say about them. They weren't who we fed. We had parked under the streetlight, which was harsh and made every face look either bloated or starved. Soup and sandwiches, muffins and coffee. Advice from Gina. And condoms, needle kits and bandaids from Dr. Damien.

Poor boys, I thought. Poor boys. Bad boys, perhaps, but how evil could you be when you were only fourteen? The sad ones and the ones with a sort of juvenile swagger which was heart-rending in its vulnerability. And the loud, obnoxious ones, of course, the bullies, the little bastards. We got them all and Daniel understood all of them. The boys liked the commercial chicken noodle soup more than my homemade Scotch broth, and preferred muffins to sandwiches.

I handed out food, watching Daniel move amongst the mob, patting shoulders, restraining bullies, occasionally doing that thing which Clint Eastwood does: fixing a boy with his stare, which seems to convey some very complex instructions. They hold the stare for some time, then Daniel nods and looks away and the boy immediately goes and does what Daniel wants him to do. Some sort of telepathy, I suppose. It must have evolved in the old days when men went hunting megafauna with mega-teeth and couldn't afford to attract attention by speaking or even gesturing. This time I saw the boy jerk his chin to one side and Daniel immediately followed him into the darkness under the railway bridge.

He came back carrying a figure which lolled. He had slung the boy over his shoulder and carried him without effort to the back of the bus, where Dr. Damien received him into his arms and laid him on the floor.

'Not dead?' said Daniel.

'No,' reported Dr. Damien. 'But very ill. I saw a lot of this in the Sudan.'

'You don't mean he's been shot?' I asked, leaning forward to look at the boy. His face was as white as a sheet, with yellow overtones and black shadows. His hair was perhaps brown, dry as straw. He was wearing black clothes, with no jewellery except the black rubber band doubled around his wrist.

'No, he's starving,' said Damien. 'You need to call an ambulance, Daniel. If they can get some fluids into him fast they might save him.'

'Starving?' exclaimed Sister Mary, horrified. 'How can anyone starve here? There's food enough, God knows!'

'Wait a moment,' I said. 'I'm getting the beginnings of an idea.'

'Are you?' asked Sister Mary, staring into my face with her bright, birdlike gaze. 'Good. Tell me when you know, and we shall do things about it. Meanwhile, an ambulance, Daniel dear, and I shall talk to the boy who brought our poor little brother here.'

'Me,' said the boy resignedly. I brought him another cup of soup and a muffin to compensate. 'I knew you'd want to know about him. Only I don't know much. He's been here about a week. Longer'n me.'

'What's his name?' asked Sister Mary, toying with the lid of the chocolate box.

'Toby,' said the boy. 'That's all I know.'

'And what's your name?'

'Jacob.'

'And was Toby eating anything?'

'Never touched a crumb while I knew him,' declared the boy. 'Said he wasn't hungry. Doesn't drink. Or take pills. Just sat under a tree and said prayers. Can I have some chocolate now?'

'Of course.' Sister Mary gave him two milk chocolate bunnies. 'Anyone Gina can call for you? Want to go home, perhaps, now Toby is going to hospital?'

'Yes,' said the boy, and crumpled a little. 'My dad will be mad at me,' he said.

'Let's see,' said Sister, and led him into the bus, where we had a phone paid for by the church, dedicated to returning the lost and the strayed. Any father who continued to be angry with his son after being talked to by Sister Mary was a man of adamant evil who ought not to have a son—at least that was my view.

I was longing to know what or who the Sunnies were, but this didn't seem the time to ask Sister Mary. Daniel didn't know, nor did Gina or Suzanna. Dr. Damien was coaxing a little warm water down Toby's contracted throat. The boy swallowed. A little more water was offered and accepted.

'A terrible thing, starvation,' said Damien gently, so as not to alarm the patient. 'Sooner or later it destroys the mind. First you can't think about anything but food, then the will is blunted, the body starts to consume itself, the mind becomes dull, the reflexes sluggish, the patient isn't even hungry anymore. The urine is full of acetone from muscle destruction. Gradually the tissue wastes. Bruises form spontaneously...'

'But how could anyone get that hungry in a city like Melbourne?'

'Perhaps he was held in captivity. Perhaps he is in the terminal stages of anorexia, or liver failure. We just need to get him onto a drip before his arteries collapse...aha. Here comes the ambulance.'

With great efficiency, Toby was loaded onto a stretcher and Dr. Damien instructed the paramedics in short sentences which they seemed to understand perfectly. As the ambulance drew away I saw a small hand waving from the soup bus window. Jacob was saying goodbye to Toby and the life of the streets.

We took Jacob with us on to the next stop, the most nerve-racking of our evening, though it wasn't usually too rough this early in the night. King Street is not my favourite place. It is all nightclubs and rich kids making a statement about how free they are, which is always tiresome. They, however, are not our clientele. They just jeer at us and occasionally throw bottles as they pass on their way to being picked up by Daddy in the four-wheel drive and taken home to Toorak. God bless their little hearts and may their private school ties revolt, writhe around and strangle them one night.

Too early for the rowdies, thank God. One night I might leap down and do them some violence. They annoy me out of all charity, not that I ever had much.

Jacob sat inside the bus, next to Gina, while we handed out soup and sandwiches, coffee and muffins, to the working girls. There are few children and no old people in King Street. Mostly our clientele are professionals. They rather rely on us for supper and they love Sister Mary. One pimp who unwisely raised his hand to the sister, saying that she had reformed one of his girls, was smashed down and pounded into the pavement under the spike heels of all the prostitutes within hearing. They didn't kill him only because Sister Mary made them stop. I gather that he recovered, but we never saw him again. And no one has objected to Sister Mary's presence since.

Tonight the mood was sad; one of them had died. 'Poor bitch fell under a bus,' said Delia, the Prostitutes' Collective rep for King Street. 'Told her not to wear them bloody platforms on wet pavements.'

'She will get her reward in heaven,' said Sister Mary. 'Her sins have been washed clean and she sits at the feet of the lamb in joy and content.'

'Now?' asked Delia, her voice like an old crow's.

'Now, this very moment,' said Sister Mary with such complete conviction that just for a moment, even in King Street, we all believed.

It didn't last, of course. I listened to the King Street gossip as the food left my hands. Which club was tolerating the sellers of various illegal substances. Which had cracked down. And one funny story.

'She was picked up by the cops with a bag of leaves,' said Ann, Delia's best friend. 'They charged her with possessing cannabis. But Mandy, she said, it isn't cannabis, you just have to look at it, I demand an analyst's certificate. She got legal aid onto it, they demanded an analyst's certificate. So they finally got a bloody analyst's certificate, with the cops bitching and moaning the whole way, of course it's cannabis, you can't trust whores. And you know it wasn't leaf after all? No one had believed the poor cow.'

'So what was it?' I knew that it took almost six months to get an analyst's bloody certificate—Gina had been complaining about it that very night.

'Some sort of leaves.' Ann shrugged. 'Threw the case out. Cops were dark, I can tell you. Mandy's gone home to Hamilton, she reckoned she wasn't safe on the streets here. They'd get her for something, just for making fools out of them. Well, thanks for the soup. Gotta be going. Men to do. We've got a new motto: the customer always comes first.'

I laughed politely and the women drifted away. Leaves, eh? If they were the same sort of leaves as either that weight loss tea or the datura smuggled in the Fair Trade goods, someone ought to be told about it. But who? And what, in fact, would I say? And was that starving boy Bo's Tobias?

I finally got Sister Mary by herself and asked the question that had been gnawing at me: 'What are the Sunnies, Sister? You seemed to know what that cop meant.'

'Oh,' said Sister Mary, 'yes, of course. They are the Sunshine Sisterhood, Mission to the Miserable. God bless their good hearts.'

'You,' I told her, 'are pulling my leg.'

'I wouldn't dream of it,' she said a little indignantly. 'They have a centre in Flinders Lane, dear, up towards Exhibition Street. Haven't you seen it? It has a big yellow sunflower painted on the door.'

'Oh, yes, I suppose,' I said, having vaguely noticed the painting on my forays in search of Chinese food. 'I thought it was organic food or something healthy.'

'Oh, they are terribly healthy,' she said with a smile, 'nothing but vegetables—and how the old men complain and demand roast beef! Still, they make a wonderful carrot cake. You should ask for the recipe. You'll be along to talk to them tomorrow, I guess? Give them my blessings. They are fine women.'

'Yes, but what do they do?'

'They feed the hungry,' said Sister Mary. 'Clothe the naked. You'll see. Now, it's time we took Jacob and the bus back to Flinders Street where, with the blessing of God, his father will be waiting to take him home. I have explained the situation. I think it will be all right.'

Nothing more to do than pack up, pick up the rubbish, start the bus and proceed very discreetly through the city and back to where we began. Ma'ani, the Maori who was rostered as driver and heavy on the next run, was there with the new crew and a fresh load of food and supplies. Ma'ani is over two metres tall and about the same wide, and somehow there's never any trouble on his run. If there was, he might step on it and not notice, and Trouble has a way of knowing things like that.

We debussed, stretching. I always get a backache from stoop-ing over the counter. I greeted Ma'ani, who gave me a hug. I emerged partly crushed in time to see a car skid around the corner and a frantic man throw himself out, run across to us, and drag Jacob into his arms.

'You all right, son?' he whispered, over and over. 'You okay? We've been looking everywhere, everywhere. I swear he'll never come near you again, son. The bastard. I never knew. But you'll never see him again, son, I swear. I swear.'

Jacob, who had burst instantly into tears, began to calm down. Sister Mary beamed. The father looked up at her.

'You brought him back, didn't you?'

'God did,' she replied. 'Now you can take him home and keep him safe.'

'You want to come home, Jake?' asked his father.

Jacob nodded, wiping his wet hand over his wet face.

'I thought I'd lose his mum as well,' said the father. He reached into his wallet and stuffed a handful of money into Sister Mary's hands. 'You give that to God and say thanks.' Then he led Jacob into the waiting car, and drove away very quietly and carefully, as though he could buy off fate.

Daniel and I went home very silently and put ourselves quietly to bed. It had been quite a night. And tomorrow I was going to meet the Sunnies. I was in the middle of some pro-found remark about cannabis and datura when I fell heavily and instantly asleep.

The man who was becoming a murderer tried to walk away. He found himself in a dark alley before sunrise. None of them were watching him. He could escape. But then a boy on a bicycle nearly ran him down, and two cats rushed around him. He hated cats. He fell in with the others.

Chapter Thirteen

Sunday is not as much fun as Saturday because the following day is Monday, which means I have to get up at four, but it is a pleasant day nonetheless, for a woman with a silent breakfasting partner and a snuggly cat. Daniel made the toast, I made the coffee, Horatio supervised and drank milk. The jam was strawberry and the coffee Fair Trade East Timor Arabica.

Bliss. Silence. Only the rustle of the Sunday papers and the occasional exclamations of horror at the news. And the oddly loud Sunday morning purr of the stripy cat, who seated himself in loaf formation on the big kitchen table between us and radiated contentment, in the way that only a well-fed male cat can do.

After an hour, I padded off and had a shower. I dressed in suitable clothes to visit a Mission to the Miserable. A bright blue jumper with parrots on seemed to be the right thing. Daniel wore his usual leather coat but added a patterned scarf. We bade Horatio take care of the house and went down into the cold street.

Flinders Lane used to be the garment-making heart of Melbourne. You wanted schmutter—old clothes, new clothes, fur coats, tailored suits—Flinders Lane was the place to get it. Now there are a few tailor's shops hanging on but most of it consists of strange little apartment buildings, the back of the cathedral, souvenir shops and little café s selling odd ethnic specialities. It made a nice walk on a cold day, since it is uphill and exercise keeps you warm.

In my case, far too warm. I am built for endurance. I am not built for speed. I stopped at a corner to get my breath and saw it ahead of me. The Sunshine Mission to the Miserable. It had been a mechanics' institute perhaps, or a school; it had an educational look about its stained red bricks and gothic windows. The sunflower on the door was big and bright yellow. I opened it into a hall. Everything was going to be bright, by the look of it. I put on my sunglasses. So did Daniel.

No one seemed to be about. But hark! In the distance I could hear singing. And I knew the song and found myself singing along.

'Jesus loves me this I know, For the bible tells me so,' carolled a mixed ensemble. The Kings Singers they were not. I was reminded of the old Salvo joke about drunks singing 'stir up this stew—stir up this stew—stir up this stupid heart of mine' as I listened to a choir of reluctant bass voices ruined by whisky and tobacco. Over them were firm female voices, alto, contralto and one very strong soprano, singing as though they weren't singing something trite and foolish and written for children when people thought children were stupid.

'Yes, Jesus loves me! Yes, Jesus loves me! Yes, Jesus loves me! The bible tells me so.'

Daniel was looking puzzled. As well he might. I explained. 'This is a children's song,' I told him. 'Not usually sung by adults. And not a lot of them sound too happy about singing it, anyway. This is an odd place. Shall we go on?'

'By all means,' he said. 'As long as you promise to protect me from the Christians.'

I promised, crossing my heart and hoping to die, and we went further down the corridor towards the singing. It got louder, but not more tuneful. Boldly, I thrust open the door to a large room where a lot of men were seated on benches. Opposite them a lot of old women were sitting on identical benches. There was a brunch laid out on the tables: nice fresh

fruit, muesli and toast with non fat spread and organic jam, jugs
of milk and, by the scent of it, steaming hot carob to drink with
your healthy meal.

The hymn ended and there was a clatter of cutlery, an out-
break of grumbling and five of the women who had been singing
moved through the crowd to greet us. They were wearing a sort
of modified nun's gown in the form of bright sunflower yellow
smocks with JOY printed in blue on the bosom.

'God bless you!' exclaimed the first. 'I am Sister Bliss. This
is Sister Delight, Sister Content, Sister Joy, and Sister Blithe is
just helping Mrs. Gossens to cut up her apple. How can we be
of service to you?'

'Sister Mary sends her blessings,' I said, to establish our
credentials. Sister Blithe, having helped Mrs. Gossens with her
apple and rather markedly taken the knife with her, clasped her
hands.

'What a woman,' she said. 'She gives joy another meaning
altogether.'

Sister Blithe was a stocky forty-ish woman with short, curly,
butter coloured hair, bright blue eyes, a rosy face like one of her
own apples and an air of honest pleasure in life which was very
attractive. She was obviously as healthy as a horse, as strong as
an ox, and as merry as a grig—whatever grigs are. There was
something rustic about Sister Blithe. You could imagine her
milking a cow and washing her face in the dew on the way home.
Daniel was much taken with her.

'We are Daniel and Corinna,' he said, taking the offered
hand. 'We are looking for Corinna's father. Two rather unpleasant
policemen told Sister Mary that he might be here.'

'Can you see him? These are all the men we have for the
moment,' said Sister Blithe, as though she was sorry not to
have more specimens for our inspection. I really didn't know if
I would recognise my father immediately, so I gave Sister Blithe
the picture. The other sisters went about their business, coaxing
old grumps to eat the nice muesli and persuading them that carob
was just the same as coffee but without that nasty caffeine.

'Oh,' she said. 'Yes, I remember him. He's not here now, I'm so sorry. Come along and sit down and have a cup of carob with me and I'll explain.'

We accompanied her to a small room lined with books. Sister Blithe poured us all a cup of carob, which I did not really dislike, since I had drunk litres of it as a student. Coffee cost much more than the wholefood collective's carob with honey and soy milk. It was quite good unless you thought of it as coffee, because it isn't. Coffee, I mean. In any case it was hot and wet. The small room was agreeably warm. Sister Blithe was looking so uncomfortable that I decided on a few pleasantries.

'This is fine work you are doing. How long have you been here?' I said.

'Just on a year now,' she replied, sipping her carob. 'We are feeding quite the five thousand these cold mornings. That's why the heating is good and the food is nourishing. The poor and the old feel the cold. We're not licensed to have more than ten sleepers-in and our places always fill up long before dark. But we can provide food and a bath and some clean clothes to most of them. Joy is our creed. So much of the world is dark and despairing. Someone has to remember joy and delight. God wants us to laugh as well as cry.'

'True indeed,' murmured Daniel.

'God is a true refuge,' she said, almost as if speaking to herself. 'If you lose your only love, as I did, if you despair and weep all day, God is not pleased and fate cannot be turned aside. Only when I began to laugh again—at a kitten, as I recall, chasing her tail, so small and fluffy and determined—did I know to what God was calling me.'

'How sad,' I said conventionally. 'How did he die?'

'Die?' she said, startled. 'I never said he died. I lost him, that's all. Lost him. He followed another path. One where I could not go. I inherited quite a lot of money from my grandfather. I came here, found some like-minded friends and formed a community. We bought this old school and refurbished it, and we have been doing God's work ever since. We have a small cinema, you know, and we show movies,' she told us, a little proud of her innovation.

'What sort of movies?' I had to ask.

'What the old people like. Ealing comedies. My favourite is *Whisky Galore*. But there is a strong groundswell in favour of the Marx Brothers. And you know—they laugh! Some of them haven't laughed in years. It is so touching to see them laugh. Their life is spent entirely in finding a place to sleep, something to eat, a way of surviving another day. There aren't a lot of laughs in that. It's a grim business. So here, for a couple of hours at least, they aren't dirty or hungry or cold, and they can laugh.'

'That's wonderful,' said Daniel sincerely.

'But your cuisine isn't getting rave reviews,' I pointed out.

Sister Blithe laughed aloud. 'No, but they need the vitamins. Some of our regulars get used to it, even prefer a nice apple to a lolly. There is the problem of teeth, of course. We shall have to do something about that. Now, it is kind of you to have listened to me for so long. You are looking for your father. But you were not sure if you would know him?'

They were innocent blue eyes but it would not do to fib to them. 'I don't know him very well,' I said. 'I was taken away when I was five and adopted by my grandmother. I have seen him perhaps ten times since. I don't know what he looks like now—besides, he must be considerably bruised.'

'Yes, he was. Well, he came here with a couple of Salvos. He didn't like being in their shelter because there were rude men there—very likely, of course, one's society cannot be select in homeless shelters. Also he said the food was greasy and he was a vegetarian. So they brought him to us, which was wise. We can easily cater for vegetarians. In fact we use very little meat, just one meat dish for each dinner. Protein is good for the old people, despite what Sister Joy says about lentils. One can have too many lentils in one's life, don't you feel?'

I nodded. One certainly could. Lentil soup is cheap and filling and I had already eaten as much of it as I was ever going to eat.

Sister Blithe took a strengthening sip of carob. 'So you didn't actually know your father very well?' She was endeavouring to tell me something. I tried to find out what, because she was drying up.

'No, but by the time you met him I am willing to bet that he was thoroughly out of control and extremely annoying,' I said, wondering if that was what she was hinting at.

'Just so,' she said, pinkening like a Gloucestershire sunrise. 'We gave him a bath and some new clothes, and then offered him a nice meal of bread, cheese and fruits. He said that this was not what he was used to. Apparently he only eats organic fruit, and ours isn't organic. It won't be in the foreseeable future, either, unless the prices go down.'

'Indeed,' I agreed. 'How provoking, and how very ungrateful. I would not blame you if you showed him the door, you know.'

'Even Christ only got a thank you from one ex-leper out of ten, and we are not in his class,' she told me, smiling again. She had a most beautiful smile. 'We are not in this for the gratitude, which is fortunate, because there isn't a lot of it about, as you say. Sister Joy gave him her own lunch, which was an organic apple and an organic pear, and he accepted them and settled down in the common room to read some of the literature. A lot of them sleep there, you know, all day, because they will have to walk about all night. We have an application in for forty more beds, but we haven't heard back from the Fire Department yet.'

'The poor are always with us,' I said. 'You do what you can in the circumstances. That's what Sister Mary says. And God is aware of what you do.'

'Indeed,' sighed Sister Blithe. 'Well, he drank some of our water and accepted peppermint tea made with fresh peppermint. Sister Bliss was wondering if he had perhaps some residual concussion, though the hospital had discharged him. But they discharge people so early these days. It's all right if they have a home and loving care to go to, but not in this case…Anyway, Bliss couldn't get him to talk to her at all and she's a nice woman. He seemed to think that we were too frivolous. He didn't like the bright colours and the singing and he didn't like the film. It was *The Titfield Thunderbolt*, too, I always like that one. We put him to bed but the night nurse said he didn't sleep. It was Jenny, she's a strong woman, and she caught him at the door in his pyjamas and put him back to bed and told him he could leave in the morning, so he stayed there. But in the morning out he went, wouldn't eat a mouthful, and I'm very much afraid that he was carrying a pamphlet from the Discarnate Brotherhood.'

'Haven't I heard that name before?' asked Daniel.

'The fleshless friars,' I told him. 'We make their famine bread out of lentil flour, which for some reason smells like sawdust. The creepy dudes who scare Jason.'

'Oh,' said Daniel. 'Well, what's wrong with them?'

Sister Blithe looked concerned. 'Your Jason is right,' she said. 'Though I would call them alarming and their doctrine quite vicious. But you will see for yourself. They, at least, are not interested in feeding the poor and the lost.

They aren't interested in feeding anyone at all. I'll see if one of their pamphlets is still in the common room. Someone must have snuck them in. If so, you will oblige me by taking it away.'

We followed her into a big, warm room which contained the cinema screen and projection apparatus, a lot of comfortable chairs and couches, and shelves of books and magazines. There was even a smokers' corner for the intractable nicotine addicts with a kitchen extractor fan above it. Only the Sisters of Joy would have done that. I entirely approved of them as I saw the reluctant breakfasters fumble their way in, take up a magazine or book, or just slump quietly down and close their eyes. Everything was made of easy-clean surfaces, but they were new and soft. Soft music was playing. Bach, simple and pure. It was soothing and serene. Rare commodities in a city the size of Melbourne. The old thick walls would probably keep the traffic noise down to a low, rather soothing hum. An old lady in a red woolly gown yawned, showing clean pink gums. I yawned, which made Daniel yawn. We had to get out of there before we joined the sleepers.

Sister Blithe came back and showed us into the corridor again. 'Here it is,' she said, putting a grey leaflet into my hand as though she was passing me a soiled nappy. 'I hope it's the only one.'

'I apologise for my parent,' I said. 'He was ungrateful and foolish. You are doing very good work. Let us give you some small token of how much we appreciate you. We work on the Soup Run. We know what we're talking about.'

This time Daniel slid a few notes into Sister Blithe's work-worn hand.

She blushed again. 'Thank you. And I'm so sorry he found that thing here. And—I hope you find him,' she said.

And we were out into the ordinary street with the sunflower door closing behind us. I looked at Daniel. He looked at me.

'Won't find anything stranger today,' he said.

'Or better,' I added.

We walked on in the Sunday streets, so quiet and still. It was early. Not too early for what Pooh Bear would call a little smackerel of something, however. Honey, in his case. In ours, coffee. I needed to take the good wholesome taste of carob out of my mouth.

When we found a small café with the right sort of brass shrine to the Goddess Caffeinia, Daniel and I sat down to absorb some unexpected sunlight and look at the leaflet for the Discarnate Brotherhood.

'Fat?' it demanded in big black letters. 'Hate it?'

'Well, that's saying it like it is,' observed my beloved. We read further.

'Obesity not only kills, but damns you to hell,' it went on. I put the leaflet down and fanned myself. Daniel read aloud.

'Greed is a sin! Gluttony is a sin! The love of food comes from the Devil!! Join the Discarnates and be cleansed. Join the Discarnates and be purified! Join the Discarnates and lose five kilos a week!'

I wished I still smoked so I could have lit a cigarette to the Goddess Nicotinia.

'A weight loss cult?' asked Daniel, smiling.

'Not funny,' I told him. 'Sort of thing that had to happen. God, no wonder poor Sister Blithe found them vicious. This is definitely not feeding the poor, is it? It's starving the rich, which isn't the same thing at all.'

'He hath filled the hungry with good things; and the rich he hath sent empty away,' said Daniel, still not taking it seriously.

'Look, this is really nasty stuff,' I tried to convince him. 'People risk death to be thin—look at the girls and that weight loss tea from the Mollyhouse. I wonder if the Discarnates are the source of it? The Professor said that he didn't trust anyone who said that they were fleshless.'

'And I don't trust anyone who says that they are pure,' said Daniel, 'or can become pure just by not eating. Purity isn't as easy as that, you're right. But austerity is always attractive. For a while, at least.'

'I don't like this at all,' I said, sipping. 'On the other hand, this coffee is wonderful.' It was. Hot, dark, with a swirl of crema on the surface, redolent of volatile oils and giving rise to visions of dark forests full of dazzling birds. To sip it was to glimpse a macaw flashing past on blue and yellow wings. I can get quite romantic about coffee. And Daniel, of course. At the moment he was annoying me.

Just when I was about to renew my argument, his mobile phone rang.

I do not like mobile phones, but sometimes they are useful. When Daniel's phone rang it did not play the Ride of the Valkyries. It did not, as far as I knew, vibrate. It did not emit that crazy frog tune which has been the cause of so many otherwise law-abiding people snatching the phones of perfect strangers and flinging them out of tram windows to the detriment of good order and at considerable danger to the public. It just rang. He answered it.

All mobile phone conversations tend to be the same. Except for the ones where the person on your end has an earpiece and is therefore walking along having an interesting argument with, apparently, the air. Ever since people got those remote control phones it has been very hard to distinguish a respectable businessman from a wandering loony. Who can tell, in the absence of other clues, whether 'Sell Timeo and buy Dona Ferentes' is a sane stock exchange instruction to a secretary back at the office or an attempt to deflect the attentions of mind-reading Martians?

Daniel's conversation went, as they usually do, 'Yes, it's me. You did? Where? And you are…okay. Be right there.'

'Drink up,' said Daniel, now back with me. 'Jon and Kepler have caught their smuggler. We're going to pick him up. I'll just call Timbo and have him bring round the car. You don't have to come,' he added. 'Do you want to tackle the Discarnates first?'

'No,' I said. I was not all that enthusiastic about finding my father. What was I going to do with him when I did? Jacqui was all right for the moment with Therese Webb, on whom I hoped that the Goddess Arachne was shedding blessings by the armload. But what was I going to do with Sunlight, who was evidently not in a good frame of mind after his adventures, if the two of them didn't want to go home to their commune?

I shuddered briefly and returned to the coffee and the macaws. They really are gorgeous birds. The vision of those wings lasted right to the bottom of the cup.

Walking down hills is always preferable to walking up them, and we were back at Insula in a few minutes. There we met the charming Timbo, who smiled. Good, he had obviously forgiven me for putting stinking blankets into his sacred boot. Jon and Kepler were waiting. They looked both excited and grieved.

'I would have said he was a good worker, too,' said Jon, getting into the back of the car and making room for me and the willowy Kepler. 'Where are my manners? Hello, Corinna, Daniel. Nice to see you again, Timbo. Meroe has reported on the herbs. They are not all poisonous, and some grow perfectly well here. Can you have a look at the list, Corinna?'

'Certainly, but I won't know much,' I said. 'I only know about herbs you can cook with.' I scanned the list. 'And most of these are,' I said, surprised. 'Why would anyone import thyme? Borage? Bay leaves? Mint? Mint doesn't even dry properly, and we've got acres of it. Forests of it. Trudi keeps us all supplied with peppermint, she rips it out of her garden in armfuls. Says it's nearly a weed. Jon dear, this is mad.'

'I reached the same conclusion, but continue reading,' he said equably. I did so.

'Right, here's the dangerous ones. Monk's hood. That was the murder means in a Brother Cadfael story—it's wolfsbane. And datura, that's the thorn apple of Kipling's Jungle Book story about the King's Ankus. Castor oil beans—source of ricin, which killed that poor Bulgarian in the umbrella murder in London. All of which would grow in Australia, I assume,' I said, scanning the rest of the list. 'Here's some old-fashioned laxatives, and—dandelion leaves? Did I mention mental derangement as an explanation of this mystery?'

'Yes, and I have to agree,' said Daniel. 'Still, we ought to be able to clear it up once we ask this young man what he thinks he is doing.'

'What are you going to do to him, Jon?' asked Kepler.

'We'll have to sack him,' said Jon. 'I know that it's just such a relief that they aren't smuggling anything awful that I feel like letting him off, but he's a major breach of security.'

'I suppose so,' said Kepler.

Jon took his hand. I leaned back in the seat. Timbo was very skilled and the car was warm. I closed my eyes. Just for a moment.

And when I opened them again we were in a nice quiet backwater of West Footscray, stopping in front of an oval on which a lot of young men were playing an informal game of something with a round ball, possibly soccer.

'I'll just wander along to the end of the ground,' said Daniel, getting out and slouching casually away. For a tall man in a leather coat, he can almost vanish, making himself into something which no one needs to notice. It's a remarkable skill. The soccer ground was suitable for trapping our rabbit. It had a high cyclone wire fence around it. There were two gates, one at each end of the ellipse. The other one looked to be locked. I could see a chain and padlock.

'Where's your man?' I asked Jon.

'There,' he said. 'Red baseball cap. I'll call him. He'll know the jig is up when he sees me.'

'Right,' I said. Jon is noticeable. He walked to the gate and called 'Chris! Hey, Chris!'

The red baseball cap's bill slid around to point at us, then briefly spun as the boy hauled it off his head. He looked around wildly for a place of safety, failed to find one, glanced at the back gate and saw Daniel there, looked at Jon, looked at me, looked at his puzzled fellow soccer players, took a breath, and gave up. He hauled off his cap, stuck it in his

back pocket, flipped the ball to a friend, and plodded out to the gate.

'Chris,' said Jon as he approached, 'what have you done?'

'Nuthin',' said Chris, but his heart wasn't in it.

'You want us to take the security video over to your mum?' asked Jon.

Chris acknowledged defeat. 'Nah,' he said.

'You've got two choices,' Jon told him. 'You can come and tell us all about it, and though we do have to fire you we'll find you another job, or you can just resign and we call the cops.'

'Not the cops,' gasped Chris. He was a weedy, undersized creature with a fine natural crop of acne. Not an attractive prospect for an employer.

'Have you got more of the weeds at home?' asked Jon severely.

'Yair,' said Chris. I could tell he was going to be difficult to interview, even when he was cooperating. He didn't seem to own many words.

'Then let's go to your home,' said Jon.

'All right,' said Chris. 'Mum's at work.'

He led the way across the road to a well-preserved white weatherboard cottage. Someone had planted roses and geraniums and lovingly watered the hanging baskets of fuschias every morning. There were other plants, but those are the only ones I know, as well as daisies. If the plant isn't one of them, then it's just a leafy botanic thing.

Chris let us into a sparely furnished clean hallway and parlour.

'I live in the bungalow,' he told Jon. 'Jon?'

'Yes?'

'It wasn't drugs, was it? Only he swore it wasn't drugs.'

'No, it wasn't drugs,' said Jon, looking down at the frantic hand clutching his sleeve. 'Who got you to do this, Chris?'

'Just this dude,' he muttered. 'Offered me a hundred. Need the money.'

'Why?'

'Just do.' Chris squirmed. Jon flicked up the boy's sleeve to expose his elbow and he indignantly pulled it down again.

'No! I'm not on the gear!' he cried.

'Then what did you need the money for?' Jon has a sort of gentle patience which will sooner or later wear down any male-factor. He isn't angry or shrill, there's no escalation, he never gets louder, but he never gives up.

'I'll give you the rest of the stuff.' Chris opened the back door of the house, dived out, and emerged from his bungalow with a large plastic bag full of miscellaneous veg. 'This is all of it.'

'When is more coming in?' asked Jon.

'Next month. On the first.'

'All right. Now we are going to sit down at the kitchen table and you are going to tell me everything you know, Chris. And then we shall see.'

Something slightly indulgent in Jon's tone made Chris prick up his unwashed ears. And gradually, picking up broken threads of narrative and knotting them together, Jon extracted the whole story.

Some seven months earlier a dude had leaned on the fence and watched the soccer match until he could speak to Chris. He had then asked him if he needed to earn some extra money, and

Chris had said yes because he needed the money. Because, all right, his dad was gambling and his mum couldn't earn enough to pay the mortgage. And he had two little sisters still at school. So Chris and the dude agreed on a hundred every delivery. All Chris had to do was remove the monster pots to the car park. There he would take out the herbs and stash them in the bushes for the dude to pick up. Except that he hadn't picked up the last lot so Chris had brought them home in case someone found them. And his hundred would be posted in his letterbox. Except that it hadn't been.

'Who was the dude? Didn't he give you a name at all?' asked Jon.

'Mollari,' said Chris, concentrating hard. 'Londo Mollari.'

I looked at Daniel. Daniel looked at me. Londo Mollari was the Centauri ambassador on *Babylon 5*. I decided not to say anything. The name didn't mean a thing to Chris, obviously. Or to Kepler or Jon.

'What about a phone number, any way to contact him?'

Chris shook his head.

'What did he look like?' Jon persisted.

'Short hair. Sort of brown. Bit bigger than me. Ordinary.'

Not one of nature's great observers, this boy. We got up to go. Jon put his hand on the boy's shoulder and shook him slightly.

'I'm not going to sack you yet,' he told him. 'You stay where you are and tell me the moment this Londo calls you. He'll want his herbs back, I expect. And see me tomorrow for some leaflets on Gamblers Anon. Your dad needs counselling.'

'What do I do now?' asked Chris, seemingly astonished.

'Go back and finish the game,' Jon suggested, and smiled.

We watched him run across the road to the game as we got back into the car. Timbo set it in motion and we slid away.

'I do love you,' said Kepler to Jon.

The murderer had decided his deed but not his place and time. When could he best strike down his tormentor? Not when he was praying, for then he would go to heaven. The murderer knew that his victim deserved to go to hell, and meant to send him there.

Chapter Fourteen

After we had dropped Jon and Kepler at Insula, Daniel went to a meeting on another matter and I took Timbo and the car to the headquarters of the Discarnate Brotherhood. As we swept down towards Studley Park I reflected that it was no wonder Megan, my courier, had charged me extra for delivering their pitiful excuse for bread. This was a long pull for her little pedal-assisted putt-putt. I tidied my hair and examined myself in the mirror. I looked very respectable, as befitted a woman visiting missions. I was conscious of a squirming feeling somewhere just above my waistline, as though I was about to give birth to a gerbil. It was probably the carob.

Timbo stopped the car and said, 'Jeez!'

It was a fair comment. The home of the Fleshless Friars was a folly. A very big and elaborate folly. In about 1890, to judge by the meticulous brickwork, some citizen of Melbourne, as richly endowed with gold as he was poverty-stricken in taste, had decreed that an Englishman's castle was his home and had actually caused one to be built. I couldn't imagine how I had missed seeing it before. It was not precisely concealed behind a screen of genuine yew trees and a high box hedge of immemorial density, because you can't conceal a castle like that, but somehow I must have repeatedly, as a student, walked right past it and never blinked. Which was like walking past an elephant in your third floor bathroom and not noticing. A purple elephant, complete with howdah and tiger.

I had to agree with Timbo. 'Indeed,' I said. We looked at it for a while.

The brickwork was red, with sooty overtones. There were crenellations. There were battlements. There was a great door and a gothic porch. Horace Walpole would have clasped his hands with glee. No flowers or even grass in any of the beds, I noticed, just a writhing of dark green ivy, hauling itself bodily up into ilex trees with iron thorns and leaves of the darkest green any plant can have before it gives up on photosynthesis altogether. A few irregular lumps, heaved up under the vines, marked where statues or gravestones—or possibly unfortunate canvassers—lay fallen.

There would have been a carriage drive in a real castle, but in this case there was just a gravelled road which was broad enough, at the end, for a car to turn around. Several cars were parked behind the corner of the stone wall. Some of the brothers were allowed modern methods of transport, then.

I got out. Timbo emerged and leaned on the door.

'You want me to come with you?' he asked.

'No, thanks anyway,' I told him.

The big soft face looked worried. His curls sagged. 'Only Daniel told me to take care of you or he'll —'

'You stay here and mind the car,' I said. He took out a packet of cigarettes, hesitated, and put them back again, still looking at me. The castle had really spooked Timbo, who had been unaffected in that dreadful Braybrook slum which reeked of evil. Thus architecture can make cowards of us all.

'Won't be long,' I assured him. 'If I'm not back in an hour, you come in and rescue me.'

'Okay,' he said. This time he took out the smoke and lit it—a watchdog with his proper orders.

I turned and went up the great steps under the gothic porch. The stones were slightly hollowed under my tread, like the steps of every authentically ancient building I could recall. Had they been specially carved that way? The person who had ordered that this place be built probably had that sort of lunatic thoroughness.

The door was a dread portal, studded with nails. A stretched eagle was more or less outlined in metal studs.

I could not see the piece of Viking skin which I had expected under the hinges but doubtless it was just a matter of time. The latch was appropriately overwrought in iron.

I looked around for a method of attracting attention, as a serviceable battleaxe would not have made much impression on that door. Fortunately there was a long chain, which I pulled, and an unusually dismal bell gave one solid clunk.

Inside the great door a wicket gate opened and a hooded figure looked out.

'We are sequestered,' it whispered. 'Nothing disturbs the fast of the sabbath.'

'I need to speak to the proprietor,' I said.

The hood tilted a little and I caught a glimpse of horrified, disgusted eyes. 'He won't see you today,' said the voice. 'He won't see anyone today. Or you at all. Go shed some of your flesh,' it said, dripping with loathing. 'Food belongs to the devil! Come back in penance and he may see you!'

I was taken aback by the force of this hatred. What had I done to this little brother? Nothing, except be fat and exist. I stepped away a little and the door started to close.

That wouldn't do. I grabbed for the figure's arm and with no exertion dragged it practically into my arms. It fought frantically. It was like trying to hold on to a spider, all legs and venom.

'Let go!' it panted.

'I got this leaflet,' I said patiently. 'It says, come here to lose weight. I'm here.'

'Tomorrow night,' said the figure—I still hadn't seen its face. My grasp had weakened. It dived back into the castle and a skinny hand extended and thrust another leaflet at me.

I took it.

Then a sweet voice said, 'What is the trouble, brother?'

'I've given her the leaflet,' whined the little voice. 'But I can't help it, brother, they're so disgusting, like pigs, all sweaty and gross and...' The door closed on the sound of retching and sobbing.

I stared at the eagle rivets for a while, shaken to the spine. I could not recall being so shocked. I was not used to being hated. Well, since school, and that was school. That child had not just disliked me, I had made it sick.

I gathered myself together and went back to the car. Timbo had been inspecting the cars. He, too, was deeply disturbed.

'You all right, Corinna?' He took my arm and helped me into the car next to him, a great honour. 'They tell you to bugger off?'

'More or less,' I said, still shaken.

'Them cars,' he said, starting the engine with less than his usual finesse and roaring backwards down the gravel drive, 'them cars...'

'What about them?'

'They been killed,' he said. 'Wires ripped out, steering rods smashed, broken radiators—on purpose,' he added, eyes wide with horror. 'What kind of people are they?'

'Not nice people,' I said, wishing I had a drink. 'Not nice people at all, Timbo.'

I felt like vomiting all the way home. Timbo let me out of the car outside Insula. He actually stopped the car in Flinders Lane and helped me down as gently as if I had been a geriatric aunt. He leaned me on the door while he rang my doorbell and summoned Daniel to come down and get me. Then he glared into the face of an outraged parking officer and said, 'Can't you see the lady's sick?' so menacingly in his usually soft voice that the grey ghost backed off, possibly for the first time in history.

Timbo surrendered me to Daniel, bestowed a shattering pat on my back, and drove off. Daniel put his arms around me.

'What on earth has happened, ketschele?' he asked, drawing me into the atrium and shutting the street door on the screams of the disappointed parking inspector. 'Here, sit down on the edge and say hello to the nice fishies. If my mother could only get her hands on you, fish, you would be gefilte. Or maybe not. Perhaps they don't make gefilte fish out of carp. Could be a lucky escape. Though Horatio will get you if you don't watch out. And one day Lucifer might find his water wings. Or learn to scuba dive. I can see him doing that.'

He kept talking and his voice was very soothing. I found my tongue. It was just where I had left it, in my mouth.

'Daniel, that monk hated me,' I exclaimed, not very coherently. 'He actually hated me. I made the little monk sick just by existing. I've never heard of such a thing. I'll never be able to eat again.'

'It's early,' said Daniel judiciously, listening to this nonsense. 'But not too early for a snack and a drink. Several drinks, perhaps. Come along,' he said, and after a blurry interval I found myself inside my own apartment, sitting on the sofa. There was a blue mohair rug over my legs, my shoes had been removed, my jacket hung up, my severe hairdo loosened and my lap weighted down with a large tabby cat. In my left hand I held a gin and tonic and in my right a small plate of tiny smoked salmon sandwiches, in which Horatio was showing a refined interest.

'Eat up,' said Daniel, taking a sandwich. 'I am just going to sit here for about ten minutes and listen to the music.'

The sandwiches, on rye bread, had cream cheese and capers in them. They were lovely. I sipped my drink, trying to shed the feeling of dreadful blubbery loathing which had washed over me—for my own body.

Start somewhere and examine it, Corinna. I wriggled my toes. They were nice toes. An admirable fringe to the foot, stopping it from fraying. The ankles held the feet on well. Knees were essential for flexibility. Thighs and hips for solidity. In between the parts which gave Daniel and me delight. I had always liked my breasts and in the black dress they had floated like waterlilies. I did have a double chin, but what of it? What if I had three chins? They were all mine and I had paid for them. My arms and shoulders were strong enough to knead dough all day if I had to. My admirable tastebuds were informing me that the smoked salmon was probably Spring's and the cream cheese Meroe's homemade, with extra cream. I had created the bread which even now was giving me pleasure. How could I hate myself in the way which I certainly had, all the way home? I had been in a fury of passionate self-loathing. I had only come out of it when some imbecile started wittering on about gefilte fish. Oh yes, that was Daniel, my beloved, and the music was 'Weep O Mine Eyes' and other madrigals and I was home and sane again.

Then Horatio, despairing of my courtesy, took the last little sandwich gently but firmly out of my grasp and ate it in a very pointed fashion, reproving me for my lack of generosity to beautiful cats who charitably sat on the laps of the afflicted. And I laughed.

Daniel turned the music down. He raised his eyebrows.

'I'll explain,' I said, and did, to the best of my ability. He was shaking his head by the end of the recital.

'Something gave Timbo a serious turn, too,' he commented. 'He's got a lot of courage, that Timbo, and so have you. This is clearly black magic of some sort, strong enough to unnerve both of you. I'll just ring and make sure that he got home to his mum all right. If Horatio would like another sandwich, I'll fetch some more. I thought we might invite the Prof and Meroe to drinks, so I started making cocktail snacks and after a while you can't stop, have you noticed that? You got back just in time to prevent me from making celery curls and tomato roses, ketschele. But they can all go in the freezer for another day if you'd rather.'

'Ten more minutes,' I said, and leaned back, sipping my drink and stroking the affronted Horatio. Eventually he elevated his chin for a seriously intimate scratch and I believed that he had forgiven me. I felt as I had when, as a child unused to electricity, I experimentally stuck my little finger into the lamp socket above my bed. I managed to drag back the finger, but the after-effects had been like this: lassitude and a strong sense of astonishment.

What would it be like to be thin? Had I ever seriously envisaged it? I closed my eyes and tried to see her: Corinna the slim, in high heels which accentuated her racehorse ankles, in short skirts which showed her straight thighs, in tight belts which showed off her slim waist, her…sagging throat, her wrinkled face, her scrawny arms, her fried-egg breasts, her limp wrists, her strengthless body? A Corinna who couldn't haul a sack of flour across the floor? A Corinna who bruised her lover with her hip bones? A Corinna whom nobody knew—not even me? Erk.

I took a gulp of my drink and resumed caressing Horatio. No, I did not want to be thin. And this Discarnate Brotherhood's spell was, as Daniel had said, evil. And had to be stopped.

By the time Horatio and I had eaten the rest of the smoked salmon sandwiches I was better. I got up to admire the array of cocktail snacks which Daniel had constructed. They were lovely. Little piped cheesy things. Tiny little quiches. Little meatballs on toothpicks. Pinwheel sandwiches. They could not be wasted.

'Instead of dinner,' he said, waving a dismissive hand. 'Sometimes it's good to sample a lot of different tastes.'

'You knew this might happen,' I accused, dipping a meatball into sweet chili sauce. 'Mmm, very nice. You suspected that contact with the Fleshless Ones might freak me out.'

Daniel disclaimed second sight and smiled. 'No, I just had an urge to make a few little sandwiches, and then I got carried away. I found that book on mezes. Nothing like truffling around someone else's kitchen to give an old party caterer ideas.'

'Were you really a party caterer?' I might never get to the end of the fascinating professions of the amazing Daniel. And he had lied about the celery curls. There they were, chilling in their bowl of iced water.

'An old friend of mine started a business and one weekend all her staff got food poisoning,' he said. 'So I came along to help and it was quite amusing, really. Though I soon got sick of stoning olives. Not a pastime for an impatient man. We used to do tea parties. And drinks parties. It was fun for a while. But I came home and I found you. And you are beautiful and I love you and I want to make that perfectly clear, all right?'

'Right,' I said. Then I sniffed. Something was burning.

'My curry puffs!' and Daniel dragged open the oven. They were only a touch singed. He slid in a tray of little pizzas.

'Did Timbo get home okay?' I asked.

'His mum said that he was real upset but she'd make him a nice dinner. She's settled him down in front of *Cannonball Run*, his favourite movie, with a couple of bags of crisps and a beer. He'll be all right.'

'She'll roast him a nice sheep,' I commented. 'Couple of gallons of ale and a few gateaux for dessert. Poor old Timbo, he was really shocked.'

'He'll recover,' said Daniel. 'What about people? Or do you feel like barring the door and watching *Babylon 5*?'

'People,' I decided. 'Just Meroe and Professor Dion, I think. And Jon and Kepler. It's Sunday. I have to go to bed early.'

'And I can't stay,' he said ruefully. 'Got a surveillance job.'

'No matter,' I said airily. 'Horatio will accompany me to bed. And without you, I do get more sleep.'

'But it's not anything like as much fun,' he grinned, and kissed me. 'Why does *Babylon 5* ring a bell?' asked Daniel, getting down the company vodka in case Meroe was feeling like drinking.

'That kid said that the dude who tempted him into indiscretion was called Londo Mollari.'

'And we don't think that the Centauri really have landed at last?'

'No, we don't.'

I stole a little pizza as he took them out. They were fantastic. How could I ever have thought that I could not eat again? Ridiculous.

I rang around and found that I could indeed have Meroe and the delightful Professor, who brought Mrs. Dawson, who had called on him to enquire about a Latin quotation and had been beguiled into playing string games with Nox. Jon came alone. Kepler was working on an antidote to a vicious computer virus.

'He's only got twelve hours to find it and kill it,' said Jon, accepting a glass of red. 'It might be anywhere and he doesn't know what it looks like. And if he doesn't find it, every major airport is going to lose its air traffic control. He's got nerves of steel. I'm a wreck and he just suggested I find someone else to worry about.'

'Good,' I said. 'Come and worry about me.' He gave me a hug.

'You must have been cooking for hours, Daniel,' said Mrs. Dawson, looking at the array of treats. 'Remarkable how scent flows around these old buildings. I could smell crisping bacon on the stairs.'

'I know,' I said. 'I've been smelling caramel all week, and when I made onion rolls once, the whole of Insula woke up ravenous and started frying.'

'Yes, Mrs. Pemberthy complained,' said the Professor.

'But then, it makes her happy,' said Meroe, taking a glass of vodka and orange juice. We wandered into the parlour. Rain was falling outside. I switched off the TV and with it the news that was showing someone shooting someone—somewhere.

'The world has certainly changed,' commented Mrs. Dawson, a picture in a dark terracotta shawl thrown over her chocolate leisure suit. 'But in most respects it remains sadly familiar.'

'Too true.' Professor Dion had a line of small scratches across his neck, which he was dabbing with a very clean handkerchief. I took over. 'Thank you, m'dear. I'm afraid that Nox becomes rather overenthusiastic when she is playing with string.'

'She got you,' I said, patting the little beads dry.

'She did,' he sighed.

We sat down. Meroe, who had been unpacking magical apparatus all day, was freshly rinsed and hungry. She was delighted by the celery curls, which she had not seen for years. 'Nice!' she crowed, crunching a third. 'Thank you, Daniel. This is a civilised idea. Corinna, you're looking pale. Have you had a shock?'

Not much gets past those bright gypsy eyes. I explained as best I could, though now the spell had faded my reaction appeared foolish to me. To my surprise, the rest of the company appeared to understand.

'You aren't used to being hated,' said the Professor gravely. 'Daniel understood it, didn't you, my dear fellow?'

Daniel nodded. 'Because I'm a Jew,' he said to me. 'I can be hated for existing. I know what that's like.'

'And I recall very well being in Petra, with my first husband,' said Mrs. Dawson, putting a little pizza and a quiche on her plate with great care. 'I left the party to look at some carvings, and when I turned around I stared straight into the eyes of an outraged Bedouin man. There I was, a woman, a foreign woman, unveiled, alone, a horrible thing, a monster.

I felt that identical shock to the solar plexus, as though someone had punched me.'

'I've been in places in China where my skin and my eyes made me a demon,' said Jon and drank some more wine.

'I was an Englishman in some very anti-English places,' said the Professor.

'And I'm a gypsy,' said Meroe simply. 'Everyone hates gypsies. It's a natural reaction, Corinna. We know how you feel.'

'But that these people are deliberately fostering such hatred,' objected Mrs. Dawson, 'that is wicked.'

'So it is. Let's see who they are,' I said, unfolding the second pamphlet the little monk had given me. It was nicely printed— desktop publication, I would have said. The screamer was the same: 'fat? hate it?' But it was followed by the startling statement, 'so does god'.

Mrs. Dawson fanned herself with the end of her shawl. 'My goodness!' she exclaimed.

'One rather hopes for a large hairy foot from above, does one not?' asked the Professor, patting his lips with his handkerchief. 'Or a good old-fashioned lightning bolt. That would do just as well.'

'God has a plan for you,' the pamphlet told me. 'Book your place in a seminar on the subject and God will reveal, through his minister, his plan to make you thin. The love of food comes from the Devil! No more sweating, no more blubber, no more disgust! You will be forgiven your state of sin, and you will be delivered from the foul prison of your flesh.'

'I wish I knew a bishop,' said Mrs. Dawson, as silence fell.

'You want them exorcised?' asked Meroe, interested.

'No, I want them put under an interdict. Or simonised. That always sounded painful. But surely this 'minister' can't have any followers,' she said.

'That I don't know. I've only seen three. I need to find out if my father is there. I'm just not sure how to go about it. Anyone got any ideas?'

'Start with a tenancy search, that sort of thing,' Daniel suggested. 'That will tell us who owns the building, who rents it. Talk to delivery people, neighbours. Tell you one thing, anyone who could make the owners break up their precious cars has a lot of sway. I never thought I'd see the middle class destroy a car.'

'It's all of a piece with his philosophy,' mused Meroe. 'They are totems, and he is asking them to cast aside their totems. To throw away possessions as well as despise the flesh. There were a lot of ancient Christian saints who talked about the body like that. All those desert fathers, starving together.'

'And all those female saints who existed on holy communion and air,' I said bitterly. They had always annoyed me most when I had been forced to admire them at Sunday school. I couldn't see anything holy about anorexia, which was a form of suicide, and wasn't that forbidden?

'He seems to have tapped into one of the more unfortunate veins of spirituality,' commented Meroe. 'But it explains his appeal. Join him and get thin. That's sold a lot of books and potions and gym memberships. Made a lot of fortunes.'

'And not only thin,' put in Jon, 'but virtuous.'

'People,' said Mrs. Dawson, eating her little quiche with a snap of white teeth, 'really are most peculiar.'

'I think I can help you get in to see the reverend father,' said Jon.

'How?'

'I can make you an acting unpaid freelance journalist for our newsletter, *Life and Times*,' he said. 'I'll make you a card. Such people always want publicity. You can try interviewing the reverend father—what is his name?'

'I can't see it here,' I said, turning over the leaflet. 'Lord, he's charging $2000 for that seminar! Oh yes, here's his name. Hungerford, that's him. How very apt.'

'Are you sure you want to go back there again?' asked Meroe.

I thought about it as I watched Horatio enter the room with the elegance of Beau Brummel in a new blue coat and an especially inventive stock. He greeted the company politely and chose his lap. The lot fell on Mrs. Dawson, who appeared sensible of the honour and provided him with a dab of cream cheese. He licked it complacently off his whiskers.

'Yes,' I decided. 'I do. As much as I don't know what I am going to do with my father when I find him, that is not a good place for him to be. Somewhere else must be better. Thank you, Jon, I'll come and pick the card up tomorrow.'

'And have you got any further with those poisonous herbs?' asked the Professor.

'We found out where the girls got the ones that made them sick,' said Daniel. 'They may well be the same leaves that kid smuggled in. We're still on the track of the sellers. I've got a few people watching. We should find something soon.'

'Good,' said Mrs. Dawson, setting Horatio politely aside and getting to her feet. 'Thank you very much for your hospitality, my dears. I shall be going now. Coming, Dion?' she asked, and the Professor joined her, gallantly offering his arm. Jon decided to go out, to avoid bothering Kepler. Daniel and Meroe cleaned up and after about an hour I shut the door on all of them.

Which was rather a relief. I put myself to bed in my own bed, and I slept like a baby.

The murderer prepared his tools. His knives were as sharp as sunlight. He was only hampered by the incised wound which the snapping elastic band had made around his right wrist. It was deep enough to expose the tendons and hampered his grip. But it did not hurt anymore. Nothing hurt.

Chapter Fifteen

I must have dreamt of baking because when I woke I knew I was in the mood to make rolls—onion, bacon, poppy seed, garlic, herb. With this in mind I took my coffee and toast downstairs and met Jason, bidding him start slicing as soon as the usual array of dough was in preparation. The daylight came in a flurry of activity as we rolled, glazed, fried, cooled, blended, mixed and scattered.

In a few hours we had as beautiful a collection of savoury rolls as any baker has ever laid out on trays and Jason was so tired that he just mixed ordinary sultana and spice, chocolate and jam muffins for the shop. Not that they weren't superb.

I let the Mouse Police out into the cold alley. They scampered off, tails high. I leaned at the door for a moment, saturated in delicious scents, and the smell flowed out into the darkness. A passing security guard sniffed, swallowed and stopped in his tracks.

'Onion rolls,' he breathed. 'My grandda used to make onion rolls.'

'Have one on me,' I said, and gave him the hot roll. He flicked one finger to his cap in a salute.

'Your good deed for the day,' he said. 'Thanks, Miss.'

Well, nice to start the day with a good deed. Who knew how many bad ones might follow?

Jason was so filthy from all that chopping and slicing that he had taken a shower. He was re-clad in a baker's overall and was now eying the rolls with undisguised lust. Hard work made Jason hungry. Then again, so did breathing.

'One of each,' I warned. 'You don't want to spoil your breakfast.'

He grinned at me. The Mouse Police skidded back and flung themselves in abandoned attitudes on their flour sacks to sleep out the winter. A bicycle whirred towards us. I fielded the flung paper and went upstairs to make myself more coffee while my apprentice took care of the rest of the bread.

What a luxury. I spread out the paper and toasted some more sourdough. There was a scrape left in the bottom of the jar of cherry jam. The coffee was good. And the news was no worse than usual—misery, pain, betrayal, mass murder, that sort of thing. And well, well, the Discarnates had taken out an ad. It hit me in the face afresh.

'FAT? HATE IT? SO DOES GOD.' They had a nerve. Someone ought to tell the far-too-well-named Father Hungerford where to get off. I toyed with the wording of a reply: HYPOCRITICAL? HATE IT? SO DOES CORINNA. But it didn't have the same punch. And I wasn't so secure in my virtue that I was about to make decisions for God.

I went back to the bakery to allow Jason to go and engulf a Del Pandamus breakfast. Megan came for the deliveries and we stacked them all into her rickshaw. She demanded and got a bonus in the form of a bacon roll. The day dawned.

And the morning went on as usual, which was soothing. Lots of my favourite people dropped in. Jenny P for the tomato rolls and gorgeous Ika for the chocolate muffins. Frank Mattea, a mathematician with a non-Euclidian moustache, buying iced queen cakes for Gemma, his beautiful daughter. Cat-loving Karina threw herself on Horatio as Peter and Vanessa bickered amicably and bought onion rolls. The only time I ever saw their discussion grow grave was when Pete suggested that John Howard had a heart and I had to remind Vanessa that the sourdough batard was banned as a weapon under the Geneva Convention. Horatio usually will not tolerate familiarity, but sees Karina as some form of relative. He even allowed her to kiss him. Joy Finnes tied Raz, her elderly border collie cross, to the doorknob and purchased crusty bread. Raz is too old and amiable to unsettle Horatio. Mary Mou bought a bacon roll and came back for another. Tristina bought sourdough. Amanda bought muffins. Leila Kaunitz brought me a Bosch figurine, the odd creature in the egg. All the regulars. I liked having regulars.

I retained some rolls because the scent was dragging in the famished hordes by the nose and they were bounding off the racks. Our soup was a strong chicken broth, with vegetables and pearl barley, and it seemed that half of the workforce had woken up undernourished and chilled this cold morning. My savoury rolls were a perfect accompaniment to the soup. By one, the last drop and crumb had gone.

Kylie had drunk her cup of soup and eaten a cheese roll, her choice. I had, of course, truthfully informed her that there was no fat in my soup, as I had gone to considerable trouble to skim it off. Kylie was actually wearing a jumper which covered all of her—a skimpy, fluffy jumper which appeared to be knitted from cat fur, but a jumper. Perhaps my girls were growing sense, after all. Stranger things had been known. If only in the Fortean Times.

And then it was closing time. Daniel came in as I was putting the shutters up and kissed me on the back of the neck.

'Lunch?' I asked.

'Nice,' he said. 'You have been baking up a storm.'

'Jason's staying for a while to mind the soup,' I told him. 'At double rates,' I added, at which his mutinous frown cleared. 'And since all he has to do is mind the pots to make sure that they don't boil over, then strain the stock before placing it in the fridge, it will be a nice quiet afternoon for him. He can experiment with new muffins or improve his reading skills with the recipe collection.'

'Sweet,' said Jason, entirely reconciled to an afternoon's pot watching. 'I reckon I can get those date ones right. They're too heavy so far. Maybe I ought to mince the dates…'

We left him, a happy young man.

I was just about to allow my sweet Daniel to lead me to higher and happier regions when I remembered something I hadn't done. And I had spoken about it to Del Pandamus only yesterday. Damn.

'Daniel,' I said, resisting his pull on my hand, 'we forgot about the Lone Gunmen.'

'So we did,' he said, unenthusiastically.

I took a good look at him. Unshaven and a touch haggard, though on him it looked good. It must be nice to have the sort of face on which adversity just brings out your cheekbones.

I thought of a new plan.

'So I will go see the nerds while you go up to the apartment, have a shower and a shave, and pop yourself into my bed for a nap. I'll join you as soon as I can. Shouldn't take a moment,' I said airily.

Daniel went where he was bidden and I skipped down the steps to the street, not having a mind to waste any more Daniel time on Nerds Inc than I had to.

On the steps I encountered Meroe, who was holding a limp bouquet of dead leaves. Seldom had I seen such depressed veg. Not since the last time I had tried to grow anything, in fact.

'Just going to see if the Lone Gunmen are all right,' I explained. 'Del said their shop was shut. I hope you aren't going to eat those,' I added.

Meroe was wearing a bright green wrap patterned with golden wheat and it billowed around her so that she looked like an offended Ceres, denying agriculture to men until she got her daughter back.

'I have been comparing the two herbal potions, the ones sold in that club and the ones smuggled in the monster pots,' she said.

'And?' I hung on to the ends of her wrap as it tried to carry my witch away.

'They are the same,' she said. 'Whoever smuggled that mixture in is using some if not all of it to make the weight loss tea which nearly killed Kylie and Gossamer. And no one can tell me who it is,' she said.

'No?'

'I have tried all the herbalists I know,' she said. 'No one has heard of such a thing, though two of them have encountered the results. Overdoses, both of them, and one ended up in intensive care.'

'Stands to reason it isn't a real herbalist,' I said. 'No real herbalist would put those different leaves together. It's an amateur with her grandma's old recipe. You said so yourself.'

'So I did,' agreed Meroe, looking more like the goddess after her interview with Zeus. 'I shall pray for guidance,' she said, swathing herself in her wheat sheaves, and went into Insula.

I continued down the steps and along to Nerds Inc, which I found open. Not for business, perhaps, because the closed sign was still on the door and dust was filtering down on the stock. But open for deliveries. Boxes of abstruse games in decorated containers were being handed down from a truck to Taz and Rat. I was pleased to see that they looked no sicker than usual. Their t-shirts bore no more than the normal freight of chili sauce and their complexions were nerd vibrant, ie, a pale shade of ivory, almost ecru. A colour which would have been nice in silk.

'Gentlemen,' I greeted them. They turned on me the faces of complete wholehearted horror that nerds turn on any woman. Had I been Sog Succoth from The Depths I would have got a more enthusiastic welcome.

'Hi, Corinna,' said Taz.

'Buying up big?' I asked as the delivery man lowered another carton of games. 'You remembered to put that BAS statement in, then?'

'Oh yeah, you can do it online,' Rat told me, barely visible over the box lid.

'Del said that your shop was shut so I came to see if you were all right,' I said.

'We just shut for a couple of days,' explained Taz. 'We took a holiday. Test out the new stuff.' He dragged up a lesson in polite behaviour which his mother must have gone to some effort to impress on the growing nerd mind (probably by removing the fuse from the household electricity supply and refusing to give it back until he listened): 'Thanks for asking, Corinna,' he said.

So that was that, just nerds being nerds, and I had a Daniel awaiting me in my apartment. No need to stay here in the cold street any longer. I bade the Lone Gunmen remember to eat some vitamins occasionally and left them. Now for lunch.

I reported the nerds' healthy condition to Del, bought some of his beef lasagna, and got in out of the cold as fast as any Le Carré spy.

When I arrived in Hebe Daniel was asleep. I sat down to do some minor accounting tasks and drink a glass of gin and tonic. Horatio walked to the door and indicated his willingness to ascend to the garden, but it was too cold and I was tired. He paused there for a moment, then seemed to agree with me, reassuming his place in the small of Daniel's back and curling up, head on paws. Outside Insula the city went on its way, hooting and shouting and seething with life. In here the little scratch of my pen on the paper could be clearly detected. I could almost hear Daniel's heart beating.

I was so fortunate. My good luck took my breath away as I sat there, adding up my little columns of figures, glowing with happiness.

After an hour I called the number on the Discarnate leaflet and got an authoritative male voice. 'Brother Simon here,' it said. 'How may we help you?'

'I'd like to interview your reverend father for *Life and Times* magazine,' I said, inventing freely. 'Would six o'clock be convenient?'

'Five would be better,' said Brother Simon. 'We keep God's hours here. I will consult the table of appointments...yes, the father could see you at five. You know where we are?'

'Yes,' I said.

'Good. Come to the front door and tell the porter that Brother Simon has given you an admit. Your name?'

'Chapman,' I said. 'See you soon, Brother Simon.'

Jon had put my new identity card through my letterbox. It was a nice job. I wondered if Kepler had managed to demolish his virus. I assumed that he had, because no headlines screamed 'Air Traffic Control Lost!' in the news kiosk

I could see from my window. If I was going to get to the castle before five I would have to leave now. I wasn't going to wake Daniel up to see me off. I changed into clothes suitable for a newspaper person, grabbed my notebook and a pen, and called a taxi. Poor Timbo had received enough shocks in his young life. I wasn't going to take him to that graveyard of slaughtered vehicles again if I could help it.

This time no one was to be allowed to upset me. My black suit was formal, my white shirt professional, my wide collar a miracle of the lacemaker's art. I had put on several silver rings which Daniel had given me, amethyst, moonstone, opal. I had sprayed myself with Yardley April Violets. I was, as far as feminine defences were concerned, unassailable.

The little wicket door opened and another of those skinny robed figures poked its nose out. This time I announced, 'I have an admit from Brother Simon,' before anyone could start retching. The bony hand and thin wrist, ringed with black rubber bands, gestured and I stepped boldly inside. And stopped.

Oh, my. It was a castle inside as well. I was standing in an entrance hall with a very high ceiling, but beyond me opened out a real great hall. It had a proper Y-shaped staircase mounting to the upper floors. A gallery ran around the whole circumference. There were two massive fireplaces, suitable for tree trunks or Yule logs, and the hall was hung with the heads of the stags which I presumed had once been roasted on those hearths. I suppose that one might as well do something decorative with the rest of the beast. If one can call cutting off something's head and sticking it on a wall decorative. I, personally, didn't.

Hundreds of glass eyes stared out at me. They looked blank, as well they might. Someone in the Depression had ordered the whole of the interior, including what looked like linenfold panelling, to be painted a colour called 'light stone'. Unique in making the painted surface look dirtier than it had before the painter began, it was a kind of contaminated cream in colour. And flaking. The floor consisted of stone flags innocent of any carpet or mat, swept painfully clean. It was freezing. I sniffed. No scent of cooking. But then, one would not have expected that.

The little acolyte had vanished, leaving me stranded in the middle of this waste of floor. I had no idea where I might find Reverend Father Hungerford. Thinking that this might be a ploy to disconcert visitors, I drew up a kitchen chair, the only portable-looking furniture in all this huge space, sat down, and began to write a description of the hall. That ought to produce some action. Nothing upsets a bully more than someone who hasn't noticed that they are being bullied.

I started to hear sounds and they were very pleasant. Plainchant. A Kyrie eleison. Lord have mercy. I hummed along. Plainchant follows rules and isn't hard to busk. I was just beginning to enjoy myself, anticipating the rise and fall of the chant, when I heard footsteps and stood up to greet whoever was coming.

Imagine my surprise when I found myself looking into that Savonarola face which had so disconcerted me one morning at my bakery. But my surprise was as nothing to that of my interlocutor, who was staggered. For a moment he was utterly at a loss. His violet-dark eyes widened, his soft kiss-me-quick mouth gaped, he gave a gasp and he was so attractive that my knees went momentarily weak.

'Corinna Chapman,' I said, holding out my hand. No use attempting to pass myself off as anyone else, though I could still credibly be a reporter for *Life and Times*. 'I am pleased to meet you, Reverend Father.'

'Miss Chapman,' he said, regaining his voice. It was a sweet voice. 'I thought you were a baker.'

'I am that as well,' I said, giving him my card. 'Shall we talk?'

'Come in here,' he said, opening one of the small doors under the gallery. 'You might find it too cold out here in the great hall.'

He had recovered. Rats. I might find the hall too cold. He, by inference, wouldn't. Indeed he appeared to be clad solely in one of the order's thin black garments, judging by the way it hung on him. I dragged my mind away from contemplating this. He resembled a Greek statue far too closely for comfort. I wondered how old he was. The little lines around his eyes indicated he must have been at least forty. Starvation had not damaged him too much yet. But it would.

His office was a small wood-panelled room which had escaped the general awfulising that had damaged the great hall. It also lacked dead stuffed animals, which was a plus. On the wall was a small icon of a ravaged looking saint, probably Simon Stylites, because he was holding a pillar. And next to him an incongruous Madonna, a modern painting of the Mother of God as a strong, rosy-faced country girl with the child on her ample knee. There was also a fine gold encrusted gothic cross next to one made of black wood tied together with tarred string, like the cross given to Joan of Arc by an English soldier who was required to watch her burn at the stake.

I sat down on a (padded) visitor's chair while my host assumed his (unpadded) bench. The office had the usual office stuff, including a new computer. There were neatly stacked leaflets with that headline on them. FAT? HATE IT? SO DOES GOD.

'How do you know?' I asked.

'I beg your pardon?'

'How do you know God hates people to be fat?'

'There we stray into doctrine,' he told me.

'Let us stray,' I suggested.

'Very well.' He set the tips of his fingers together and began to expound. Whenever I see that gesture I settle back and wait for Nanny to tell me a big, fat lie. I tried not to be distracted by the man's sheer physical beauty, a haunted face which might have been painted by El Greco, Lestat from the last frames of *Queen of the Damned*. 'The desert fathers believed that only in simplicity and austerity could true virtue and enlightenment be found. This is shared by most of the leading faiths, which all employ fasting; Ramadan of Islam and Yom Kippur of the Jews. Buddhist saints subsist on sunlight and die in mudra, preserved forever by their own austerity. Food and drink are distractions from the contemplation of the infinite, and what person can call themselves virtuous who is dripping with gross heaviness, wallowing in the fleshpots?'

'And so…' I prompted.

'Here we eat little, just enough to support life. The food is sustaining but not palatable. We work hard at uncongenial tasks, to learn humility. We learn the value of silence.'

'I see. And your seminars?'

'Those who cannot partake of the life of the community can come in, though it disturbs our peace. They can be partly initiated into our mysteries. For this they pay a lot of money, which purges them of some of their excess goods, and they can continue with our practices out in the world. Though not as well,' he added. 'The world has too many distractions.'

'The rubber bands?'

'Are to remind them of fasting and purity. They are graded, from white for a neophyte to black for a brother or sister.'

'So you have women in your order?'

'Oh yes,' he said, smiling a little. 'Women need to purge themselves of grossness even more than men. Vanity, vanity. Some little vanities, like cosmetics. Some large vanities, like sexual love.'

'Sexual love is a vanity?' I asked, making a note.

'The only love is the love of God,' he told me. 'Human love is fallible, it wanes, it ceases, it stops, it is denied,' he added. That about summed it up for earthly love, I thought. And remembered the naked man asleep in my bed, cat curled into the small of his back. I must have smiled because Father Hungerford's expression became markedly more austere. 'You may think that it will last,' he said coldly, 'but only God knows eternity.'

'True. Perhaps you would show me around?' I asked. 'If my presence is not too upsetting for your community?'

'There will be time before collation,' he said, consulting a Phillip Patek watch—vanity, eh? I stood up and shut my notebook.

He led me up the main stairs to the series of small rooms all around the gallery. Each one had a camp bed, a single blanket, a small table and a cardboard box, which probably contained what few personal belongings members of the community were allowed to keep. They seemed to consist of a toothbrush and a razor. No books. Not even a tin of sweets or a handkerchief or a flower.

'We are still at work,' said Father Hungerford, leading me down back stairs to a large room in which perhaps forty people in brown robes were sitting on the floor and stitching tapestries. A thin woman in a black robe was supervising, handing out new threads and occasionally fixing mistakes. I was obscurely pleased that the front of her robe was stuck with threaded needles and she was at that moment asking, 'Who has the good scissors?' Some things about needlework never change. The tapestries were not exclusively religious, though several people were working on pastel Raphael Madonnas. I caught sight of that unicorn and Pegasus one which Therese Webb had been working on. So this was why her prices had gone down. She had said something about slave labour.

There was no buzz of conversation in the room as there would have been amongst any usual group of people all doing the same thing. Just the plainchant, which was coming from another room. No one looked up as we came in except the needlework sister, who gave a brief smile and abandoned her search for the good scissors.

'Why tapestry?' I asked her.

'It isn't too hard to learn for those who have never so much as sewn on their own buttons,' she said briskly. 'It requires concentration. It is a good discipline. And we can sell the tapestries to support the community. These acolytes are only here for the two-week retreat. By Friday they will be back in the world, much thinner and more at peace with themselves.'

My father, as far as I could tell, was not in this room.

I caught the eye of a portly gentleman who was stitching easily at a sunset over a country cottage of unusual frightfulness. He winked. This cheered me. That one would be back on the port and cigars as soon as he shucked his brown robe.

'And here,' said Father Hungerford, leading me on, 'are the singers.'

Another room, this time smaller and therefore warmer. Twenty people were singing from an overhead PowerPoint projection. It was an authentic medieval music manuscript, with those square notes which I suspect might be called neumes. They were doing a pretty good job, which argued that they had been singing together for a while. 'Credo in unum, in unum Deum,' they sang. 'I believe in the one God.' One God, perhaps, but an awful lot of sects, of which this was not the least peculiar. In his own way, Hungerford had stolen the ideas of someone like Fox, who established the Quakers—silence, work, plainness—and embroidered them with decorative St. Anthony features like that famine bread and complete rejection of human love. At least he wasn't asking anyone to sit on a pillar, I suppose...

No father amongst the singers. We went on, down and down, and came to a cavernous kitchen in which it would have been proper to prepare a massive banquet for a hundred or so like-minded friends. There were huge slow combustion ovens, cold as charity. There were several cooking hearths, with pot hangers and treadmills for little dogs to turn the spit—how Mrs. Pemberthy's Traddles would have adorned one of these! There were huge unpolished tables running down the middle of the cavern which had once groaned under haunches of venison, saddles of beef, mounds of potatoes, hundred of pies, game and larks' tongues and pork—and mounds of butter and cheese and breads and bowls of bitter salad and marzipan castles and iced cakes and fruit jellies oozing with cream.

The three electric light bulbs swayed over a meagre repast. Huge pots held what I thought was a vegetable stew, mainly turnips and potato, with a few carrots, parsnips, and maybe an onion to eke out the broth. Famine bread lay already cut into chunks on wooden trays. No spices, no salt and pepper, no butter, no cheese, no meat, no herbs. I must ask about those herbs, I reminded myself. Several of the brown-robed were cutting up yet more turnips. One of them was my father.

He looked straight at me and did not react. He didn't recognise me. I didn't know what to say. I stayed silent. Silently, I began to fume. I had chased him from pillar to post, whatever that meant, exposed myself to shock and fear, and finally found him and he didn't even know me!

Father Hungerford was introducing a black-clad monk. 'Brother Amos,' he said. 'Our brother was once a famous chef.'

I almost put out my hand and then didn't. In view of Father Hungerford's statements about sexual love, touching was probably forbidden.

Brother Amos had been fat. He now sagged. His eyes were red. His hands shook. He nodded. 'Have a taste,' he offered, and gave me a spoon. One of the huge pots was placed on a trivet on the table. I tasted. Turnip stew. Not unpleasant. Brother Amos brought out a bottle of vitamin concentrate and measured an amount into the pot.

'Sustaining,' he told me. Then he opened a small box and put a heaping teaspoon of something which smelt foul beyond belief into the innocent stew. 'But not palatable.'

'Black broth,' I said, enlightened. The Prof had told me all about how the Spartans mortified their flesh with appalling soup in order to prove that they were the hardiest soldiers. He thought it was a silly idea, mind, and added that they had in the end been beaten by the Thebans, who ate their soup without contaminants. 'That's asafoetida, isn't it?'

Brother Amos nodded and went back to the vegetable cutters. I was shocked. The idea of making a good soup and then deliberately spoiling it offended the core and root of my own philosophy.

Father Hungerford took me further, and we were out in the open again. More of the brown-robed were stacking crates of bottles.

'Our spring water,' he said blandly. I examined the bottle he handed me. It made no claims about being a weight loss product. It was just water in a blue bottle.

'One allows sunlight to fall through the coloured glass, which affects the water inside,' he said. 'On the same principle as homeopathy. Wristbands and this water maintain our acolytes in the right way when they go out in the world.'

'At five dollars a bottle,' I said tonelessly.

'Indeed,' he said.

'And how lucky you were to find a spring on your own property,' I said, maintaining my poker face.

He matched it easily. 'It did seem like an incidence of divine grace,' he agreed.

'And what about your other products?' I asked. 'The herbs?'

'We do not sell any other product,' he said flatly. 'Just water. Supplying herbs is a dangerous business. People will misuse even the most innocent of God's gifts. Now, if you will excuse me, it is time for collations. Brother Timothy will see you out. And I may see your piece before you submit it?'

'Of course,' I said. I watched his admirable back move away from me. Brother Timothy was a rangy, elderly welterweight. He hitched up his robe and led me around the castle, through a graveyard of dead cars to the great hall door, where he supplied me with an armload of leaflets and a free bottle of the blue water.

'Do you like it here?' I asked him. He produced a dog end and lit it with a wary glance inside.

'It's quiet,' he said. 'I used to be on the street. Food's crook but there's enough of it. I sneak out sometimes for a smoke and a drink. And the singing's nice,' he added. He butted out the stub of his cigarette and shut the door on me.

I walked out into Studley Park Road so distracted that I was halfway home before I thought about getting a taxi. My father didn't even know me. I saw his blank face turned to me over and over in my mind. He didn't even know me. And the brotherhood didn't distribute herbs?

When I returned to Insula I could hear banging and swearing from the undercroft. Of course, Monday night. Rubbish collection tomorrow. That was Trudi reasoning with the skips.

Every apartment in Insula has a rubbish chute, and all of them end up in the basement where the old kitchens and wine cellars are. Every day Trudi sorts out the rubbish and puts the nonrecyclables in a skip and the recyclables in a council bin. We have several skips in case it has been a big week for rubbish. By the noise it seemed that we had a bumper crop.

I went to the small door which leads out into Flinders Lane and grabbed an ascending skip which Trudi was pushing from behind. Together we hauled it up without much trouble. Then we went back for the other. Trudi leaned on the wall and caught her breath, then delved into the first skip, pulling on a string as though she was fishing and saying very rude Dutch things loudly enough to make any passing Dutch person blush.

And up came Lucifer, his little orange head breaking through the plastic bags, absolutely stinking, smeared to the whiskers with what could have been spoiled smoked trout pate. It was my day for smells, it seemed.

'Bath for you, bad boy,' scolded Trudi. 'Corinna, you give me a hand?'

Together we secured the little door. Trudi found a torn towel and contrived a sling for the besmeared kitten. He was delighted with himself. Trudi wiped him as clean as she could. Then she reached in her pocket.

'Have one?' she asked. It was a paper bag of bullseyes from that really good confectionery shop which sells, for instance, several hundred flavours of jelly beans. Peppermint, another strong scent, which might ameliorate rotten fish and garbage, our present ambiance. Yum. I love that clear peppermint burn through the sinuses.

'Usually I don't eat lollies,' said Trudi. 'But somehow I felt like some. Thanks for the hand. I will take this bad cat up in the goods lift,' she told me, passing me in the atrium. 'Not fit for company, him.'

Holding the complacent Lucifer at arm's length in his twist of towelling, she persuaded the goods lift to start and ascended out of sight.

I had a lot to think about and plodded up the stairs, sucking my bullseye.

Chapter Sixteen

Daniel had woken, shaved, dressed and fed the cats. He had laid the table and made a salad and I was suddenly hungry. Oh, yes. No lunch. Beef lasagna was just what I had in mind. I really didn't know where to start in describing the community of the Discarnates so I settled down to absorbing hot, garlicky, tomatoey and cheesy tastes to rinse the idea of asafoetida stew and spoiled fish pate à la Lucifer out of my mouth. The red wine helped. So did the rocket. Meroe's, I could tell, sweet and tender, not old and bitter as rocket is when picked for more than twenty-four hours. It reminded me of Florence.

Daniel talked while I ate: 'The castle belongs to Hungerford himself, not the Discarnates. He bought it a year ago for a couple of million, outright. The neighbours think he's very odd but they haven't got a lot of complaints. Even the usual ones—parking, noise. The visitors are as quiet as mice and they never leave cars or litter on the street. Reverend Father buys all his vegetables from an organic grower. I talked to her. She says he pays top dollar for top produce, but he gives her the willies.'

'Me too,' I said, with my mouth full.

'He also buys loads of bottles,' said Daniel. 'Blue glass. I asked if there was really a spring on the property but no one could tell me.'

'I suspect it is tap water,' I said, managing to swallow. 'But I don't know that, it's just a strong suspicion. What I do know is that the whole set-up is stranger than anything I have ever seen and I really don't know what to make of it.'

'Did you find your father?' he asked, spooning out more lasagna.

'Yes,' I said, and burst into tears. Unexpectedly. I waved away Daniel's concerned embrace and wiped my face on my napkin. 'He was working in the kitchen and he looked right at me and he didn't know me. That's always a shock.'

'Have some more wine,' said Daniel.

'A good notion. Anyway, that lets me out of it. If he doesn't even know me I can't see that I owe him anything. So tomorrow I'm going to sic Starshine on him and then he'll know he's been in a fight.'

'Did he look happy?' asked Daniel.

'No, just blank,' I replied. 'But Reverend Father Hungerford, Daniel dear, there's another kettle of thingies altogether. I can't decide if he's a complete fraud or an authentic fanatic. Complicated by the fact that he is absolutely beautiful.'

Daniel shifted uneasily and ran a hand over his chin. 'What sort of absolutely beautiful?' he asked.

'Vampire chic. Red-lipped mouth in a desert father's face. Ravaged in a highly aesthetic way. A nonforeshortened El Greco.'

'Oh,' he said. I had learned a new thing about Daniel. He did not know how beautiful he was, and he was either envious or jealous. I would know by his next statement. I did hope it wasn't going to be jealousy. 'The beautiful have it easier in life,' he said ruefully. Aha. Envy, and the noncorrosive kind.

'Oh? Have you found your life helped by people finding you gorgeous, beautiful man?'

'Me?' he said, surprised. 'Corinna, you aren't saying —'

'Of course I am,' I cooed. I don't usually coo, but sometimes you just have to. There was the most comely man I had ever seen, disclaiming his own beauty. It was so cute.

I wiped my lips before I kissed him. He was still looking bemused. 'And of course you may take it as read that I wouldn't go near the Rev Father if my foot was in a trap,' I told him. 'I am talking aesthetics, not lust. I have never known anyone I wanted more than you. Now let's get back to the story.'

I told him all I could remember about the Discarnates. The brown-robed tapestry makers, the singers, the horrible stew, the organic produce and the vitamins, the pictures on the wall, the bottles of blue glass containing the spring water. In the process I drank another glass of wine and ate two ripe Josephine pears and a chunk of matured cheddar.

I felt better after I had unloaded my day but that meant I had loaded it onto someone else. Daniel was thinking hard.

I left him cutting cheese into ever smaller pieces and feeding them to Horatio, and went down into the bakery to check that Jason had obeyed my instructions about the stock. He had. Two big pots of robust beef stock had settled fit for skimming. I skimmed them, heaved them onto the all-night cooker and added the mounds of chopped vegetables and herbs on which Jason had toiled at double time. The gentle heat of the cooker would simmer my soup just under bubbling all night and tomorrow there would be broth again for the hungry multitudes. I was freshly affronted by the idea of adding a flavour destroyer to a perfectly good pot of stew. Somehow it struck me as wicked. Spoiling good food, I heard Grandma Chapman's ghost whisper to me. A middle class thing, a deliberate perversion of appetite and hunger, just as depraved as dining on nightingales' hearts in aspic.

I distributed a pat or two and a few kitty treats to the Mouse Police, who were just waking up after a good day's nap to start their nightly patrol, when I suddenly thought of bullseyes and smelt burned sugar and revelation came over me in a flood of light.

I ran up the steps, calling for Daniel. He jumped, scattering cheese, which Horatio was happy to harvest for him. Then I grabbed the phone and started calling.

By the time half an hour had passed I had assembled what, in a Western film, would have been called a posse. I had Meroe. I had Jon and Kepler, with his digital camera. I had the Professor and Mrs. Dawson, who had just come back from dinner at the

Thai restaurant. I had Trudi with Lucifer on her shoulder and her keys at her belt. Lucifer was unusually subdued. One bath, it seemed, had not been enough to remove the scent of old fish, and he had not only endured two but had been blow-dried. He looked fluffy and a little light-headed as he clung to Trudi's shoulder-mounted kitten rest, an old leather glove thrust through the strap of her overall. I had Daniel. What else could I possibly need? I was going to be very embarrassed if I was wrong. But I could handle that.

'Very well, m'dear,' said the Professor genially. 'We're at your disposal. What are we going to do?'

'Clear up one mystery,' I said. 'I hope. My mistake was in thinking that all these strange happenings were connected to each other. No reason why they should be. Not everything is connected. What we have are two mysteries: the mystery of the herbs and the Mollyhouse, and the mystery of the Discarnate Brotherhood and my missing father, and they don't have anything to do with each other.'

'All right,' said Jon slowly. 'With you so far.'

'The one which is the most dangerous to the general populace has to be the herbs,' I said. 'So we'll go and solve that one now, and then we can decide what to do about the other one later.'

'All right,' said Mrs. Dawson, smiling. 'Lead on.'

'Where are we going?' asked Daniel.

'Down,' I told him, and led the way to the goods lift. Here Daniel left us. Trudi operated the machinery and the rest of the posse sank, like Don Juan, into the depths.

When the door hissed open I waved everyone out. Kepler raised his camera. The air was thick with the smell of burned sugar. Two figures were working at the old gas stove, relic of Insula's serviced apartment days. One turned, an apple speared on a bamboo skewer, and I saw a mouth gape in the gloom.

Then it dropped the apple and fled.

There was a flash as the camera went off repeatedly. There was a scrabbling noise. Then Trudi found the overhead lights, everyone stopped moving, and I heard a door clang. Daniel, who had doubled around to the back door, came in leading Rat by his tail of hair.

'Hello, Londo,' I said.

Jon removed Taz from under the sink and Mrs. Dawson escorted Gully out of the cupboard into which he had wedged himself. They came quietly. The jig was comprehensively up. The Lone Gunmen were sprung.

We lined them up against the rubbish chutes and glared at them as Kepler took photographs of the baskets of leaves, the beige paper packets, the pot of boiling toffee, the skewered apples, the flasks of cheap essential oils and the hobby-shop soap moulds and unscented bath fizz.

'You idiots,' I started.

Taz held up a hand. 'But —'

'Don't but me, son,' said Daniel roughly. 'You poisoned Kylie and Gossamer. You put two others in intensive care. When Meroe finishes laying a curse on you I'm booked for making you eat your way through your stock, leaf by leaf.'

'That would be amusing,' commented Mrs. Dawson. She moved to the boiling toffee and began to dip apples.

'You corrupted that boy Chris,' said Jon in a cold, distant tone. 'You might have ruined his life and you certainly ruined his character.'

'Er…' said Rat. Daniel pulled his hair. I had never seen him so angry.

'We get chairs,' said Trudi to me. She was keeping well away from the stove. 'We all sit down. I get drinks. Then we decide what to do. First,' she confronted the Lone Gunmen, 'you give me those keys. You must have stolen my keys and copied them. Give me.'

Gully took out a bunch of keys and detached three with trembling hands. He broke two fingernails doing it. Trudi checked them against the ones hanging from her chain. Then she nodded briskly and I followed her to a recess, where we unearthed a lot of wooden chairs. A bit of a dust and they were fine. We brought them in and everyone took a seat, except the Lone Gunmen and Mrs. Dawson, who was still dipping apples.

'Sorry, dear, I really can't let them all go to waste,' she told me, and I understood at once that she really couldn't. Besides, she dipped a very smooth apple.

Trudi went into the wine cellar, down two little steps, and came out with several bottles, which she opened with her clasp knife. There was a tray of tasting glasses and we rinsed them. The wine was a good robust red which someone must have forgotten about. It was twenty years old and in its prime, tasting a little of blood and a little of flint; a big, striding red, very suitable for judgment.

By now the nerds were a collective nervous wreck, quod erat demonstrandum, which was what was wanted. I could not imagine the depths of idiocy to which they had sunk. And there were still things I didn't know. I began with a brief summary of the facts.

'The leaves came in to Australia, entirely illegally and in violation of quarantine, through someone ordering them packed into those very ugly pots in India, right?'

'Right,' said Jon.

'So someone must have either corrupted your outfit or just got into contact with an Indian supplier and arranged it through them. I don't think you have a lot of corrupt people. I think it was done easily from an internet order.'

'All right,' said Daniel.

'Then the dude who suborned poor Chris just had to arrange the delivery when they got here,' I said. 'Simple. Only the Lone Gunmen would give Londo Mollari as an alias. Lesser fans would be using a *Star Trek* alias. *Babylon 5* is for the cognoscenti.'

The nerds exchanged a glance in which some complacency was mixed with the terror. At least someone had noticed that they were sophisticated. I continued my peroration, refreshed with a glass of the red wine.

'Nerds Inc was in financial trouble. I know, I helped them with their accounts. Not entirely their fault. The collapse of the dotcoms and the rise in home loan insanity has meant that people have less money to spend on elaborate computer systems and games. So they were making reasonable money out of research on the internet. They did the research for a nice gentleman who wanted to make his club as authentically eighteenth century as he could. He paid for his research and they did it—they are good researchers. In the process they hit on a way to make money. They would go to the club in suitable period costumes and sell charms and soap and toffee apples—fairytale things. They had the costumes from all those sci-fi conventions and were used to acting a part. So far so harmless. Except that five dollars for a toffee apple verges on criminal. But someone came on a recipe for a weight loss tea and they thought that all their Christmases had come at once. They were right. It's a licence to print money. They're friends with Kylie and Goss. They have heard all about how much one has to be thin. Probably at wearying length,' I added.

Taz dared to roll his eyes in agreement but Jon glared him back into frightened immobility.

'Then they closed for two days,' I said. 'Even though I knew that they were skint. And today they bought a lot of new games. I squibbed it earlier. I should have known then.'

'But how did you know they were making the stuff down here?' asked Mrs. Dawson.

'People kept saying that scent moves around the building, and it does,' I said. 'My onion rolls made everyone want a fry-up. Even if you don't actually register the smell it has an effect—it made Trudi go and buy bullseyes, it made me think of caramel sauce. And I smelt it through the dumb waiter. Therefore it was coming from below. I knew about these old kitchens. Though it took me long enough to put it all together.'

'You sent a couple of addicts to beat us up,' said Daniel. 'That night at Vlad Tepes.'

'I just thought they'd scare you off,' stammered Gully.

'You thought wrong,' Taz pointed out.

'So did you,' snarled Rat. 'You found that recipe. It was your idea.'

'You went along with it. You said we should make a really rough package. You said we ought to charge fifty for it.'

'Shut up,' suggested Daniel. They shut up.

'The thing I don't know is why go to all that trouble? The herbs could have been bought or collected perfectly well here,' I said. 'Meroe was puzzled too.'

'Show her,' said Gully. Taz reached for his pocket and handed me a folded sheet of paper in a plastic sleeve. I put it down on the table and all heads moved to read it. Except Daniel, who had never looked away from the Lone Gunmen. Under his eye, they did not dare to try an escape.

In increasing horror and wonder, I read a facsimile manuscript. It was written in pale grey on pale grey and had been picked out in biro later. To assist the short-sighted, Meroe read it aloud: 'The Reverend Doctor Ellis' Oriental Balsamic Infusion is guaranteed to purge the flesh of grossness and cure bruises strains scalds green wounds and the most obstinate bleeding (which will be with Difficulty believed) without ligature. Even a Brain quit thro' either Length ways or Breadth ways or an Eye pierced or tendons cut quite asunder this Balsam will agglutinate the Parts and defend them from Corruption.

'To purge the flesh of grossness and superfluousness take one wineglass twice a day fasting. Infused in vinegar it clears the head and drives away heaviness.'

She stopped. She stared. So did we all.

'So you made up the herbs as it says in the recipe,' I said. 'Why did you have to buy them from abroad?'

'Read the rest,' said Taz. Meroe puzzled out the smaller letters and began to laugh, which was not the reaction I had expected.

'The best senna is to be obtained from Goa,' she quoted. 'Your Bombay datura or thorn apple is the finest...' She sat down in a gale of merriment which made her hold her sides. We all looked at her. Mrs. Dawson put her final apple down on the greaseproof paper and poured the last golden swash of toffee onto the marble confectioner's slab. I watched her knot and twist the warm toffee into shapes with a skewer. Her hands were so old and so graceful that I could not look away from them. Finally Meroe conquered her mirth and sat up, accepting a glass of wine from a puzzled Jon.

'Only you idiots would have done such a thing,' she exclaimed. 'You could have gone out and picked your ingredients and no one would ever have caught you. Now what in the name of the Goddess are we going to do with you?'

'Call the police,' suggested the Professor. 'Comic or not, they have behaved very badly. What if those leaves contained some dreadful plant disease? You can't just bring in handfuls of undifferentiated vegetation from somewhere like India and expect it not to harbour a few extras. Fire blight? Citrus canker? Could have wiped out whole orchards with their foolishness.' He snorted and poured another glass of wine.

'Not to mention the damage to their customers,' added Daniel.

'And to my staff,' said Jon.

'They are in big trouble,' I agreed.

'And there is the matter of a nice, solid, well thought out curse,' said Meroe gently. 'The Goddess is not mocked lightly.'

'We never meant to upset the Goddess,' protested Taz. 'We didn't mean to…we didn't mean to do all that stuff.'

'That you did,' prompted Daniel.

'That we did,' he confessed miserably. 'But it was all going downhill, the shop, even though we were working real hard, and…well, it happened.'

'If we call the police your young man Chris will be implicated,' said Daniel to Jon.

'And if we call quarantine they will be fined to their utter ruin. We'll destroy all the remaining herbs in the incinerator,' I suggested. 'What about this. They apologise to Trudi for stealing her keys and give her a nice present. They apologise to the Goddess by…what would you like, Meroe?'

'They can clean and rearrange my stockroom,' she said placidly, like Belladonna with a mouse securely under her front paw. 'And in return I will sell them suitable herbs for a refreshing, cleansing tea which no one can abuse.'

'They will apologise to Jon and Chris by…?'

'Oh, a suitable little present for the boy, perhaps, but they are not out of the woods with me. I am keeping these photographs, and if you so much as think about approaching one of my staff again, to the police they go, and you too, clear?'

'Clear,' said Rat.

'They can apologise to Daniel for attacking him by…what?'

'Oh, like this,' said Daniel, and delivered a stinging cuff behind each nerd ear. They hopped and ouched.

'They can spend at least five evenings playing games with Kylie and Goss, and paying for their drinks,' I added. 'And they can apologise to me by hiring someone to do their own accounts in future. Including the money you made from the Vlad Tepes scam, which I assume you have not declared? Plus instant computer help whenever requested. You can continue charging five dollars for your toffee apples at the Mollyhouse. But no more weight loss tea. All right?'

Taz looked at Rat. Rat looked at Gully. They breathed a collective sigh of relief. 'Deal,' they said in unison.

'Now,' said Mrs. Dawson. 'Let's have a toffee apple. For some reason, I have been thinking about toffee apples all week.'

We had another glass of wine. And a toffee apple each. They were very good. When I left the cellar the Lone Gunmen were asking Mrs. Dawson to teach them how to make those elegant candy plaits, Trudi was attempting to remove toffee from Lucifer's front paws, and Jon and Kepler were drinking wine and discussing herbs with Meroe. Daniel and the Professor were discussing the sad opinions of Marcus Aurelius. I liked us all very much.

◇◇◇

The murderer fell upon his victim in a balloon of red air and light in which he kicked, screamed, punched and stabbed clumsily, like an angry child. Curiously, the knife did not seem to want to penetrate. He bit and kicked instead, catching a flailing hand and listening to the dry stick sound of bones breaking.

Then the cloud of unknowing was gone, and he was empty; he stood a moment looking at the human wreck. He ran and hid, whimpering.

Chapter Seventeen

It was late before I got to bed and consequently my four AM awakening was not pleasant. I have never really loved four AM and today was not going to produce even a passing affection for the loathsome hour. Coffee. More coffee. Into the vein, if possible.

Jason looked downcast too. He flared up at me when I asked what was wrong.

'My nose is all stuffed up,' he whined. 'I can't breathe. My head hurts. And my elbows. And come to think of it my knees and my eyelashes.'

'You have caught a cold,' I told him, putting on the kettle for a hot lemon drink. Fortunately Jon had given me a swag of lemons from his mum's tree. We were self-sufficient in lemons. 'I feel lousy too. Let's get the bread on and we'll just do the minimum today.'

'This never happened when I was on the gear,' he mumbled, hauling and pouring with none of his usual elan.

'No, then all you had to worry about was waking up dead,' I said tartly. 'Come on, Jason, tote dat barge, lift dat bale.'

He looked at me as though I was speaking fluent Molvanian. Never heard any gospel tunes, eh, techno boy? Well, he was about to hear some. I opened the lentil flour for some more famine bread and began to sing 'Old Man River'. It was the sort of singing one expects after a night on that red, which was robust enough to stand a fork in; deep, gravelly, and entirely unlike Paul Robeson.

Oddly enough, Jason got the idea, and we went on to sing some more spirituals. He picked up the tunes very fast and we vamped the words when I couldn't remember them. They were work songs, after all. And both of us were longing to be able to stop working and take some more aspirin.

'Deep river,' I sang. 'My home is over Jordan —' pause for breath—'deep river, Lord, I want to cross over into camp ground.'

'By and by, by and by,' sang Jason, flicking switches on the dough mixers, 'I'm gonna lay down my heavy load.'

Singing, of all things, was working. In two hours we had laid the foundations of the day's baking and were refreshing ourselves with hot lemon and honey. I went up to the apartment and got the brandy. We were going to need some extra assistance to get through this particular Tuesday. I felt Jason's forehead. He was hot and very uncomfortable and I wasn't going to keep him a moment longer than I had to. His recently grown-out hair was curly and wet with sweat.

'Do you want to do the muffins or shall I?' I asked as he drooped onto his baker's chair to watch the pasta douro oven.

He replied listlessly, 'No, I'll do it, have to be blueberry, though, I can't remember what I was going to do with all them dates.' This was pitiful indeed. He must have been feeling really awful. I had heard that heroin addicts tended to catch anything going around, due to their depressed immune systems.

'The dates will wait,' I told him. He compounded his muffins and cooked them—perfectly good muffins, even if the maker thought he was dying—and then I led him protesting feebly up the stairs to my apartment, where I tucked him up on the sofa under the blue mohair rug. He had my personal box of soft tissues and a lemon drink to hand and I noticed that even in his semiconscious state he had a firm grasp of the TV remote control.

'Just close your eyes,' I said.

'But how are you going to do all that work by yourself?' he asked.

'Did it before,' I said, 'can do it again. Push Horatio off if he annoys you. I'll be back in a couple of hours.' I heard the TV go on as I went down stairs.

Drat. I had gotten used to being helped and now I was on my own again and not at my best. No matter, I had indeed done the lot before. All the real bread was now baking, the famine bread was mixed, the pasta douro was about to come out of the oven and I had made a lot of crusty rolls to compensate for no Jason herb bread. I had forgotten to get the herbs the night before and my one attempt at making them with dried herbs hadn't worked. Edible but not, as Brother Amos would have said, palatable. I mused on Brother Amos for a while as I tried to remember another song. He had been a chef, Father Hungerford had said. How could a chef deliberately ruin good food?

The Mouse Police zoomed out into Calico Alley, collected their snack of tuna pieces, zoomed back in as though their tails were on fire and then raced up the steps to my apartment.

I heard their paws hitting the treads in perfect unison. Doubtless they had gone to join Jason in his unaccustomed luxury.

I leaned on the door for a moment. It was about seven. My paper came flying in. Then the same security guard came past. The onion roll man.

'Sorry, no onion rolls today,' I said.

He grinned a nice white grin in the gloom. 'Ordinary will do me fine,' he said.

I handed over a crusty roll and he bit it with pleasure.

'Where's your boy?'

'Got a cold.'

'Lot of that going around,' he said. 'Thanks,' he added with his little salute, and then he went on and I started sorting the orders.

Megan was late and she, too, was sniffing and dripping and complaining. Today, I could tell, was not going to be a day which even Rebecca of Sunnybrook Farm could view optimistically. Then the Discarnates arrived for their famine bread and had to wait because I was running behind and it wasn't ready. The three of them loomed in the doorway like a visitation of the Inquisition and they made me so nervous that I dropped an egg on the floor and had to grovel at their sandalled feet to clean it up.

Father Hungerford was not with them. That was a mercy. I finally boxed the bread and shoved it at them and they went away, cowled and mysterious and exceptionally irritating, into the darkness.

I began to think that the day wasn't going to dawn at all. But I had progressed. The deliveries were all done, the shop bread was all in the oven, I could start the clean-up which I was going to do on my own for a change, and the muffins, at least, were very good.

I washed down all my surfaces and dried them. I rinsed out the mixers. I stacked the shop trays. Morning must arrive soon. But it was still dark outside. So I got out the old mop and bucket, took another dose of aspirin with the last of the coffee, and began to clean the floor and sing. 'Oh, Lord, what a morning,' I sang. 'Oh, Lord, what a morning, oh Lord, what a morning, when the stars begin to fall…'

'We'll weep for the rocks and mountains, we'll weep for the rocks and mountains,' sang a clear elderly soprano at the alley door. Mrs. Dawson. I might have known it. We carolled merrily to the end of the verse: 'When the stars begin to fall.' Nice and apocalyptic. I was feeling better.

Mrs. Dawson laughed aloud. 'A long time since I sang any spirituals,' she told me. 'All alone today, Corinna?'

'Jason and his cold are upstairs,' I said. 'He really is sick.'

'Poor boy,' she said briskly. 'Just give me a loaf and I shall go and make him some breakfast, if that would be of any help to you.'

'That's very kind of you…' I began.

'Not at all,' she assured me. 'I take an interest in that excellent young man. What does he eat?'

'Everything,' I said. 'There's eggs and bacon and lots of fruit and vegetables. Thank you,' I said, as she ascended the stairs almost as fast as the Mouse Police, but with a lot more grace.

What a woman. I hoped she would remember to give herself some breakfast as well.

I heard Gossamer rattling around outside as I opened the shop door and took down the shutters. Amazingly, she was clad in a very big jumper knitted, apparently, out of pink string. She was wearing adorable little black fingerless gloves as well. She dived into the shop and shivered theatrically.

'I know. And it's still dark,' I agreed. 'Turn up the heat and then help me with the soup urn.'

'Where's Jason?' she asked, turning up the thermostat and standing under the hot air blower until her pink curls fluffed.

'Sick,' I said.

She clutched my sleeve. She actually looked worried. 'Not… he hasn't gone back on…?'

'No, he's just got a cold,' I said, touched. 'I put him on my sofa and Mrs. Dawson is making him breakfast.' Then I remembered I had gossip to impart. 'Now let me tell you a tale, young woman, and I want to see your hair curling—guess who was responsible for your weight loss tea?'

'Who?' she asked, eyes widening.

I told her the whole tale of the Lone Gunmen as we prepared the shop and it took so long that the customers had started to arrive before I reached the end.

'So they're going to play games with us and buy us drinks?' she asked.

'If you want,' I said. 'That was the offer.'

'That'd be nice,' she said. 'They have the latest games.' Then she giggled. 'I wonder which one was the witch,' she said. And I really hadn't enquired.

When I could leave Goss and Horatio to mind the shop I went back into the bakery and found that Mrs. Dawson had carried down a tray on which reposed a fine cooked breakfast: fried eggs, bacon, grilled tomato, toasted sourdough and a whole pot of fresh coffee. She sat down on Jason's chair to watch me eat it. I obliged. I was now starving.

'I had forgotten how much young men eat,' she said, a little taken aback. 'Still, it is feed a cold and starve a fever, I believe.'

'What did he eat?'

'Two bowls of muesli, a cooked platter like the one you are eating, another three slices of toast with plum jam and a bottle of Coke. Then he actually thanked me, lay back and smiled, and now he is asleep, sneezing occasionally, with those two scruffy cats reposing, one either side of him. I hadn't the heart to shoo them out.'

I didn't tell her that the Mouse Police were notoriously difficult to shoo. I could tell that they were on that sofa for the duration of Jason's visit. I speared a succulent bit of tomato, cleaned the plate with the last crust and sighed. She got up to take the tray.

'Mrs. Dawson, I do not deserve you,' I said. 'But thank you very much.'

'It was nothing,' she said. She returned the tray to the apartment and half an hour later—I feared she had also done my washing-up—she left through the shop with her own muffin and loaf, neat and elegant as ever. Having made the world a much nicer place to be in.

Light finally arrived. Not very much of it and not very clean, a dirty brownish gloom, but it was daylight and I appreciated it. Goss offered to enlist Kylie to work for the day and I accepted with pleasure. I was just thinking it was time I went and had my shower and changed out of my baking clothes when who should stalk in but my two least favourite policemen, Kane and Reagan. I knew that getting up on a Tuesday was a mistake.

'Good morning,' I greeted them, with as much of a smile as I could manage. 'Cold morning.'

'Where were you at six o'clock?' demanded Reagan, putting out a hand to seize my upper arm. I backed away.

'I was here,' I said. 'All this bread didn't bake itself.'

'What about your junkie toy boy?' asked Kane.

'Corinna, you want me to call Daniel?' asked Goss, highly incensed at this imputation. I held up a hand.

'Why not knock off the insults and tell me what this is all about?' I asked calmly. 'Before I start complaining and don't stop until you are back on traffic duty in East Wallaroo. Yes?'

'You were out at the Discarnate Brotherhood yesterday,' said Kane.

'I was.'

'And you were shown over the place by the head bloke,' said Kane.

'I was.'

'And someone has attacked him and left him for dead on the street,' said Kane.

'God, really? Is he badly hurt?'

'Hospital said two broken ribs, bruises, shallow cuts. Blade must have turned on the bone. They'll probably send him home in a couple of days. But it could have been murder.'

'And you think it might be me?' I could not follow their reasoning at all.

'Was anyone with you at six am?' Reagan persisted.

'No. I sent Jason upstairs to nurse his cold. Hang on. I gave a crusty roll to a security guard at about six.'

Kane whipped out his notebook. 'Name?'

'I don't know his name. He passes down this lane at about six every morning, or has the last two mornings. Wears that snazzy black and white uniform. Tall man with white teeth.'

'Anything else about him?' asked Kane wearily.

'His grandad used to make onion rolls. Come on, guys, you can't really imagine I was out on Studley Park Road beating up Father Hungerford when I had all this bread to make.'

'We'll check,' said Reagan

'We'll be back,' said Kane.

'What is it with those guys?' demanded Gossamer, putting down the phone as the door swung shut behind the policemen.

'They've got the fixed idea that Daniel is a dangerous criminal, Jason is a druggie, and I'm either their dupe or their accomplice.'

'Oh,' said Gossamer, slamming back an intrusive shelf.

'I see. Idiots.'

That about summed it up for the constabulary. I had not had time to gather my thoughts, so when Kylie came down to add her talents to the selling of bread, I excused myself and went up to check on the patient and have my long delayed shower.

It was a pretty sight which met my eyes when I came in to my own parlour. Jason was fast asleep with Heckle under one elbow and Jekyll curled up close with her nose in his ear. They were all snuggled under the blue blanket. I heard only a faint wheeze from Jason and a faint purr from Heckle. I turned off the TV.

Mrs. Dawson had done the washing-up. I would have to think of some way of repaying her. I got my shower, lavishing rose petal soap on my exterior and finding that my hair was now just long enough to make a creditable twist on the crown of my head, thus getting it out of my eyes. I dressed in warm clothes. And for once I really didn't want any more coffee.

The sofa was occupied, so I lay myself down on my freshly made bed and shut my eyes. And I dreamed a sharp, vivid dream. I saw the beautiful Father Hungerford come out of the castle on a filthy morning when the darkness had an assassin in it: I saw him struck down and beaten and stabbed by someone so beside themselves that they could not insert a knife between bones. Then for some reason I saw him sitting in his office, talking about the failure of earthly love, with the Madonna on the wall behind his head. Savonarola face, Madonna's milkmaid face. Fanatic's face, saint's face. Over and over again they alternated. My subconscious was trying to get something through to my terminally addled mind, but I couldn't see the connection.

And then someone was kissing me awake. It was Daniel.

I dragged him down into my arms and kissed him back.

'We seem to have Jason,' he pointed out.

'So we do,' I groaned. 'He's got a cold. I'm letting him sleep up here until he gets better. I can't send the poor boy back to a backpackers' when he's sick. Oh, and we've had a visit from the police. Someone has beaten Father Hungerford to a pulp. I hope you've got an alibi for six this morning.'

'As it happens, I have,' he said, laughing. 'I was in a police station. Best alibi there is, apart from being dead or in prison.'

'I've sent them off to find my onion roll man,' I told him sleepily. 'I need to get back to the shop,' I added with vast reluctance.

Daniel demurred. 'No, I dropped in, Kylie and Gossamer are managing beautifully. Supervised, I might add, by Horatio. I suggest that you remove those shoes and have a little nap with me, because I can't keep my eyes open any longer and I'm very cold.'

So he was. I took off some of my recently donned clothes and tucked us under the doona until he thawed. Then he fell asleep, and so did I.

I woke at three and arose. Daniel rolled over into the hollow left by my body and curled up like a cat. I reclothed myself and set about finding out what had happened to Earthly Delights. Jason was sitting up on the couch, reaching for the remote control and coughing like a Wilfred Owen poem about the Great War. I called Kylie's mobile phone. If I wasn't there to confiscate it, there was no way it would have left her person. She, of course, answered at once.

Kylie reported that it was all fixed, Goss had even done the banking, and they were off to talk to the Lone Gunmen about playing games. I went down and shut up shop, thanked and paid my assistants, and wondered what I was going to give Jason for lunch. The shop had sold out of soup, though there was a new pot ready for the morrow. On reflection I went to Del Pandamus' Café Delicious and bought a lot of miscellaneous food left over from lunch. With this and a bag of bread I climbed again to Hebe and found that the natives were restless.

Daniel had dressed and was carrying on an irritated phone conversation while trying to remove Jekyll from the sofa. Jekyll was not cooperating. She liked the sofa and she was staying. She had dug in all available claws and was daring Daniel to try something.

'Lunch?' I said to Jason.

He turned a fevered face to me. 'Not hungry,' he croaked.

I put the bag on the table and flicked up Jekyll's front claws, freeing the boy's legs. Jekyll surrendered and moved aside.

'Put your shoes on,' I said. 'We're going to the doctor.'

Now I was close I could hear a gasping wheeze as poor Jason laboured for breath. This wasn't just a cold. He must have caught bronchitis or—horrible thought—that viral pneumonia which the street kids had. Jason did not fight. He rose and followed me to the door, stopping twice to recover his breath.

Daniel finished his phone call and caught us. 'I'll take him,' he said. 'And I'll pick up some of his clothes and stuff. He can't go back to that hotel in this state.'

'I'm all right,' said Jason, then coughed like a consumptive for five minutes.

'Yeah,' said Daniel. 'You're a picture of health. Come on.'

They left. I wondered how I could make Jason comfortable on the couch. Just as I was thinking this, Meroe and Mrs. Dawson came to the door. Meroe had a jug of some infusion and a basket of various comforts.

'How's Jason?' she asked.

'Sicker. Bronchitis, I hope, not pneumonia. Daniel's taken him to the doctor. I'm just wondering how I can fit him in. If I give him my bed…'

'I have a solution,' said Mrs. Dawson. 'I still have permission to use the empty flat, Pluto. It has all the things he will need, it's warm, and we can pop in and make sure he's all right during the day. Meroe will make him tisanes and infusions and Dion and I will feed him. Then you can take over at night. Oh, and while Jason's sick, I know Cherie Holliday would like to help in your bakery. After finding each other again she and her father are now needing to separate a little. She's getting a little restless now that he is so much better. There is a limit to the number of excursions one can take, you know. She's been to the zoo so often she tells me she's on first name terms with the meerkats.'

'But that's such a lot of work…' I began, overwhelmed.

'Oh no, dear,' said Mrs. Dawson. 'How will he know we love him if we don't look after him? Why don't we just pop up there now and see what needs doing?'

So we popped. Apartment 7B, Pluto, was fully furnished and needed very little work to make it a nice cosy nest for a sick boy. Meroe and I moved the TV into the bedroom. The flat was supplied with all the usual luxuries. We made the bed, put on the electric blanket, renewed the toilet paper and Meroe laid out her stores. We left her there making infusions and went downstairs to claim poor Jason. He had a bag of clothes, a collection of pills, a bottle of that frightful medicine which is supposed to taste of cherries and a diagnosis of bronchitis. He was staggering.

Daniel half carried him into the lift and supported him into the flat. There we put him firmly to bed. With Mrs. Dawson supervising, Jason found himself sponged clean, clad in the former owner's blue silk pj's, and bedded down with four pillows and a comforter. His medicines were within, washed down by a strong lemon and honey drink. Meroe's sweet rose-scented tisane was on his bedside table. He had the remote control under one hand. He allowed me to feed him a cup of thin beef bouillon. His eyes closed and he snuggled back into the pillows.

We started to leave, but he croaked and we looked back.

'I thought you had to be dead to feel this grouse,' he said, and then started to cough again. 'Thanks,' he said. 'Just. Thanks, I guess.'

'We'll leave the door on the latch,' Mrs. Dawson decided. 'Now, if you want to talk to Cherie about some baking, Corinna dear, I'll just tell Trudi what we've done with Jason and arrange with Del to have some of the Pandamuses sit with him for a while. This can be managed,' she said, and went off to manage it.

I looked at Daniel.

'What a woman,' he said, anticipating my very next words. 'Come along, Corinna, you need to see Cherie, then we need some food. I slept through lunch, and so did you.'

Cherie said that she would be delighted to rise at four and help me until Jason was better. She had been reunited with her father after a long and desperate time. Now they were beginning, ever so slightly, to get on each other's nerves. Andy was mostly off the bottle and had just got a part-time job with a real estate agent. Cherie also needed something to do until her RMIT fabric class started in September. Baking might fill in a small gap and would be good experience. Even if it just instructed her that the last thing she wanted to be was a baker.

She agreed to go right upstairs and sit with Jason until Mrs. Dawson got back with a selection of Pandamuses. She took her constant companion, Pumpkin Bear, with her. I was sure that Jason would find Pumpkin Bear consoling.

Everyone was getting involved. Jon and Kepler, concerned, said that they would provide tomorrow's soup and company.

Mistress Dread, encountered on the stairs, agreed to go up late evenings when she came home from her dungeon and listen for coughing. Therese Webb, calling to find out if I had located Sunlight yet, tutted and said that she could always take her knitting and sit with the poor boy, now that Jacqui was so much calmer.

And then I remembered that I had indeed found Sunlight, and I would have to decide how to arrange the meeting of my two irritating parents so that neither of them would fly off the handle again. I was utterly fed up with both of them.

I hadn't the remotest idea how to arrange this touchy rendezvous. I swore Therese to secrecy, told her the situation, and begged her to think about it. She said she would and departed, taking the royal dog Carolus for a walk. I watched his magnificent tail sweep past me as Daniel and I finally got back into Hebe and shut the door. And locked it.

'Food,' he said avidly. 'Silence and food.'

I could not have agreed more. We ate most of the Café Delicious leftovers with gusto. I had rather overdosed on wine and we drank apple juice.

Then we went to bed and slept all night in each other's arms. Sometimes you have to leave the world to get on with it all by itself.

Chapter Eighteen

I woke in luxury and bathed and dressed in pleasure and even the toast tasted better than usual. Daniel came with me as unskilled labour and we let Cherie into the bakery at four to begin Wednesday.

She knew nothing whatever about the work but she was strong and willing and we managed. Better than I had on my own, anyway. I instructed and directed until everything was humming or chugging, then wondered what on earth I was going to do about the muffins. Cast your burden upon the lord, Grandma Chapman had said—though only as a last resort.

'Cherie,' I said. 'Here is a recipe. Make it.'

Daniel gave me a conspiratorial glance. There was plenty of time to make another batch if Cherie turned out not to be able to make muffins.

I opened the door for the Mouse Police to go out, and Cherie giggled at their turn of speed in the rain. It was almost sleeting down. There were little bits of ice in that rain. Ma'ani loomed up suddenly, making my new staff member squeak. He collected the bread for the Soup Run, asked about Jason's health, invoked a prayer for all poor souls abroad this morning, and trudged off. The Mouse Police skittered around his ankles as they returned and flung themselves panting up the stairs.

But I had shut the inner door. They sulked down again and slumped to wash themselves on their flour sacks, which were not as comfortable as my blue mohair rug. If they weren't keeping

Jason company then they could stay in the bakery and do an honest day's mousing, was my view.

Bread was happening. Cherie was beginning to understand the magical, alchemical process by which all that pallid dough transformed itself into the staff of life. She had mixed her apple and spice muffins and was watching anxiously for them to rise. I was sorting deliveries and drinking coffee when the day returned, the drizzle stopped and there was my security man expecting another free roll. I dragged him into the warmth by one surprised arm.

'Hello,' I said. 'Do tell me your name and your address so I can get the cops off my back. You're my alibi. And in return I will give you a free roll. Or would you prefer a muffin?'

'The muffins smell very good,' he said greedily. I like greed in a customer. He gave me a card with all his details on it and Cherie tipped one of her muffins into his cupped hands. He tore off a bit and gave his little salute.

'Very nice,' he said, and walked out into the dimness again. His name was George Venn and he had a respectable address in Caroline Springs. Also, I now knew who he worked for. That ought to detach Kane and Reagan from their theory about my criminality.

I sampled Cherie's muffin. It was a good, workmanlike muffin, perfectly saleable. Not a Jason muffin, but one could not expect that. I complimented her skill and she blushed.

'I like feeding people,' she said breathlessly. 'It's a real buzz when they smile like that.'

'So it is,' I said, feeling benevolent.

And we did the day's baking in good time, without any dramas. Kylie and Gossamer came in to operate the shop.

I went up to see how Jason was doing as Daniel counted off the deliveries to the sick Megan's temporary replacement, a gormless little brother who needed to be told everything twice. I heard Daniel instructing him for the third time where William Street was as I went up the stairs. If that bread got where it was going it would be a miracle.

I heard coughing as I opened the door. A gust of eucalyptus vapour met me. I love that scent. Even so one can have too much of a good thing. The scent came from a humidifier. Jason had breakfasted on cereal, it seemed, and was now lying back and breathing like a broken-down horse. I hated to see him so ill.

Ellie Pandamus came in from the kitchen with a cup of hot infusion.

'He looks bad,' she whispered. She is seventeen and intensely motherly. Her older sisters have to struggle to get their babies back from her.

'No, he's going to get better,' I said firmly. 'This is very kind of you, Ellie. Make sure you get some breakfast, too,' I said.

I watched her feed the tisane to Jason without spilling it on him. She is a very good girl. Del is worried that she wants to be a nurse and thus delay marriage, but I can't see Ellie waiting too long to find someone to give her lots of babies. She loves having something to look after. 'How will he know we love him if we don't look after him?' Mrs. Dawson's words echoed in my head. After this, Jason would have to know that we all loved him.

I left Jason and began to walk downstairs. Watching that gentle girl had triggered all the things which had not been otherwise triggered and gelled the ones which had refused to gel. But I did not run this time. Sometimes revelations require planning.

Shamelessly, I left Daniel and Cherie with the baking. Nothing left to make but extra muffins—cheese ones, for the soup. Cherie could do that. Daniel could grate the cheese for her. I had to get into some respectable clothes and go calling on a mission. I had to get my parents back together but there was something even more important than that and if I did not go right now, I might miss my chance. I was repeating that quote about the tide in the affairs of men all the way up the hill to Exhibition Street. As Tolkien said in the voice of the hobbit Merry, too late was worse than never.

◇◇◇

Reverend Father Thomas Hungerford hurt all over. His eyes were swollen shut, his bruises caught and stung as well as ached, and his broken fingers and broken ribs throbbed. He bit his lip. No one must hear him complain. These things were sent by God. He had been collected from the hospital and conveyed back to the castle. He knew the scent of cold stone and dust, and the wooden smell of his own office. No one had spoken to him.

He lay and ached and contemplated the measureless abyss of his unforgivable folly. Pride, it had been his own puffed-up pride: not discipline and austerity but vanity, vanity. He had walked away from love and comfort and all things human, seeking ever greater union with God by denying all of God's gifts. His punishment would have been just if all his bones had been broken. His punishment would have been just if he was now standing, bodiless, shivering, in the whistling gale before the judgment seat. He had forgotten mercy, and compassion, and love, and Christ himself, and his soul had shrivelled to the size of a pea. He had brought this assault upon himself and he deserved it. Feed my lambs, the lord had said, and what had he fed them on but dry bread and bitter gall? Only repentance could justify his continued existence. And he repented with all his heart.

But now he could smell something other than cold stone. Something sweet. Flowers. Roses, perhaps? He put out an experimental hand and found that he was lying on a springy mattress, rather than his camp bed. The covers over him were light and soft, not the scratchy blanket of his own bed. He listened. Someone was breathing, quite close to him.

'Brother Simon?' he tried.

'Brother Simon is minding the acolytes,' said a voice.

A female voice. He struggled up on one elbow and groaned, battered by the pain.

'No,' he began. A firm hand came down on his shoulder and pressed him back against the pillows. He knew that strength, too.

'Yes,' she said. 'You drove me away once, dear Thomas, but you won't drive me away again. I never forgot you. You never forgot me, either. My picture is on your wall. I did not know that you had been hurt until Corinna the baker came and fetched me. "How will he know you love him if you don't look after him?" she asked me, and I had no answer. So I am here to look after you and I will not leave you until you send me away. Do you want to send me away?'

The voice was perfectly calm. This, he knew, was his moment of decision. His body shrieked with pain. His austerity was under threat. He ought to demand his camp bed and his old blanket and send this loving woman away. But it all seemed faintly ridiculous now, since he had seen his attacker and realised the magnitude of his own vanity. Human nature could not be forced too far from its path. No, he would accept her kindness. Her scent of roses.

'No,' he said. 'Don't go.' He gathered his resolve and said, 'Never leave me.'

She gave a sharp gasp. He wondered that she had so little faith in her own virtues. Then Sister Blithe lifted him up on her broad shoulder and gave him first a kiss, and then a cup of strong sweet tea. He had drunk it like that once, with milk and sugar. She remembered.

Tears pricked his wounded eyes as he fell asleep.

'But how did you know?' asked Sister Blithe as we sat down to more tea in the small room into which she had imported a real bed and an electric fan heater. With the door shut one could hardly feel the chill winds which whipped around the gallery.

'He had your picture on the wall,' I said. 'The milkmaid Madonna. But it was because you both said the same thing—from your own perspectives. You said sadly that he had gone where you could not follow. He said that all human love was vain, transitory, and unreliable. So I decided that he must have become more and more distant and more and more like Savonarola and you couldn't do that, Sister Blithe, really you couldn't. You're one of the world's optimists.'

'I am,' she said. 'Though it's a philosophy that takes a bit of a battering in the real world.'

'No shit,' I agreed. This wasn't a good time for optimists, what with politics and cruelty and detention camps. 'I'd better go,' I said. 'I've left my bakery in the hands of the willing but unskilled. Will you be all right?'

'Oh, yes,' she said, with a smile that Raphael would have painted. 'He will moderate and perhaps I will acquire more discipline. We shall do well,' she said. 'Come back in a week and see how we are getting on.'

'Sooner, sorry,' I said. 'I have to bring my mother to see my father, who is working in the kitchen here. And I have to talk to Thomas as soon as he can manage it.'

'Three days,' she said placidly. 'It's Wednesday. Come back on Saturday and we shall arrange things.'

'Deal,' I said, and went home, full of tea and relief.

I had taken a huge chance, dragging that good woman out of her sunflower bedecked life and into the cold world of the Discarnates. But it looked like it might work out after all.

I was so relieved that I shouted Daniel dinner at the Japanese restaurant which makes the very best sushi and sashimi, and regaled myself with teriyaki chicken, one of the world's great dishes.

Thursday was a nice day in which nothing whatsoever happened except the things which ought to have happened. Bread. Cherie's muffins (poppyseed and lemon). Café Pandamus food for lunch. Jason coughing like a hag but seeming to feel a little better. Mrs. Dawson sending the Professor up to tell him tales of Ancient Greece because the harsh light from the TV was beginning to hurt his eyes. I would long remember the scene: Jason propped up and wheezing, holding Pumpkin Bear in one arm, and listening with awe to the story of Odysseus and Circe. The Professor's silver hair, beautiful profile, elegant hands as he gestured, his bard's voice telling of the sailors turned into pigs by the enchantress. Not a long journey for most of them, I fancy.

On Friday Kane and Reagan came back and reluctantly agreed that my Mr. Venn had cleared me of any complicity in the assault on Father Hungerford, which was still unsolved. And I went up to try to prepare my mother for meeting my father again.

I greeted Carolus, who was enthroned on a silken cushion. He condescended so far as to lick my hand, a mark of favour. I greeted Therese, nearly invisible behind an almost finished knitting project. It must have been an elephant cosy. In green and orange wool. I greeted my mother and she actually said, 'Hello.'

'I've found Sunlight,' I said, sitting down. She did not leap up and scream at me. She clutched her hands together but she said quite quietly, 'Where? Is he alive?'

'Yes, he's alive and unhurt, though thinner. He's living in the Discarnate Brotherhood, and I can take you to see him tomorrow.'

'Good.'

'Is that what you want me to do?'

'Yes,' she said, a little doubtfully. 'How did you find him?'

'I looked everywhere he wasn't,' I said grimly, 'until I found out where he was. This was not an easy task. What do you want to do now, Jacqui? Do you want to go back to the commune?'

'I don't know,' she said. 'I have been thinking. Therese has been so kind to me and I never did one thing to deserve it. You've been kind, too,' she added, to my complete astonishment. 'We only have a biological bond, and it isn't very strong, is it?'

'No,' I said. 'Not all that strong.'

She sighed as if to acknowledge that this was true and sad. 'All right. Take me to him tomorrow, and we shall see.'

'Come down to the street at ten,' I said. 'I'll have a car.'

And no outcry about that, either. Starshine had certainly changed.

And Jason was definitely on the mend. He was sitting up and breathing much more easily. Jon was warming one of his amazingly nourishing spicy stews in the kitchen when I popped in. Kepler was teaching Jason to play chess. The air was full of that Middle Eastern cinnamon and cumin scent which made Morocco the gourmet's playground.

Jason was in excellent hands. I refrained from kibitzing on the chess match and went back to Daniel. Earthly Delights was closed for the weekend, we had supplied all our regulars even though disaster had landed upon us, and I felt wonderful.

Except that tomorrow held enough mystery for ten detective novels and I didn't want to think about it. So, resolutely, I didn't.

Saturday and Timbo conveyed us to the castle where the Discarnate Brotherhood purged the wealthy of their excess for the good of their souls. This time I was not greeted by a retching acolyte but a cheerful Sister Blithe in her yellow smock, who conducted us inside. Therese walked just behind Jacqui, presumably to catch her if she fainted. I walked with Daniel and tried not to feel anxious. Then the day became surreal.

Passing us was a long line of the brown-robed ones, each carrying a stag's head. It looked vaguely pagan and entirely strange. They filed past out into the street, where the heads were being packed with great care into a large furniture remover's truck. Each moth-eaten relic was being swathed in bubble wrap as if it was a Da Vinci. Odd, I thought.

'Sister Blithe?' asked Daniel, making a sweeping gesture.

'No reason why a religious order should live with a lot of unsanitary old taxidermy,' she said. 'I sold it all to a collector—for a fine sum. Which will be enough to lime-strip the linenfold panelling and repaint the walls. This way,' she said to my mother, taking her arm. Jacqui leaned on her.

We came fully into the great hall and found that the whole community was assembled. Father Hungerford, wrapped in a bright red comforter, was sitting in a wheelchair. His face was still sadly battered and all his Greek beauty was marred, but he was still beautiful, as a work of art is beautiful even though vandals have damaged it. His injured hands lay in his lap.

'Oh,' said someone in the back row. The man I had identified as my father came forward, slowly, moving as if his bones hurt. Jacqui stiffened and looked straight into his eyes. There was a long silence as they examined each other.

Jacqui was dressed in an embroidered tracksuit and her hair was tamed into a plait. She was clean and clothed and in her right mind. Sunlight was shivering in a brown robe on which someone had spilled paint. His face had thinned, his eyes were hollow. Some of his bruises were still there as yellowing patches on his forearms and throat. Still they did not speak. The congregation looked on and murmured.

'Do you want to come home now, Sun?' she asked, very softly.

He took the offered hand. 'I'd like that, Star,' he said.

Without another word they turned and walked out of the castle, hand in hand, as I had always seen them walk. Therese Webb dabbed at her eyes. Daniel chuckled.

'Brothers,' said Father Hungerford. The voice was the same, compelling and sweet. 'One of you needs to confess.

I urge it on you. I require it of you. I saw the skirts of a black robe when I was struck down, though I saw nothing else. One of you has done this, acting perhaps as God's instrument to punish my intransigence and lower my pride. But I need to know who it was. God already knows. Do you fear me more than God?'

It was a good argument but it wasn't carrying the audience. The brothers and sisters shifted and rocked. They whispered. They stared at each other. Father Hungerford was right. They all needed to know who had beaten him.

And I knew. I sidled into the crowd and drew him forth by the sleeve. He stood shivering as though he was very cold.

'They should never have made you do it,' I said, because I was full of sympathy. 'It was a terrible thing to make you do. Twice a day, to poison the food, to ruin good food. No cook could stand it forever and you were a really great cook. There has to be a cracking point. It was the asafoetida, wasn't it, Brother Amos?'

He fell to his knees and buried his face in Father Hungerford's red doona and burst into wails and lamentations and tears.

Sister Blithe took me and Therese by the hands. 'That was a good deed,' she said. 'Now off home, kind people.'

'What are you going to do about the food?' I asked as we were led away.

'Oh, it will stay more or less the same. Just not poisoned. Except that bread. No one should have to eat that bread. I'm sure we can bake something better for ourselves—oh, sorry, Corinna dear, I'm sure that you can bake something better for us. Wholemeal, you know, but with a little yeast and sugar and salt.'

'Yes,' I agreed. 'I will not be sorry to see the last of the famine bread.'

'And as for the other food, we will stay simple. There is a great virtue in tasting a single ingredient. Vegetable stew tastes wonderful if you are hungry enough to appreciate the humble swede. I'll call on you in a week or so. Nicely done, Corinna.'

Timbo took us all home to Insula. That afternoon, Sun and Star packed their meagre belongings, borrowed fifty dollars from me, and went home to Sunbury. Therese Webb watched them walk off to the station, hand in hand.

'All's well that ends well,' she said. 'Now I can get on with my Knitting for the Needy and other projects. That dark blue jumper for you, for instance, with the Florentine colours. And perhaps a matching one for Daniel? And while it was nice to have someone to look after, Corinna, I think that in future I shall confine myself to Carolus, what do you think?'

Carolus looked up from his snoozing position in the dumb waiter and gave a short but majestic whuffle.

'Carolus seems to think so,' I agreed.

It was so nice to get back to normal. I like normal. I like boring. Jason spent a week in bed and came gradually back to work, at first only descending to compound his muffins then returning for a strengthening walk with Mrs. Dawson or a game of chess with Kepler. Mrs. Dawson saw no reason why he should move out of the borrowed apartment. No one was using it, so he stayed in Pluto on the understanding that his housekeeping had to be first class. And it was. He had lived for so long in small rooms and then on the street that he was careful with his belongings. He also liked things tidy and clean.

After a fortnight Cherie gratefully retired, though she said that she would always be happy to earn a little pocket money helping out if I needed her. She started her fabric class and went into huddles with Therese. Daniel solved a very unpleasant stalking case and was congratulated by the bench. Star and Sun sent a free postcard advertising aloe vera saying that they were very glad to be home and they'd pay back my fifty any day now.

Then one morning, just when I began to believe that everything had settled down, I heard a scream from the bakery and ran in, thinking that Kylie or Goss had spilt a pot of boiling soup over themselves. Mrs. Dawson, the Professor, Meroe, Jon and Kepler, who were in the vicinity or passing at the time, also came in. But it wasn't an accident. It was a woman and she was shrieking for her son. She was dressed in a parachute silk tracksuit. She had high heeled shoes on her grimy feet. Her hair was straw yellow in places and black at the roots. Her cheeks were raddled with drinking and her voice was sodden with brandy.

'Jason!' she screamed. 'Where's my son?'

I began to get some insight into why Jason had left home. I stepped forward.

'Be quiet,' I said loudly. 'Why are you making all this noise? Who are you?'

She goggled at me with pure hatred in her eyes. 'You stole my son!' she shrieked, clawing for my face with filthy chipped talons.

I held her easily enough, though I was fighting down an urge to clip her ears. This harridan, the mother of my tidy Jason? Genetics is a minefield. I gave the woman a shake and she struggled.

'You aren't my mother,' said a cold voice from the bakery door. 'You just gave birth to me. You couldn't even tell me who my father was,' Jason went on. He was as white as chalk.

'My baby!' screamed my prisoner.

'They took the babies away again, didn't they?' accused Jason. 'That's why you come for me. They took the babies away and now you got no family allowance. Just the dole, and that ain't enough for what you drink.'

'Jase!' she cried, in what sounded like real pain.

'No,' he said, in total, flat denial. 'You've made a mistake. You can't make me come back. You don't want me back.'

'I do, I do,' she cried again.

'No,' said Jason, and gave the sort of smile I ought not to have seen on a boy's face. He held up a piece of paper. It was his birth certificate. 'You don't get a dollar for me now,' he told the woman, speaking right into her face. 'I'm sixteen today. No more money from the government for you. And this is my family now. Your family is where they look after you.'

Jason moved until he stood between Mrs. Dawson and the Professor, who put a gentle hand on his trembling shoulder.

This being a perfect time for Kane and Reagan to come in, they did, and I surrendered my prisoner into their professional grasp.

'Take her away,' I said, disgusted. 'Don't come back,' I added.

Dumbfounded, they did just as I asked. We heard the woman begin to scream again as she reached the street. Then no one moved. I was terrified of saying the wrong thing.

Jason looked like he might cry, or swear, or faint. Jon looked at Kepler.

'So, shall we have the party tonight?' he asked. 'What do you think, Jason? Party?' Jason was looking dazed. Kylie and Goss had both kissed him, one on each cheek. Then moved away in case he got any ideas.

'For your birthday,' said Kepler. 'Your birthday party, of course.'

'Of course,' said Jason, a little hysterically.

'We'll have to start preparing right away,' said Jon. 'Can we ask Therese and Cherie to do the draping and decorating? Go ask the Pandamuses to come, Jason, and the Lone Gunmen. Eight o'clock in the atrium.'

And light of foot and a bit dazed, Jason went. I kissed Jon. So did Meroe. He did not seem to mind.

Chapter Nineteen

Consulted, Cherie and Therese had gone into a complicated discussion which lasted far longer than my attention span. The upshot of it was that they and Trudi were busy all day, trailing bolts of calico and hammering. Jason shut himself in the bakery with a book called *Wonderful Cakes* and wouldn't let us in. Jon and Kepler allowed us to do a little chopping and preparing but Daniel and I found ourselves at a loose end quite quickly. It was a bright day and we went for a long walk, through the art gallery and all over the hills and dales of the gardens, coming home cold and pleasantly tired and ready to be amused.

In furtherance of that we took a lush bath and a little nap. Then we dressed in our dining clothes. I wore my black Spanish dress, and Daniel was sleek in a silk shirt the colour of blood plums and a waistcoat I had embroidered with silver birds. As we approached the front door a sheet of paper was slid under it. It directed us to bring a blindfold each and assemble at the lift. We collected scarves and did as we were bid. Anything for a weird life.

I held Daniel's hand as we heard the lift rumble down.

A door opened, we were led forward by the hand, and the door shut again. Then we went down until we reached a floor where we were led out again, me by someone who was giggling.

I diagnosed Kylie or Goss. I had the sensation of people all around me and I heard the Professor say, 'Hmm!' in a way that only he does.

'Unmask,' cried a voice, and we did.

We were in what seemed to be a firelit cavern. It smelt wonderfully of fruit, wine, spices and flowers. The walls were draped in dark fabrics. Big vases of flowers stood on the floor and a huge table had been set up, flanked by lots of chairs. In the middle of it was a small fountain with a Medusa's head.

I laughed and took the cup which was offered to me and tasted. The fountain contained not water but wine.

'Oh, lovely', I cried. Jason gave me a fast hug. 'Happy birthday,' I said, handing him a box. He put it on the small table which was filling up with presents. The Pandamus family, who had cared so devotedly for Jason, were delighted with the firelit cavern. Everyone, from Yai Yai in her armchair to the smallest girl in her fairy costume, was sipping and nibbling on the delectable little munchies with which the table was littered. Nuts, olives, little frittatas, little pizzas. 'Aha!' I said muzzily through the next glass of wine, 'some of these are yours, are they not, beloved?'

'Just my recipe book,' said Daniel. 'I have spent the day in blameless company, dear love.'

Trudi went to the end of the room and the goods lift trundled down, revealing Jon and Kepler carrying a dented aluminium vat which smelt of lemon and cracked pepper.

'Lentil soup,' said Jon. 'Do sit down, ladies, gentlemen.'

I was sitting next to my lord D'Urbanville. He was dapper and pleased. His mundane name was Tarquin, it appeared. We discussed Georgette Heyer as we sipped soup. It was the essence of fresh tastes.

'Trudi, how did you do all this?' asked Daniel, impressed.

'Therese and Cherie, they told me what to nail, I nailed it,' she said simply. 'In the old days they used to have wine tastings and parties down here, we thought, why not again? Just needs some work, seal the chutes, put out the rubbish, clean up a bit. We maybe got better ideas when we found someone left a whole case of that red wine and also bottles of good Dutch genever. I think better in Dutch,' she informed me, lifting the little glass full of colourless liquid.

'And we did the flowers,' said Kylie and Gossamer. They had borrowed goth clothes from Cherie and all three of them looked erotic, overdressed, and terribly pleased with themselves. Mistress Dread approved, but was observed pulling all their corset laces much tighter.

Soup was accompanied by my pasta douro. Then Jon and Kepler hauled in a mountain of boiled new potatoes the size of golf balls, sprinkled with fresh herbs, a smallish vat of beef stifado—I wondered at their daring, cooking a Greek dish for Greeks—and trays of stuffed eggplant. The whole was accompanied by Meroe's fairy leaves in a delicate lemon juice dressing.

I was picking at the eggplant filling trying to work out what made it taste better than any other eggplant. Tomato, yes, and pine nuts, and—cheese? The Magnificat came to mind. 'He hath filled the hungry with good things and the rich he hath sent empty away.' Those Discarnates were even now dining on turnip stew. Very proper. But possibly not to be said to any devout people. I smothered my chuckle and ate more eggplant. Cumin, maybe?

'But which of you was the witch?' persisted Kylie. She swished her long black skirt and tapped Taz on the cheek with her fan. He blenched.

'It was him,' he said cravenly. Rat ducked his head.

Kylie said, 'I think that's very clever of you,' and he began to smile.

'And I was the apothecary,' boasted Taz.

'You're clever too,' said Goss.

'Can I get you another drink?' asked Gully.

Jon and Kepler were at last able to sit down and collect a crumb or so of the feast they had so carefully prepared. Just as Jon picked up his spoon, a little Pandamus girl came and whispered in his ear. Considerably startled, he followed her to where Yai Yai was sitting in her armchair, safely out of the way of any draughts. She laid a claw-like hand on his wrist and said something to him. He came back and Kepler said eagerly, 'Well?'

'She said I cooked as well as any man could,' said Jon, quite overcome.

Dinner trailed very agreeably away to a languid dessert of fine cheese, oriental fruits and coffee in the Hellenic manner made by Del himself over a primus. I spooned up a liqueur soaked fig, really not able to eat much more. It burst in my mouth, sweet and tart and voluptuous.

The company relaxed. All's well that had indeed ended well. I was full and a little drunk and delighted. Both my parents had gone home. I had had the confrontation which I had avoided all these years and I hadn't been struck by lightning. Nerds Inc was still solvent but they wouldn't be selling any more poisons or corrupting any more boys. Father Hungerford was back with Sister Blithe, Therese could devote herself to Carolus, and how I looked forward to Carolus snubbing Mrs. Pemberthy's rotten little doggie, Traddles. Daniel was still with me and Jason had fought off his family. All in all, a pretty good result.

Jason was opening his presents. I had given him a cheap watch. Baker's watches always get ruined. Jon and Kepler had given him a chess set. Meroe had given him a book on positive dreaming, and the others had largely given him money, which was always acceptable. He beamed. His CD collection was going to get a boost. It was the only male birthday of my acquaintance where someone didn't give the birthday boy socks. But we are a select company.

Then the lights dimmed and we saw candles. Jason bore his birthday cake into the room. He set it down carefully. It was a huge chocolate cake, covered with licks of ganache, and it looked delicious and completely inedible after the dinner we had just absorbed.

Then again, dessert goes into a different stomach. The children sang 'Happy Birthday' four or five times to make sure that they got it right, then everyone had to have a go at blowing the candles out. Finally Jason sliced it. Unusual. Inside, it was not chocolate brown, but red.

'What sort of cake is this, Jason?' I asked.

'Devil's Food,' he said, and grinned.

Recipes

Lemon and Lentil Soup

The admirable Mark Deasey's lemon and lentil soup. I have never tasted better.

2 cups brown lentils
olive oil
2 medium–large onions, peeled and chopped
bunch of silverbeet
juice of 2 large lemons
salt and whole black peppercorns

Soak the lentils overnight or, if time presses or you forgot, cover with cold water and bring to the boil, cover and turn off the heat and leave for an hour.

Drain, cover to two centimetres with fresh water (this reduces the flatulence quotient), bring to the boil and simmer until tender (which won't be long, don't overcook them)—maybe five minutes. Keep tasting.

Cover the base of a heavy pot with olive oil. When hot, throw in the onions, stir, and leave to braise until they turn golden. While this is going on, wash the silverbeet well. Chop off the manky ends of the stems only, finely slice the rest and leave in a colander.

When the onions are ready, throw in the silverbeet, turn the heat to high and stir until the onions and silverbeet are mixed together. Cover closely, turn the heat down to medium and cook, stirring occasionally, until the stems are tender.

Add the lentils and enough water (if needed) to come barely to the top of the mixture. Add the lemon juice and about 20 peppercorns, coarsely cracked (do this with a mortar and pestle. Taste the difference with freshly cracked pepper and henceforth your preground pepper will gather dust at the back of the shelf). Add salt to taste and simmer the lot together for about 15 minutes. Serve with bread or cheese scones.

Oriental Fruits (Persian Delights)

6 cups dried fruit (for example, figs, stoned dates, stoned prunes, apricots, apples, pears, etc)
a cinnamon stick
2 pieces star anise
1 long piece of lemon peel, removed with a potato peeler
1 cup dry sherry
water

Cut the fruit to an agreeable size and chop the stem off the figs. Put all the pieces into a heavy-bottomed saucepan with the cinnamon stick, star anise and lemon peel. Add the dry sherry and enough cold water to barely cover. If your tooth is incorrigibly sweet, add some caster sugar but this syrup will be fine without it.

Bring slowly to the boil, cover, reduce flame to lowest possible. Simmer 10 minutes, take off heat, and leave to sit covered for an hour or more. Reheat just before serving. Place a knot of Persian fairy floss on top and serve with Greek yogurt.

Devil's Food Cake

This was originally a red velvet cake, which explains why some recipes still have cochineal in them. I can see no point in this as the red colouring is entirely subsumed in the chocolate. The culinary opposite is Angel's Food cake, now made with that abomination, white chocolate.

160 g butter
1 cup caster sugar
3 eggs, lightly beaten
70 g cocoa (I use Cadbury's baking cocoa)
3 tsp instant coffee
2 cups self-raising flour
1/2 cup Kahlua or marsala
1/2 cup milk (or less, see how wet the batter is)

Filling
300 ml cream
Icing
80 g good dark chocolate
80 g butter

Preheat the oven to 180 degrees or moderate. Spray two 8-inch (20 cm) cake tins with oil.

Cream together the butter and sugar. Stir in the beaten eggs and beat again. Add the cocoa powder and coffee and keep beating. Fold in the flour and the milk and marsala alternately, and if the mixture is as stiff as dough add more milk until it looks like—well, cake mix. Until it can be poured.

Pour into tins and bake for about 40 minutes, until a skewer inserted in the middle comes out clean.

When the cakes are cool, join them with a thick layer of whipped cream.

For the icing melt the butter and the chocolate in the microwave or over boiling water. It only takes a minute. Beat the mixture until it is smooth, then let it sit until it is cool enough to handle. Slather it over the cake. It will set.

Oddly enough, this cake keeps very well. The tricky bit is testing this, because it vanishes off the table really fast.

Happy cooking! *Kala orexi!*

Afterword

Please do not try to lose weight by making up your own herbal tea. It will not work. It might also poison you. Blake was not joking about Caesar's laurel crown. Just because it's herbal doesn't mean it's good for you.

I have made every effort to ensure that I haven't made any mistakes, but I will have. If they are minor, do not tell me in reproachful, or even worse, gleeful detail. It ruins my day. If they are major, of course, I apologise. Anyone who likes can email me on kgreenwood@netspace.net.au

To receive a free catalog of Poisoned Pen Press titles, please contact us in one of the following ways:

Phone: 1-800-421-3976
Facsimile: 1-480-949-1707
Email: info@poisonedpenpress.com
Website: www.poisonedpenpress.com

Poisoned Pen Press
6962 E. First Ave. Ste. 103
Scottsdale, AZ 85251